**His body t[illegible]
drew his Glock [illegible]**

“What?” Blair asked.

“Get in the garage. Now!” He reached through her open window to hit the remote on the SUV’s visor. As the door wound up, he yelled, “Go. Go!”

His urgency must have penetrated, because she pressed down on the accelerator and the SUV shot forward, and as it did, gunshots rang out. Bullets pinged off the metal of the other side of her vehicle.

“Go!” he shouted again. But once her SUV drove into the garage, he would have no cover. Nowhere to hide from the bullets. He could have followed her vehicle into the garage; he probably should have.

But he didn’t want that son of a bitch to get away like he had in the alley. He wanted to catch him this time and stop him. But first he had to make sure he himself didn’t get shot.

Dear Reader,

I'm so grateful you're back for another book in my ongoing Bachelor Bodyguards series for Harlequin Romantic Suspense. I am enjoying revisiting my fictional town of River City, Michigan, and the Payne Protection Agency with all its many franchises. I think this one, which the Kozminski brothers opened to specialize in security for valuables, might be my favorite franchise of them all. Do you love a good redemption story like I do? Not that these "bad" boys have really had much choice after all the trauma they suffered in their childhoods. Ivan Chekov might have suffered the most, but the giant of a bodyguard has a heart of gold and a code of honor like nobody else. He's just the person to protect art gallery owner Blair Etheridge, but independent Blair doesn't think she needs anyone protecting her. I love a strong, independent heroine even more than a reformed bad boy, and I hope you enjoy this book as much as I enjoyed writing it.

Please reach out to me through my website or socials and let me know what your favorite character types and characters are. I'd love to hear from you, and for now...

Happy reading!

Lisa Childs

PERSONAL SECURITY

LISA CHILDS

Recycling programs for this product may not exist in your area.

ISBN-13: 978-1-335-50279-7

Personal Security

Harlequin Enterprises ULC
22 Adelaide St. West, 41st Floor
Toronto, Ontario M5H 4E3, Canada
www.Harlequin.com

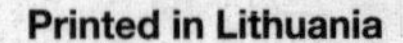

Printed in Lithuania

New York Times and *USA TODAY* bestselling, award-winning author **Lisa Childs** has written more than eighty-five novels. Published in twenty countries, she's also appeared on the *Publishers Weekly*, Barnes & Noble and Nielsen Top 100 bestseller lists. Lisa writes contemporary romance, romantic suspense, and paranormal and women's fiction. She's a wife, mom, bonus mom, avid reader and less avid runner. Readers can reach her through Facebook or her website, lisachilds.com.

Books by Lisa Childs

Harlequin Romantic Suspense

Bachelor Bodyguards

His Christmas Assignment
Bodyguard Daddy
Beauty and the Bodyguard
Nanny Bodyguard
Single Mom's Bodyguard
In the Bodyguard's Arms
Soldier Bodyguard
Guarding His Witness
Evidence of Attraction
Bodyguard Boyfriend
Close Quarters with the Bodyguard
Bodyguard Under Siege
Hostage Security
Personal Security

Visit the Author Profile page at Harlequin.com for more titles.

With great appreciation for Adrienne Macintosh,
my insightful, organized editor, who keeps me
on track with the story and with spreadsheets!
Thank you for all you do!

Prologue

Twenty-four years ago...

Blood covered Ivan's small hands as he tried to cover the hole in his father's chest and stop him from bleeding. So much blood oozed between his fingers that it ran over the backs of his hands. A pool of it spread beneath him, soaking into the living room carpet and into the skin of Ivan's bare knees, staining them red.

"Dad... Daddy..." Sobs choked his voice, and tears streamed down his face, dropping onto his father's chest. "Please, Daddy..." *Don't die.*

But he couldn't say the words. He couldn't even *think* them because he was too scared that it was going to happen. This was the most scared he'd ever been in his eight years of life. He was afraid that Daddy was leaving and that Uncle Viktor was coming back...for *him.* To shoot Ivan like he'd shot Ivan's dad just a short while ago.

The sound of their deep voices, loud and angry, had woken him up from a dream. That dream was a nightmare now.

"I... Ivan..." his daddy whispered, his voice so soft and weak. Ivan leaned closer to hear him.

"Yes, Daddy?"

"Be good, son," he whispered.

"I will, I will," he promised.

"Be a good man, too," Daddy whispered, "and protect..."

"Who, Daddy?" Ivan asked, and leaned closer again so he could hear. There was nobody else. Ivan had no brothers and sisters, and Mama had died so long ago that Ivan couldn't remember much about her anymore. Just the softness of her voice and her weak smile. Nobody had been able to protect her from whatever sickness had taken her from them.

"Protect..." Daddy whispered. But then a strange sound rattled in his bleeding chest, rose up from his throat and slipped out of his lips in a faint breath. His last breath.

Daddy died.

And then something else rattled, the knob on the door as it turned. Uncle Viktor was coming back...

And Ivan realized what his dad was trying to tell him, to protect himself. But the door opened, and it was too late.

Chapter 1

"I can't believe he's alive," Garek Kozminski mused aloud as he stared through the glass wall of his office at one of his and his partners' employees. Garek, his wife and his brother had recently opened a franchise of the Payne Protection Agency, the premier security company in River City, Michigan.

Garek's branch specialized in security for valuables, so the idea had been that their employees wouldn't be in the same danger as some of the other branches. But that hadn't proved true in the short couple of months since they'd launched their franchise.

Milek, Garek's brother, lounged in one of the chairs across from him. He pushed back his overly long blond hair, narrowed his silvery blue eyes and peered through the glass, too. "Josh? Can you blame him for putting his life in danger like he did? He was trying to get his child away from a kidnapper."

"I wasn't talking about Josh," Garek replied. But the dark-haired security specialist, Josh Stafford, was next to the man whom Garek had been staring at and thinking about and not just because of his recent close call but also because of his past.

"Ah, you're referring to Ivan," Milek said as his gaze went

from Josh to the man sitting at one of the desks in the open area of the former warehouse they'd converted to their office space. The building was so big that there was an apartment inside it, too, as well as Milek's art studio. Despite the vast size of the office area, Ivan Chekov seemed to shrink it. He was that big of a guy, like his coworkers Viktor Lagransky and Blade Sparks. While Josh was of average height and build, he looked small next to them.

But Garek hadn't hired any of these guys for their muscle, not even the former boxer, Blade. He'd hired them because he could relate to them all too well. Like him, they'd been dealt some tough breaks and had to be strong in bad situations. And all of them deserved a second chance like he and Milek had been given.

For Ivan, this was more like a third chance, his second being when he'd survived the hit put out on his life years ago. As if he'd felt their stares, Ivan glanced up and met Garek's gaze through the glass. The man was a study in contrasts, from his pale blond hair buzzed short to his dark, nearly black eyes, and his imposing size to his gentle demeanor.

"I know Ivan took a pretty hard blow to the head while protecting Josh and Josh's son and Natalie Croft, but I don't think he was in danger of dying from the concussion," Milek said. "Although head wounds can be unpredictable."

Garek sighed. "Too many things are unpredictable."

"Unless you're Penny Payne-Lynch," Milek said. "She has the ability to predict some things about the future."

Penny was the mother of the man who'd started the Payne Protection Agency, Logan Payne, who was also Garek and Milek's brother-in-law. She had a reputation for being able to sense when danger was coming.

Garek was beginning to suspect he had the same ability, at least where his team was concerned. Because at their opening-day celebration, he'd had a horrible fear something terrible was going to happen to one of their new hires and that they might even lose one. Actually, they had almost lost two of them. Josh had come under attack a few times, and Ivan had been ambushed.

"Do you think he's ready to go back out on assignment?" Garek asked.

"I don't think we have a choice," Milek said, "unless we want to lose our biggest client."

"Mason Hull." The guy was the CEO of a Fortune 500 insurance company, Midwest Property and Casualty. But there was something about the man, something that didn't feel white collar to Garek. Hull was young to be a CEO already, and even though smart, he was also more hands-on than the normal chief executive officer. Hull did things himself that others would delegate, and Garek suspected that was more than just pressuring his policyholders to hire a security company. He probably did other things himself not because he didn't like to delegate, but because he didn't want anyone to know what he was doing. Because he sure hadn't shared a whole hell of a lot with them.

"Hull wants us to protect the assets of the policyholders he's most concerned about having claims," Milek said.

"I understand why he wanted us to protect the Croft Custom Jewelry company," Garek said. "They had filed a bunch of claims..."

"Which turned out to be an inside job at the jewelry store, not inside the insurance company like Hull seems to be worried about," Milek said, his forehead furrowing beneath the hair that had fallen across it again.

Garek's hair was long, too, and he looked as much like his younger brother as the Payne brothers all looked alike, but he wasn't a painter like Milek. How did the guy see through that hair to create the works of art that he did with paint and canvas?

Thinking of art elicited a slight groan from Garek as it reminded him of the next client the insurance CEO wanted them to protect.

"But what about the art gallery? Why is he concerned about them?" Sure, it had an unsavory reputation and even some criminal charges brought against it in the past, but that had been long ago and under different owners. "The place isn't even up and running again, so they've had no claims. It doesn't make sense for him to be so concerned about it." Unless he thought they were reopening more than the art business of the gallery.

Nothing about this case really made sense, though, which was why Garek was so worried. Did all insurance company CEOs stress about losses as much as Mason Hull? And why would he specifically seek out the Kozminski branch of the Payne Protection Agency for added security for the assets his company insured? Maybe Garek was overly cynical from growing up like he had or maybe he was right to be suspicious of the man and his motives.

"For the grand reopening party, the new owner is going to borrow a lot of valuable pieces from private collectors and museums to display," Milek said.

"How do you make money if they're just for display?" Garek asked. He, of course, knew nothing about art at all. That was his brother's domain.

"The chance to see those pieces will draw a lot of art enthusiasts to the opening," Milek explained. "There are works offered for sale, as well, but only by the hottest artists around right now."

"Like you?" Garek teased.

Milek sighed and shrugged. "My agent says someone from the gallery has been trying to contact me, but we're not sure it's a good idea."

"Why?" Garek asked. "You've been giving too many of your works of art away for free, and hell, we might need some money to keep this place afloat if we have any more cases go like the last one at Croft's."

"All the stolen jewelry was recovered," Milek reminded him.

"Yeah, but some of that was stolen after we'd installed security at the store," Garek said. He was surprised Hull hadn't fired their agency then. And the fact that he hadn't made Garek even more suspicious of him.

Milek sighed. "Well, in the end, we got it all back and put a stop to any more inside thefts at Croft's."

Garek glanced back at Josh. "And he'll make sure nothing else happens there." His fiancée owned and managed the store now, so he was personally making sure that it, and her and their son, stayed safe.

But Josh had apparently, from the box he was carrying, stopped in at the office to take care of his coworkers, too, by handing out doughnuts. With one hand, Josh held up the box toward them and gestured with his other hand for them to come out and join them.

Milek's stomach growled. "I think I forgot to eat breakfast."

Garek snorted. "You forget a lot of stuff."

"Sorry about that," Milek said.

"No, I didn't mean it like that," Garek hastened to explain. "I meant when you're painting you forget. Here, what you did with that last case, I couldn't have done any better. You handled the business and kept all our employees alive."

Milek sighed. "I wish I'd kept them from getting hurt."

"Me, too," Garek said. "But with this job, there is always going to be danger. I just wish I knew for sure where that danger was going to come from..."

"What's bothering you?" Milek asked. He stared at Garek now.

Garek shrugged. "I don't know. Something just doesn't feel right about all of this."

"The gallery?"

He nodded. "Do you remember what happened with it years ago? That one of the owners went to prison for money laundering?"

And for, of all people, Viktor Chekov.

Milek nodded, too. "Yeah, that might be why my agent doesn't want me to showcase any of my art there. But I don't think there's anything to be worried about now. The old owners aren't involved and the other person that was—"

"Viktor Chekov," Garek interjected. The former godfather of River City. A ruthless killer.

"He's in prison thanks to you," Milek continued. Then he glanced at Ivan. "He probably wouldn't be here if you hadn't put his uncle away."

True. If Ivan had come back before his uncle's arrest, he probably would have been killed. He had returned for the old man's sentencing, though, as if he'd wanted to make sure his uncle was really going to prison. He'd already been working security then, so he had been the first one Garek had hired when he and Candace and Milek started their agency.

"Just because he's behind bars doesn't mean Viktor Chekov can't still be a threat," Garek reminded his brother. Despite it being a few years since the former godfather of River City had gone to prison, Garek still hadn't completely relaxed. He never knew if or when the convicted killer might get revenge on him.

Garek glanced back at Ivan again, wondering if the man's nephew lived with that same fear. That someday his uncle would come for him again.

Ivan should have been used to being watched. He was pretty sure people had been doing it for years. First his uncle had watched him, wondering when Ivan might crack and betray him, and the authorities, who'd probably been wondering the same thing. Some people had already known the truth and had done nothing to help him; he shouldn't have trusted them, either. Ivan hadn't really been able to trust anyone since the people he'd loved the most had died. His mom and then, even more tragically, his dad. What about the Kozminskis?

Could he trust them? He remembered them from when he'd lived with his uncle after his father died until Ivan ran away at sixteen. They'd been a little older than he was, a little more experienced and jaded. He'd had to work with them a few times then, as a kid, stealing for his uncle. If he hadn't…he wouldn't have survived as long as he had. But even committing crimes for the old man hadn't appeased him. He still would have killed Ivan.

After he'd run away, he'd vowed never to work with the Kozminskis or anyone like them again. But when he'd returned to River City for his uncle's sentencing, he'd found that they hadn't just changed; they were responsible for finally bringing his father's killer to justice. Something he'd wanted for years but hadn't been able to do. And so out of gratitude to them, he'd taken this job when they'd offered it to him.

But, at times like this, he wasn't sure if he'd been offered the job because he'd already been working in private security for years or because they wanted to keep an eye on him.

He'd felt his bosses watching him for a while through the glass wall of Garek's office. Finally they stepped out. While Milek headed directly toward the box of doughnuts Josh held out to him, Garek headed toward him. And Ivan drew in a deep breath, bracing himself.

"Got a minute?" Garek asked.

"Yes."

Despite the doctor clearing him after his concussion, the Kozminskis had parked Ivan at his desk to monitor the camera feeds at various businesses. They hadn't sent him out on any new assignments, and even though it had been only a week, Ivan was beginning to think that they weren't going to send him out again. That they were going to fire him instead.

"Milek and I would like to see you in my office," Garek said.

Ivan swallowed down a groan. He didn't want to lose this job for so many reasons. Being back in River City hadn't brought back just bad memories, but had also reignited the good ones from his childhood. He felt closer to his parents in River City. And maybe that was his most important reason for wanting to stay working here—it seemed like something his father would have wanted him to do, what he might have meant by the last word he'd ever uttered: protect.

While he'd worked security jobs in other parts of the country, here in River City, most of the security needs went through one of the Payne Protection Agencies.

Ivan wasn't going to give up this job without a fight. Unlike when he was a kid, he was going to stand up for what he thought was right, like working here. He jumped up from his chair and followed Garek back into his office.

Milek didn't seem in any hurry to join them. He stayed with Josh, munching on a doughnut while admiring pictures of Josh's kid, Henry, on Josh's phone.

Garek gestured at the chair Milek had been sprawled in. "Take a seat."

But Ivan shook his head; he preferred to stand. "Is there a problem with my work? It seems like you've been watching me all morning."

Garek nodded. "Sometimes I just can't believe that you're alive."

"I didn't get hurt that badly," Ivan said. "Josh's brother-in-law didn't hit me hard enough to cause more than a slight concussion."

Garek snorted. "It was more than slight."

Ivan shrugged. "Whatever. I'm better now. No more headaches." It was closer to a dull throb, but he wasn't about to admit that he wasn't completely recovered yet. He'd learned young to show no weakness, or someone, like his uncle, would use that against him.

Garek narrowed his weird silvery eyes like he knew Ivan was lying. Then he shook his head. "I wasn't talking about your concussion. I was talking about your uncle, actually—that he let you live."

Ivan's blood chilled as it did every time someone brought up Viktor Chekov. "He didn't let me. He basically held me hostage after my dad died until I was able to get away from him." And he wouldn't have managed to do that without help from a very unlikely source.

"It's not easy to get away from Viktor Chekov," Garek said, his voice gruff with emotion.

Ivan knew Garek was well aware of how dangerous and powerful Viktor Chekov was. Or at least Viktor had been until Garek brought him down.

"I'm surprised he let you live, too," Ivan said. "He had more of a reason to kill you than he had to kill me." While Ivan had tried, he hadn't been able to bring his uncle to justice like Garek Kozminski had, but when Ivan had tried, he'd just been a kid. As he'd gotten older, his uncle had begun to worry that someone might listen to him, and so he'd attempted to have him silenced forever.

Garek chuckled and nodded. "Touché."

"Why are we even talking about my uncle?" Ivan asked. "What's going on?" Maybe this was even worse than getting fired. The old man wasn't getting out of prison, was he?

Garek shrugged. "I don't know. Something about this case, for the insurance company, has me thinking about him."

Ivan snorted. "Insurance and Viktor Chekov? It doesn't make sense. He was the one who provided the insurance, at a price, to most of the businesses in River City." And if they hadn't paid his price, they hadn't stayed in business for long. Even Viktor's own brother hadn't proved the exception to his rule; he'd had to pay, too…with his life.

"The insurance company CEO, Mason Hull, just asked us to provide security for the Ethereal Gallery."

The name rang a bell for Ivan and not a pleasant one. "Viktor was in business with them." He remembered one of the partners coming by his uncle's mansion, bringing works of art in exchange for money. "They were money launderers, right?"

"While one of the partners went to prison for money laundering, no charges were brought against Viktor," Garek said.

"Of course, they weren't," Ivan said. His uncle had had too many prosecutors, police officers and judges on his payroll.

"Do you know for certain if he was involved with the gallery?" Garek asked.

During the eight years that Ivan had been forced to live with his uncle, his father's killer, he'd tried to learn everything that he could to bring him down. But the people he'd gone to for help hadn't believed him, or at least they hadn't wanted to believe him. Or maybe they'd been paid not to believe him. So he wasn't surprised that the man had escaped charges of money laundering just as he'd escaped charges of murder.

And as for the thefts that he'd forced Ivan and other desperate young kids, like the Kozminskis, to carry out, he'd never been implicated in any of those, either…even when some of the kids, like Ivan, had had to serve time in juvenile detention for the crimes he'd made them commit.

Ivan sighed. "I am pretty damn certain that it happened. But like a lot of what I saw my uncle do, it was just my word and not enough evidence. At least that was what the authorities always told me." That he didn't have enough for them to bring charges against his uncle. "So if I had believed the authorities, then nobody knows for certain what Viktor Chekov has done or will do…" Except for one thing. Ivan knew for certain that the man had killed his father. "Or who he was in business with."

Garek nodded. "That's what makes me uneasy about this assignment, about all the assignments for Mason Hull. It feels like something else is going on here, like there's a specific reason this CEO hired *our* agency."

"What do you want me to do?" Ivan asked. "Check out Hull? You think he was involved with my uncle?"

Garek shook his head. "I've already done some checking into Hull, and I haven't found anything to justify my uneasiness. So for now, we're taking the assignment. I want *you* to provide the security at the gallery."

"Why me?" Ivan asked, aware there was a reason.

"For one, Hull specifically requested you."

"Why me?" he repeated, and his stomach knotted.

"You worked the Croft case hard," Garek said. "So hard that you got hurt trying to protect Josh's son. That didn't go unnoticed."

"But is that the real reason?" Ivan asked. "Or is it my last name?"

Garek sighed. "I wish I knew. The new owner has a connection to the old owners. So maybe it is about your name and seeing their reaction to it."

"To see if the new owners are still associated with my uncle?" he asked.

Garek shrugged. "I don't know. They haven't even opened yet, so I can't imagine that they are. But you're going to need to be extra careful and alert during this assignment…if you want it…"

Ivan appreciated his boss giving him an out but knew that if he didn't take this, he would be back at that desk watching security footage. So he swallowed a groan before it could escape his lips. Even though he wanted to get unchained from his desk, this felt like going backward instead of forward—backward into the nightmare of his past.

Into the world he'd wanted nothing to do with anymore, his uncle's world.

Blair Etheridge had a million and one things to do in less than a fortnight. But the people who should have been ensuring her success seemed more intent on undermining her and causing her failure. That wasn't new; she'd had issues for several months. First with probate court and then securing loans and hiring a contractor, and with him getting the permits to do what she wanted to the old building that had been sitting empty for so long. Even the homeless community had given her grief; they kept breaking into the building and damaging the renovations the contractor had actually completed. Some of them had even written threatening messages on the exterior and interior walls:

Get out!

Leave this building alone.

Go home!

You don't belong here.

And the worst one: *Leave or die!*

A lot of other people would have walked away from the project. Several people, including the contractor and some bankers, had told her it wasn't worth it. But she had to do this, not just for herself, but for her late father. She wanted to do what he hadn't been able to do: make the gallery a success instead of a source of speculation and scandal. She wanted to make his dream, and hers, come true for the gallery. And even though he was gone, she wanted to make him proud, since she hadn't seemed to while he was alive. And maybe, even though he was gone, she would finally get close to him by working where he'd worked so hard for so long.

Despite the setbacks and threatening messages that had been left scrawled on the walls, she was getting close to the grand reopening she'd been planning for over a year. That she'd started planning after her father's funeral.

But the harassment hadn't stopped; just the people harassing her seemed to have changed. While she hadn't found any more messages, the insurance-company CEO had been calling her nonstop the past few days. But since she was focused on the contractor finishing up the building and talking to the artists whose work she was going to display and sell, she'd let Mason Hull's calls go to voice mail.

Now that the contractor's crew had left for the night, she sat in the back office at the gallery playing back his voice mails. "Ms. Etheridge, if you do not agree to having special security for your gallery and specifically for your upcoming opening-night event, your policy will be terminated."

Terminated. Her father had to deal with that threat when he'd run Ethereal Gallery years ago. But it hadn't been an insurance company making the threat and it hadn't been a policy threatened with termination. The godfather of River City, Michigan, Viktor Chekov, had threatened her father and his partner's lives if they didn't make payments for security as well.

Despite Viktor Chekov finally being sent to prison a few years ago, this felt like his shakedown all over again. Maybe she should just let the company make good on their threat and terminate her policy. But with as long as her insurance agent and the underwriting department had taken to come up with the quote and insurance for her current policy, she wouldn't have time to go through that process again with another company before she opened. Insurance was also required because of the loans she'd taken out to renovate and pay off the back taxes on the building.

So she was stuck. She would have to pay up, just as her father had, for security. And she resented the hell out of it. A growl of frustration escaped her lips, and another one echoed it. She glanced down at the rottweiler curled up under the table she was using as a desk and smiled. "Shh, Angel, go back to sleep."

She played the next voicc mail from Hull. "Ms. Etheridge, I am sending over representatives from the Payne Protection Agency to assess your security needs from installing an alarm system to providing armed guards."

Armed guards?

For what? She hadn't told the insurance company about the break-ins and the threats left behind; she hadn't even reported them because she hadn't wanted anything to raise her rates higher than they already were. So why would he insist on armed guards?

The gallery would not be open for two weeks, so valuables hadn't been added yet. And since the break-ins stopped, the only people going in and out besides herself were the contractor's crew. The building had sat vacant since her father's stroke six and a half years ago. At fifty-five, he'd been young to have a stroke, but she knew the stress that had driven him to it. Viktor Chekov had driven him to it. Despite sitting vacant for so long, it hadn't needed major updates. The electrical and mechanical had been up to code. She just needed to update the public restrooms, install more lights and paint the dingy walls. Then she would have the perfect backdrop for the art that would be arriving shortly.

Maybe that was why Hull figured she needed the armed guards, for the artwork she'd been able to charm owners into letting her borrow for the grand reopening, as well as any works she would offer for sale. She had some magnificent pieces being entrusted to her to display. So she couldn't really argue that security wasn't necessary; it was. But…

"I don't need armed guards," she said as she ran her bare foot over Angel's glossy black fur. Her shoes were lying next to him beneath her makeshift desk. "I have you."

Angel moaned in his sleep.

She chuckled. "Nobody has to know that you're more of a pussycat than a guard dog."

Her last boyfriend had left both of them, like her mother had left her father and her years ago. Blair had been more upset about the guy abandoning Angel than over his leaving her. Years ago, after her mom left and her dad shipped her off to boarding school, she'd realized it was smarter and safer to rely on no one but yourself. To be independent.

So she hadn't been upset when her ex had found, to quote him, "Someone who has more time for me than you do. Someone who makes me feel like a priority."

She couldn't deny she hadn't made him a priority because he hadn't been. Getting her art degree and master's in business had been her main focus, but having to take classes part-time while she'd worked to support herself and pay for school had made what would have taken five or six years nearly a decade instead. So she actually understood Trevor leaving her for someone who'd paid him more attention. Unfortunately for Angel, that someone had cats and hadn't wanted a dog around.

"You wouldn't have minded the kitties," she said.

He was so gentle with all creatures. But she was glad that Trevor had left the loving rottweiler with her. Angel never made her feel guilty for being busy and was always there for her, loving her unconditionally.

Nobody else, not even her father, had ever really loved Blair like that. She'd always figured that it was because, with her long, straight black hair and green eyes, she looked so much like the woman who'd broken his heart and hers. So to earn his love, she'd done everything he'd wanted, like not fighting when he sent her off to boarding school. And when the money had run out and he couldn't afford it anymore, she'd come back with dyed hair and colored contacts. And she'd never, ever asked him about her mother, knowing that the questions were too painful. For him. And for her.

But really, her mother had answered everything that mattered in the letter, which was the only thing she'd left behind besides the people who'd loved her. She'd said that she'd had to chase her muse and that being a wife and mother was stifling her talent. After everything Dad had done for her—starting the gallery, devoting all his time and energy to make it a success to showcase her talent—she'd still left them.

Maybe because she'd left, he'd never realized that success, or maybe it was because of Viktor Chekov. Or maybe after she'd left, his heart hadn't been in it anymore. It had been too broken, and eventually eighteen months ago, five years after the stroke had debilitated him, his heart had stopped working entirely.

She blinked away the tears that filled her eyes at the thought of him. Being back here, in the gallery where he'd spent so much of his life, had her missing him more. It didn't seem right to be here without him when he'd always been here even with Viktor Chekov threatening him, even after his wife deserted him, and his business partner had gone to prison. No matter what had happened, he hadn't given up on the gallery. He'd kept trying to make a success of the place; maybe he'd wanted to prove something to his artist wife despite her leaving him. Or maybe he'd wanted to prove something to himself.

Or maybe to Blair.

She didn't know why he would have, though, because she had loved him unconditionally. But perhaps she was here now to prove herself to him by making the dream he'd had a reality. That the gallery would be independent and successful and so would Blair. She didn't need a partner, business or personal, to inspire her or help her. She wanted to do this for herself, as much as for her father, so that she would be self-sufficient and self-supporting. And nobody would ever hurt her like her mother had hurt her father and her.

Angel growled again, but this wasn't an echo of hers that he instinctively uttered in his sleep. His body tensed beneath her foot. Then, his nails scraping against the polished concrete floor, he scooted out from beneath the desk. Black hair standing up on the nape of his thick neck, he ran out the office door.

"What the hell..." Her pulse quickening with fear, Blair jumped up to follow him out. He wasn't heading toward the front of the building, where the gallery was; instead he was heading down the hall toward the storage areas and the door to the back alley.

She could hear that door rattling now as someone tried to open it. Angel pounced against that door, his front paws pushing against the metal as if trying to keep out whoever wanted inside. He didn't react like this. Ever. Not to unsolicited salespeople or even the mailman.

"Angel!" she exclaimed as fear still pounded in her heart. Someone was out there trying to get in, and she wasn't sure how much protection Angel would be if that person got inside, or if she and her dog would be in danger just like all those messages had warned.

That last threat ran through her mind now. *Leave or die!*

Too late to leave now.

Chapter 2

"Isn't this kind of late to show up here?" Ivan asked from the passenger seat of the Payne Protection Agency SUV that one of his bosses pulled up to a curb outside a dark brick, two-story building. "The place isn't even open during the day yet."

"Well, we need to get the system installed before it opens for business," Milek said.

"But tonight? We're not going to get anything installed this late."

"Hull said he left her a message that we were coming here tonight to assess what kind of security system the building needs to protect it," Milek said.

"Yeah, but we have to be able to get inside to do that, and it doesn't look like anybody is here," he pointed out. It was ten at night, and while the bars and restaurants in the area were still open, the shops next to the gallery were already closed and dark, like the gallery. At least the gallery appeared dark because boards were over its front windows. "They think this place will be ready to open in two weeks?"

"The boards might be over the windows to prevent people looking inside before it's ready to open," Milek said. "But we do need to see inside..."

What was he suggesting? Breaking into houses and businesses like they used to, when they were kids?

Ivan had stopped doing that a long time ago. And he wouldn't have accepted the Kozminskis' job offer if he'd thought they were still doing it.

"So we should wait until morning and until someone is actually here," Ivan insisted. "And we should definitely make sure the owner actually wants us here." He wasn't comfortable with the way the insurance company was strong-arming clients into hiring the Payne Protection Agency for security; it reminded him too much of his uncle.

"Mason Hull tried all day to make contact with the owner, and he's concerned that he wasn't able to. So he's worried about his client as well as this place. His company is insuring the building and the collection that will be here for a lot of money. He wanted us to come out tonight to check to see if the owner is here and if the building is secure."

"Is he worried about the person? Or is he worried that they already took off with the valuables?" Ivan asked. "That makes no sense if they really intend to open up the place again." Those boarded-up windows made him wonder about that, though. "How would they even collect if they're not around to cash the insurance-settlement checks? I don't understand what Hull is so worried about that he wants us to come out here so late."

Milek shrugged. "I don't know."

"Well, I don't like it," Ivan admitted. He didn't want to do anything like he used to for his uncle all those years ago, when he hadn't had a choice. He had a choice now. When Ivan had finally gotten away from his uncle, he'd vowed to never work for anyone else that he didn't respect. While he respected the Kozminskis, he wasn't sure about this Hull person. "I don't trust this CEO guy."

Milek chuckled. "I think you let my brother's suspicious mind get to you."

Garek wasn't suspicious so much as more realistic than his younger brother. Milek was artistic instead.

"And who are the *they* who own the gallery?" Ivan asked uneasily. He could remember some of the names of the people from his past with his uncle, a past he wished he could forget, but then that would also mean forgetting people he'd loved, like his dad and his mom. Trying to keep their memories alive was why he kept his last name and why he'd returned to River City.

"Blair Etheridge," Milek said.

The name rang a bell of familiarity in Ivan's mind. He closed his eyes and tried to summon his memories of this place. While he'd never been here, he'd overheard his uncle talking about the gallery and talking about the people who'd owned it. "Etheridge was one of the previous owners. And the first name of the other guy was Blair."

"Must be an heir of Etheridge's then," Milek said. "I don't know much about them, not even if they're a man or a woman. Garek was the one talking to Hull, but since I have more experience with the art world, I'm taking lead on this assignment."

Ivan nearly snorted. Milek Kozminski was a world-renowned artist. "Yeah, you have more experience."

"I might also consider offering some of my work for sale here," he said. "But..."

"You want to check the place out first," Ivan said. And he reached for his door handle. "Let's see if anyone's around..." While he doubted there was, he headed toward the front of the building, but even the door was boarded over. "Must be a rear entrance..."

"Probably through here," Milek said, gesturing toward a space between the dark brick of the gallery building and another redbrick retail space next to it.

The alley was narrow and dark, so Ivan stepped in front of his boss. That whole impulse to protect was ingrained in him. And while Milek held his own as a co-owner of the Payne Protection Agency, Ivan didn't want anything to happen to him. Ivan knew all too well that bad things often happened in dark alleys. And he was just a few steps into the alley when he heard pounding and barking.

"Watch out!" Ivan yelled over his shoulder at his boss. And as he did, something came sailing toward him. It struck the asphalt before him, and a clanging sound bounced off the brick walls on either side of the alley as the crowbar hit the ground. He rushed forward just as someone, dressed all in black, started off in the other direction.

"Check the gallery," Milek yelled. "I'll try to catch them."

Ivan would have preferred it the other way, especially since his boss had a wife and kids. Ivan would have rather chased the person in black. But then the door, which had been pried partially open, swung out, and something big and black bounded out toward him. Its teeth were bared, and it was growling at him. Maybe Milek was safer chasing the person who'd already dropped their weapon than trying to fend off this beast.

Unlike his coworkers, Ivan could carry a weapon, and he pulled out his gun now, focusing the barrel on the beast that bounded toward him.

"Don't shoot!" Blair screamed, her heart pounding like someone had been pounding on that door moments ago. It must have been him. At the moment, she didn't care why; all she cared about was that he didn't hurt her dog. "Don't shoot him!"

"Tell him to heel," the man said, his voice deep and low, like the growls coming out of Angel. But then Angel whimpered and jumped down.

"Did you hurt him?" she asked.

"Hurt *him*?" the guy asked as if incredulous. "I didn't touch him. He attacked me."

"You were trying to break in!" she yelled, her fear turning to anger now. Was this the person who'd left the messages scrawled on the walls? But he didn't look homeless, like she'd thought the person who'd left those threats must be. He looked...clean, his blond hair shimmering in the floodlight that illuminated the alley, and incredibly handsome.

He shook his head. "That wasn't me. I'm with the Payne Protection Agency. We saw someone trying to break in. My boss is chasing him..." He gestured down the alley.

She wasn't sure if she should believe him. But how else would he have known about the Payne Protection Agency unless he was actually working with them?

"Milek's walking back now," the man said. "Alone."

She peered in the direction he'd pointed and saw the outline of a tall man with light-colored hair, similar to the man who stood in front of her. But the man walking back toward them had long hair, whereas this guy's hair was buzzed short and was even lighter blond, while his eyes were dark and big and soulful, like Angel's eyes.

But she refused to be distracted or sucked into those fathomless depths. She scoffed, "So he didn't catch him..." It seemed a bit convenient to her, like maybe the whole thing was a setup to prove that she needed security.

Goose bumps rose along her skin over how much it reminded her of the troubles her father had faced while trying to do business in River City. But she'd been told that things had changed in the years that she'd been gone, pursuing her art degree in Europe. The godfather of River City was in prison now, and the corruption in the police department had been expunged. Even Luther Mills, the notorious drug dealer, was no longer a threat, since he was dead. She wished Viktor Chekov was dead, too, because surely all the years of dealing with him had caused first her father's stroke, and then his heart failure and subsequent death.

She studied the two men again. Both were so tall and imposing. They looked more like danger than security to her, especially the one with the shorter hair and dark unfathomable eyes. "And you're both from the Payne Protection Agency?"

"Yes," the man with the longer hair said and he extended his hand. "I'm Milek Kozminski."

Instead of easing her fear, his claim increased it, making her heart pound fast and hard again. She ignored his hand and edged closer to Angel, trying to keep the rottweiler's big body between her and the men. "You're lying," she said. "Milek Kozminski is an artist."

"He is also in business with his brother, Garek, and his sister-in-law, Candace Baker," the other man replied. "Garek and Milek are brothers-in-law of the founder of the Payne Protection Agency, Logan Payne."

She narrowed her eyes and studied the man's dark eyes, trying to see if that was actually sincerity in the chocolatey brown depths.

"I really am Milek Kozminski," the other man maintained. "And Mason Hull was insistent that my agency come out to evaluate your building as soon as possible, especially when he wasn't able to make contact with you at all today. It is your building, right?"

She nodded. "Yes." She'd inherited more debt and back taxes than anything else, though, so it had taken her a while to clear probate with a clean deed, but she had that now as well as all the debt, too, just in her own name. "I'm Blair Etheridge." But she didn't hold out a hand. She didn't want to touch either of these men. "I don't understand why Hull is so insistent on my getting security now," she said. It wasn't as if she'd told him about the break-ins and the messages left for her. She'd been worried if she had that he would cancel her policy before the gallery even opened. "I still have a couple of weeks to go before the opening."

"But someone was just trying to break into your building," the other man pointed out. He gestured at the doorframe. "And he nearly got in."

She patted Angel, but her hand was shaking as she did it. That pounding on the door and the near break-in, after those messages, had rattled her, but she didn't want to admit it. Because she still wasn't convinced that these men or the insurance CEO weren't behind it. "Angel would have protected me." But the rottweiler moved away from her toward the stranger and licked his hand, as if apologizing for growling at him earlier.

The man turned over his enormous hand and ran it gently over Angel's head. Her faithful companion sounded more like a kitten purring than a guard dog as he leaned closer to the man. Then he dropped down and rolled onto his back to let the stranger rub his belly. The big man chuckled as he leaned down to scratch the soft fur.

Blair spared Angel a brief glare of irritation. But she didn't need man or beast to protect her. She could protect herself. When she was so young and her dad had shipped her off to boarding school, she'd learned to rely only on herself. "I'm sure that person was probably just one of the homeless people who'd been living inside the building while it was abandoned. Despite the contractor's crew and police getting them to leave, they keep coming back."

"If that was the case, they would have run when they heard the dog barking," the man pointed out. "They kept hammering at the door with a crowbar instead. They were trying to get to you."

A sudden chill rushed over her, and she crossed her arms. Had someone really been after her? *Leave or die.* The threat flitted through her mind, but someone was just trying to scare her into abandoning the building. Or maybe they were trying to scare her into paying a lot for security, like Viktor Chekov had forced her dad and his partner to pay, or the building had been vandalized and lives threatened. She edged a little closer to the open door behind her, ready to rush back in, and slam and lock it. "They?" She repeated the word he'd used.

"I couldn't see if it was a man or a woman," he replied. And he turned toward Milek Kozminski. "Did you get a better look?"

Kozminski shook his head. "No, they disappeared once they got out of the alley."

Again, this all felt very convenient to her. "It still could have been one of the homeless," she insisted. "They were hard to get out of the building and they keep coming back." She sucked in a breath and then admitted, "They even left some messages on the walls, saying that I should leave it alone."

"Then you are in danger," the man said.

And she hadn't even told him about the worst of those messages. Did he know? Had one of them written it to scare her into hiring them? But that was probably all they were trying to do.

"Scare. Not hurt me," she said. "And I don't scare easily." She wanted that out there, wanted them both to be aware that she wouldn't be intimidated, like Viktor Chekov had intimidated her dad and his partner. Her dad's partner, the man for whom she'd been named, had either been more scared than her father or more greedy, because he'd done more for Chekov than pay him to leave the gallery alone.

"Sometimes it's smart to be scared," the man replied. "It makes a person more cautious."

She bristled. He had no idea how cautious she was, how carefully she protected herself. That was why it hadn't hurt when Trevor left her or any of the other boyfriends she'd had over the years…because she'd never cared about them. After losing the people she'd loved the most, when her mom had left and when her dad had sent her away, she hadn't let herself get close to anyone else again. And she would *never* let herself rely on anyone.

"That's why Mason Hull requested we install a security system for you," Milek Kozminski said. "He wants to be cautious because you will be receiving the pieces you're going to display soon. Those are very valuable items."

She couldn't deny that; she'd worked hard to get those pieces on loan and available for consignment at the gallery. But she didn't have all of the art she wanted yet. "I've reached out to your agent," she said. She wasn't sure if the agent had even bothered to pass along her messages, though. Milek Kozminski could display his art anywhere. But he was here. And certainly a man like him wouldn't be trying to scare her. He had nothing to gain. But the other man…

He seemed intent on making her afraid. Of him? Or just afraid?

Even though she was tempted to press Milek to let her showcase his art in the gallery, she focused on his employee instead. "And who are you?"

"I told you, I work security for the Payne Protection Agency."

"I mean what is your name?" And he must have known that but for some reason was reluctant to introduce himself.

"It's Ivan…"

She tensed as she waited for the surname. "And?"

"Chekov."

From the way he said it, almost regretfully, he clearly knew what that name would mean to her. He had to be related to the bastard who'd terrorized this city for so many years, who'd terrorized her father. There just weren't that many Chekovs in southwestern Michigan. A gasp slipped through her lips, and she turned toward his boss. "Is this some kind of sick joke? What the hell is going on? Because there is no way I believe a Chekov is here to protect anything." *Let alone me.* Because a Chekov had pretty much ruined her life growing up and forced her father into an early grave.

"I am nothing like my uncle," Ivan said.

"He isn't," Kozminski chimed in.

But she shook her head. "I don't believe you, and I don't want anything to do with you. Get out of here before I call the police."

"You do need to call the police," Ivan Chekov said. "You need to report this attempted break-in."

Maybe nothing had changed in River City since she'd been gone because why would he want her to call the police if he was behind that attempted break-in? Unless he knew the police wouldn't do anything to him, unless they were on his payroll just like they'd been on his uncle's.

And if that was the case, she wasn't going to be any more successful than her father had been at running the gallery. In fact, it might wind up killing her just as it had wound up killing him. But not trying at all would kill her, too. She had to fulfill this promise she'd made to herself, to prove that she could do it. And she would…no matter what it cost her.

Deep in the shadows farther down the alley, the person listened and watched the two men and the woman talking outside that damaged back door to the gallery.

The person held their breath, careful to make no noise, to draw no attention to their hiding place. They didn't want to be seen, to be identified.

Damn good thing they were wearing gloves because they had left no prints on that crowbar. Nothing to link what had happened here back to them this time or any of the other times they had broken into the building before tonight. The messages they'd left had disappeared. She'd had contractors clean or paint over them. So there was no linking those back to the message writer, either.

And even if the woman actually called the police this time, as the men were urging her to do, the authorities would probably believe what the woman claimed, that the homeless were just trying to get her to go away so they could reclaim the building as theirs.

The point of those messages was to get her to go away, to abandon that building and her ill-advised plan to reopen the gallery. But Blair Etheridge and those two men had no idea what was really going on. And that was good. That was the way it needed to stay until it was all over, and the person got away with murder once again.

Chapter 3

Blair Etheridge had finally called the police; maybe more to get rid of him than to report the attempted break-in. It was an attempt that would have succeeded had he and Milek not shown up when they had. Ivan's stomach churned at the thought of what might have happened to Blair and her dog. That intimidating-looking beast was too sweet to go after anyone. Even when the rottweiler had jumped on Ivan, he hadn't tried to bite him or even snapped his teeth; he'd just slobbered on him, like he was slobbering now. Licking his hand so that Ivan would pet him again.

But Ivan wasn't sure that Blair wanted him to touch her dog or anything else right now. Even as she spoke to Milek and the officer who'd shown up to take the report, she kept looking at him with that expression that also made his stomach churn. He hated that just the mention of his surname could turn people off like it did. But he couldn't change it because that would feel like wiping out his father, just like Viktor had wiped him out. Ivan wanted to remember and honor his father, so he couldn't get rid of the only thing that Ivan Chekov Senior had left him: his name.

Doing so would make Ivan's life a hell of a lot easier, though. Yet Ivan wouldn't know what to do with easy; his life had been anything but. Maybe that was why he couldn't stop staring back at Blair Etheridge. She was definitely going to be difficult. While she had made it clear that she didn't want protection from him, she'd also made it clear that she didn't want protection from anyone else, either. She wanted to pretend that what happened tonight had nothing to do with her and the gallery.

The young officer seemed to agree with her that it had likely been a homeless person trying to break in. Apparently, he'd been one of the officers who'd helped evict the squatters from the premises. But Ivan didn't believe that had been a homeless person who'd tried breaking in a short while ago. There was something else going on here, something that might include the suspicious and overly involved insurance company and maybe even the past, when her father, her father's partner and Ivan's uncle had had some kind of arrangement.

"I should not be on this case," Ivan whispered to Milek the minute his boss walked up to him and the dog. Angel didn't pay any attention to Milek, though; he kept licking Ivan's hand until he finally gave in and petted him. "I don't know why the insurance CEO specifically requested me, like Garek said, but it's a bad idea."

Milek shrugged. "I think he wanted to see her reaction to your name."

"You saw it," Ivan said. "She wants nothing to do with a Chekov. If the CEO had any doubts that she was going into the same business her father and his partner were in with my uncle, her reaction proves she doesn't want that. And she doesn't want me anywhere around her."

"If she truly believes it was a homeless person, she has no reason to ban you from the premises, which is exactly what the young officer just pointed out to her, as well as the fact that you have no record."

Not as an adult. But his juvenile record, when his uncle had forced him to steal, like he had so many other desperate kids, was sealed.

"It doesn't matter," Ivan said. "It's her place. She should have the say in who she allows inside it." That was why, after giving his statement, he'd stuck close to that door to the alley. One, to make sure that nobody tried to get inside before it could be secured, and another, because he hadn't felt comfortable venturing farther inside after she'd threatened to call the police on him.

"Not when it's open to the public," Milek said. "Anyone can come inside then, and she needs to have the proper security because of that."

"What do you mean?" Blair asked as she joined them near that back door. She held a card with a report number on it. No crime techs had come to collect evidence. When giving their reports on what they'd seen, both Ivan and Milek had remembered that the shadowy figure they'd nearly caught had been wearing gloves and maybe even a mask. They hadn't gotten a good look at the person's head.

If only they'd seen more…

If only they'd seen enough to identify the person…

The officer had promised to pull up security footage around the building, but before he'd arrived, Milek had already called Payne Protection Agency's technical expert, Nikki Payne-Ecklund, to see what she could find, and probably hack into, in the area in the way of video footage.

"Somebody tried to get into an empty building," Milek began.

Ivan jumped in. "But it wasn't empty. She and her dog were inside." And from Angel's barking that had been obvious.

Milek nodded. "So there is no telling who might try to

get inside when the artwork is here for display. You need security for it—"

"And for you," Ivan interjected again. He didn't give a crap about material things; people mattered most. He glided his hand over Angel's big head. And animals like this sweet pet.

Blair narrowed her green eyes and studied his face.

And he held up his hands. "I know you don't want me. And that's fine—"

"No, it's not," Milek said, interrupting him this time. "You're damn good at what you do, Ivan." He turned toward their potential client. "He nearly got killed protecting a child a short while ago. He's the kind of man who would willingly give up his life for another. Who gave all he had to help another member of our team recover his son and future mother-in-law, who'd been taken hostage."

A gasp slipped through her lips. "The child from the news…from the Amber Alert?"

Milek nodded. "Henry and Mrs. Croft are safe now due to the combined efforts of our branch of the Payne Protection Agency."

Ivan knew that Garek and Candace usually handled the sales aspect of the agency, but Milek was doing a damn good job. He could see that Blair wasn't quite as tense as she'd been. Maybe that was just because of the relief that Henry had been rescued, though. The little guy had gotten to Ivan, too, and he would have willingly given up his life for the kid. Fortunately he hadn't had to. He'd just gotten that damn concussion. His head was throbbing now because of it, or maybe it throbbed over how sick he felt about Blair's reaction to his name.

He hated that all anyone remembered of the Chekovs was his evil uncle and probably his uncle's daughter, Ivan's cousin, who'd killed some people, too. Nobody remembered his father, who'd been a good, hard-working man.

Blair was staring at him, but it wasn't with that look of horror she'd had earlier. It was with consideration. But she shook her head. "I have intended all along to install some type of security system in the gallery," she said. "But I don't think it needs to be to the extent that the insurance company is demanding."

"They might demand even more when they hear about this break-in attempt," Milek said.

A curse slipped out of her lips, and that glare was back on her face. Her dog stepped away from Ivan and brushed up against her, as if trying to soothe her. "I still don't know if this is all a scheme just to get me to pay out all this money for security and for insurance and..."

"It could be," Ivan agreed.

And Milek's neck snapped as he turned toward him.

"But we're not involved," Ivan continued. "And whatever the insurance company and whoever else, even you, have going on with this place, we will do our job. We'll protect the building and the valuables and you."

Then he waited for her to claim that she didn't need anyone to protect her or to try to throw him out again. But she said nothing; she just stood there staring at him. And another feeling rushed over him, one he'd not felt for a while.

Attraction.

With her black hair and green eyes, she was beautiful. But it wasn't just her physical attributes that drew his interest. She was also smart and strong and stubborn. And for some reason he found all those traits so damn sexy. He found her so damn sexy.

Blair wanted to throw Ivan Chekov out of the building and out of her life. But she had a feeling that would solve only one of the problems she had: her strange awareness of him. Whenever he looked at her, she could physically feel his gaze on her, as if his big hands were moving over her skin instead of over Angel's big canine head. Ivan's body was big, like his hands. His shoulders were broad and his chest muscular, pressing against the thin material of his T-shirt. His thighs were muscular, too, stretching the worn denim of his jeans. She couldn't stop looking at him, like he was a work of art that kept drawing her attention. And every time she looked, she saw something different. His muscular body could have been a sculpture. And his face…

It was all sharp angles, with those deep-set, dark eyes that stared as intently at her as she was staring at him. So intently that she'd forgotten what they were talking about; she'd even forgotten to breathe because her lungs were burning. She sucked in a breath then released it in a ragged sigh.

Because she knew these men were right. About everything.

She wanted to think that whoever had attempted to get inside was one of the homeless who'd been squatting in the building, but once they'd heard Angel, they would have known the place wasn't empty and stopped. But they hadn't stopped until Ivan Chekov and Milek Kozminski had shown up. She'd also suspected they might have been trying to break in that back door or at least scare her into thinking someone was trying. But Milek Kozminski was so famous and rich that he didn't need her money, so why would he take a risk like that to his freedom and his reputation?

Now, Ivan Chekov…

She knew nothing about him but his name. But the officer had verified he had no record. The officer had even made the comment that she was lucky that Payne Protection had shown up when they had. Because they might have saved her.

She didn't like to think she'd needed saving, though, or that she'd been in any kind of danger at all. But she was also realistic. She'd seen the damage to the door and that crowbar lying in the alley. So someone had been trying to get to her. And she couldn't believe that Milek Kozminski would have stood by while his employee tried scaring her like that. But if Ivan hadn't tried to scare her, who had?

Even if he hadn't, she still couldn't bring herself to trust him, not with his being a Chekov. But as long as his boss was supervising him, maybe this Chekov wouldn't try to hurt her.

"I already intended to install a security system," she reiterated. "So I'll agree to have the Payne Protection Agency do the work for that." Because she needed to remind them and that damn insurance company that it was her choice, not theirs. This was her business now, and her life. She wasn't the kid she'd once been who'd had no choice when her mother left and her father sent her away to school.

Milek Kozminski nodded. "That was why Ivan and I came here tonight, to assess what you need. I'll do that now and secure the building until we can get the new system and a new door installed."

She glanced at the door that wouldn't close entirely now. She'd nearly forgotten how badly it was damaged. If it wasn't fixed, she really would have squatters back in the building. And getting them out had taken so long, with so many calls to the police to oust them with threats of trespassing charges. "Damn, I do need to get that door taken care of."

But it had to be pushing midnight now. The attempted break-in hadn't been a huge priority, so it had taken a while for an officer to arrive and even longer for him to write up the report of their accounts of what happened.

"Don't worry. I'll take care of it," Milek said. "You can go home. It's getting late."

"And leave you two alone in the building?" she asked.

"There's nothing here for anyone to take," Milek pointed out.

And he was right. The artwork had yet to arrive; hopefully all the promised pieces would get here in time for the opening. But she had to make sure that once they arrived, those items were secure. So she sighed again. "Okay. Go ahead. Do what you have to do."

She was suddenly eager to get home. Not just to rest. She doubted she would sleep at all with the adrenaline and the awareness zipping through her veins. She was eager to get away from *him*.

But then *he* said, "I think I should go home with you."

Her heart jumped with the shock of his words, and a laugh bubbled out of her. "Are you insane?" she asked. Was he propositioning her right here, in front of his boss?

"No. I'm being cautious," Ivan said. "As Milek just pointed out, there's nothing here for anyone to take. And I don't believe someone was trying to break down a door just to find a place to crash for the night. I think someone was trying to get to *you*."

Her heart jumped again. *Someone* was getting to her; *he* was. She shook her head, denying her own thoughts as well as his words. But then she remembered that last message she'd found scrawled on the brick of her office wall. *Leave or die*. And she had to suppress a shudder of foreboding.

"Do you have any idea who might be after you?" Ivan asked. "Do you have an obsessive ex?"

She snorted. "No."

"An anonymous stalker?" he asked. "Any enemies? Anyone who has threatened or tried to hurt you in the past?"

She shook her head even as those messages flitted through her mind again. They weren't stalking her; they were after the building, a shelter from the streets. "Seriously, nobody has any reason to go after me. I have no enemies." She usually didn't get close enough to anyone to make enemies or friends.

"Somebody was really determined to get in here," Ivan said. "And I don't think it was just to scare you. You need protection."

Somebody had tried hard to break down that door; they would have gotten inside if not for Payne Protection showing up when they had.

"He's right," Milek said to her. Then he turned to Ivan. "You should go home with her, and I'll deal with securing the gallery for the night."

"Nobody is going home with me but Angel," Blair said. "He will protect me."

Ivan snorted. "Yeah, right."

"No, he will," she insisted. "If someone tries to hurt me..."

"If they want to hurt you, they won't hesitate to hurt him, too," Ivan pointed out.

Fear gripped her again as it had earlier tonight. When he'd pointed that gun at Angel, she'd realized then that her dog could get hurt badly. Even moments before that, when she hadn't been able to get Angel away from the back door that person had been pounding on, she'd worried about him. About them both. While Ivan hadn't pulled the trigger, the other person might have hurt Angel. If the Payne Protection Agency hadn't shown up when they had, and that person had broken inside, that crowbar might have been used on her dog and on her. She flinched at the horrific thought.

"If you won't let me protect you, at least let me protect *him*," Ivan said, and his lips curved into a slight grin. Obviously, he realized how much she cared about her pet. Angel kept her from being lonely now that her dad was gone. Even though she hadn't lived in the same country with her father for years, they'd stayed in contact through phone calls and texts, and after his stroke, she'd FaceTimed with the nurse aides' help.

She shook her head again. "My house has an alarm." But only because the apartment she rented over a carriage-house garage had come with one. "I will be safe there."

"Take the SUV," Milek told his employee, "and follow her home and make sure she gets safely inside."

Ivan nodded.

Irritation pricked Blair's ego that they were talking about her like she was just an assignment, just a subject to protect and not an actual person. But maybe that was how bodyguards, or whatever they were, worked. "Again, it's not necessary—"

"But it's happening," Ivan said. "And the longer we stand here arguing about it, the later it's getting, and I thought you were tired."

"I'm not tired," she said. She was freaking exhausted. She'd been working long hours trying to get the gallery up and running, and even when she did go to bed, she couldn't sleep because her mind wouldn't stop spinning with all the things she needed to do. But she wasn't the only one who looked exhausted.

He looked tired, too, with dark shadows beneath his dark eyes. How badly had he been hurt when he'd been trying to find that missing child and the little boy's grandmother?

But she didn't want to ask him about that; she didn't want to give herself any reason to be even more drawn to him than she already was. Especially since he was going home with her.

Her pulse quickened at the thought. It had been a while since a man had gone home with her or since she had gone to a man's home. Maybe that was why she was so aware of Ivan Chekov, because she'd been so busy getting the gallery open again that she'd neglected all her other needs.

Not that she needed Ivan Chekov for *that* or even for protection. But she couldn't deny that someone had tried to get inside and had left those messages. Would they actually carry out that last threat?

If she did need protection, could she trust a Chekov for that? Hell, she couldn't trust anyone, let alone a Chekov. But she couldn't imagine that Milek Kozminski would risk his business and his reputation employing someone he couldn't trust. Maybe the only way she would learn what Ivan Chekov was really like was to keep him just close enough to keep an eye on him. Also, the police and his boss knew that he was with her, so if something happened to her, he would be their number-one suspect. Hell, their only suspect, because she couldn't think of anyone else who actually wished her harm. At the moment, though, she was too tired to think at all, and like he'd said it was getting late.

He could follow her home, but he wasn't going inside with her. He wasn't getting any closer to her than he already had. Milek Kozminski and that young officer might believe Ivan Chekov was trustworthy, but Blair didn't. That probably had less to do with his name than with the way he made her feel. Or maybe just because he made her feel again. That was a distraction she couldn't afford right now, not with the success of the gallery on the line. If Ivan Chekov was right, that might not be all that was. Her life might be on the line as well. *Leave or die.*

She'd figured that was an empty threat to make her stop renovating so the squatters could move back in. But what if someone really wanted to kill her?

But who and why?

It made no sense.

Once alone in the gallery, Milek could see the potential for the space. He could already tell what Blair Etheridge intended. She'd taken out most of the second floor, leaving the space with two-story-high exterior walls. From the five-gallon cans of paint sitting on tarps on the polished concrete floor, it looked as though the brick was going to be painted white. There were splotches of paint on some of the walls, but that looked more like the color was being tested because it was darker in some places. Or maybe it had been used to cover up the messages she'd mentioned the homeless had left for her.

The white would be a perfect backdrop for paintings, especially his, as he liked to use bright, vibrant colors.

Some of the other interior walls remained, dividing up the main floor into different areas. Those walls were at odd angles, though, so would probably have to be removed and repositioned in order to get the most display space for art.

Although the front windows and door were boarded over, the glass in them was tempered to keep out the sun, to protect the art. Milek also had to protect it. With so few exit doors and windows, it would be easy to secure the space with the proper equipment: alarms on those doors and windows, and cameras positioned around outside and a few inside as well. For added protection for the art, they would install sensors around the paintings and sculptures to set off alarms if anyone tried to touch or remove them.

He knew what kind of system to install to protect the space. But what about the woman? Was she in danger?

Ivan seemed to think so because he'd been insistent on protecting her. Milek was surprised that she'd actually agreed to his following her home. The way she'd reacted to his name…had been with such horror. Was that why the CEO had wanted Ivan on her security detail? To scare her?

But how would Hull have known about the history of the gallery concerning Ivan's uncle? How would he know any of that? Unless…

Garek was right and there was more to this assignment than appeared. He pulled his cell phone from his pocket and called his brother, which he could have done earlier but he wouldn't have been able to talk freely to him because he'd been with Ivan and Blair Etheridge. At the time, waiting for the police to arrive, he hadn't dared to leave them alone to step out to make a call. He grinned at the irony that they'd left together…even though they had been in separate vehicles.

"Damn," Garek answered, his voice gruff with sleep. "Are you in your studio and don't realize what time it is?"

"No. I'm still at the gallery."

"What? Why?" Garek asked, his voice sharp, as he was fully awake. "You were just supposed to do a quick assessment with Ivan. We didn't even know if you'd be able to get inside. What happened?"

"Someone else was trying to get inside with a crowbar," Milek said. "And the owner was still here."

Garek cursed again. "So Hull is right. There is reason to be concerned about the gallery and the owner."

"You have concerns, too," Milek reminded him. And now, so did Milek.

"Yeah, that whoever owns it now operates it like it was

in the past, as a way to launder money," Garek said. "And, like I suspected, the insurance-company CEO is probably very aware of those operations. Why else had Hull wanted Ivan specifically on this assignment? What was the new owner's reaction to hearing his name?"

"She wasn't happy," Milek replied.

"That still doesn't mean that the new owner isn't in business with Viktor Chekov, like the old ones were."

"No, she definitely reacted like she didn't want anything to do with any Chekov," Milek said in her defense.

Yet she had allowed him to follow her home.

"Well, Ivan isn't a Chekov like Viktor," Garek said. "He's a good man."

Maybe Milek and the young officer had convinced her that Ivan was trustworthy. "He insisted on sticking with her," Milek said. "To make sure she's safe."

"So you called me for a ride," Garek assumed.

"I could have called a rideshare company," Milek said.

"So that wasn't why you called," his brother said. "What's wrong? Need help at the gallery?"

He shook his head even though his brother couldn't see him. Then he sighed, a ragged sigh. "No. I'm not concerned about the gallery. I'll find a way to secure the back door for the night. But… I just have this feeling…"

"Penny Payne-Lynch's sixth sense about danger?" Garek asked.

He could have been teasing, but Milek knew that her sixth sense had been proven right more times than not. But maybe that was just because so many people in Penny's orbit put their lives in danger as bodyguards and law enforcement.

"I don't think it's a sixth sense as much as being worried about the reason that Ivan was specifically requested for this assignment," Milek admitted. "I'm hoping this isn't a setup. I don't want him getting hurt again."

"Ivan's also a pretty lucky man," Garek continued. "Or he wouldn't still be alive. His own uncle would have killed him long ago."

"The thing about luck, though, is that it seems to eventually run out," Milek said.

They had both experienced that themselves. While they'd gotten away with things, they'd also gotten caught as well. And the danger they'd faced…while it hadn't killed them, had hurt them. He didn't want Ivan getting hurt, and maybe it was Penny's sixth sense wearing off on him or maybe just logic. If someone had been trying to break into this building to get to Blair, then they would probably try again. And Ivan would do anything to protect her. Before Milek and Garek had hired him, they'd checked out his references: they all raved over how he'd put his life on the line for theirs.

Ivan would do the same for Blair Etheridge despite, or maybe because of, how she'd reacted to his last name.

Chapter 4

Protect.

His dad hadn't had time to tell him what or whom he'd wanted Ivan to protect. Himself? That was what he'd assumed for years because it had been just the two of them then. There had been no one else for him to protect. But then he'd realized that it hadn't necessarily been a person his father had been talking about; he could have wanted Ivan to protect his integrity or his heart or his soul. Or maybe even the family name.

Protect it. Make it stand for something besides pure evil like it did with Uncle Viktor.

Ivan hated how people reacted to hearing that name, like Blair Etheridge. He was surprised she'd actually agreed to let him follow her home. Once she and her dog climbed into her small SUV, he had more than half expected her to try to lose him, but she wasn't driving fast. Maybe because of the dog, she didn't want to risk him getting hurt. Her concern for the enormous rottweiler was probably the only reason she'd agreed to Ivan seeing her safely home.

He wasn't sure how safely she was going to get there because he had a feeling she wasn't the only one being followed. When they'd pulled away from the curb outside the boarded-up front of the gallery, Ivan had noticed another vehicle pulling away from several spaces behind them. Even though that vehicle was hanging back, it remained close enough that Ivan suspected it was following them. It hadn't turned off on any of the other streets they'd passed. And it would have been a hell of a coincidence for it to be heading in the same exact direction that they were at the same exact time, especially past midnight.

But coincidences did happen. Still, he would feel better if it wasn't back there, if it wasn't following him. But if he sped up or turned off on another street, he would lose Blair as well as the tail. And that tail might be the one who followed her back to her place.

So he couldn't take the risk of trying to lose it. But he kept the rearview mirror adjusted so he didn't lose sight of its headlights or of her taillights in the windshield. She turned again onto a street in one of the swankier burbs of River City. Big houses sat back from the road behind wrought-iron gates.

This was where she lived?

She had money then. Maybe the gallery business wasn't the only enterprise she'd assumed of her father's; maybe she was money laundering, too. While her father hadn't gone to prison for it like his partner, he couldn't have been totally unaware of what was going on with his business. He must have been involved, too. Ivan had been pretty young back then, so he wasn't entirely sure how the laundering had worked. But he knew that his uncle Viktor's art collection had been constantly in flux with pieces coming and going out of the house. Through insurance claims?

Was Mason Hull's Midwest Property and Casualty involved, too?

And what about Uncle Viktor?

Was he still running his business from his prison cell?

Rumor had it that Luther Mills had taken over once Garek Kozminski had brought the River City godfather to justice. Now, Luther was dead. So who was managing the crime empires that had once ruled River City? Or had the Payne Protection Agency and the new chief of police run most of the crime out of the city?

Ivan wanted to believe that, but he knew it wasn't true. Just a short time ago Henry and his grandmother had been kidnapped. And even though Henry's uncle had abducted them, it was still a crime.

Crime would never go away.

That was why any job in security was a good one, and the first one that Ivan had been able to find when he'd gotten away from his uncle. Big for his age, he'd started as a bouncer at bars while taking online classes. And then he'd moved to concert venues and up to private security for the rock stars and pop singers who'd noticed his protection at those concerts. People and things were always going to need protection. Like Blair Etheridge, even though she didn't want to admit it.

Brake lights flashed red in front of him, and she made an abrupt turn into a drive just as one of those sets of wrought-iron gates began to open. He turned in behind her, worried that she might close those gates and lock him out if he didn't get inside quickly. His front bumper nearly touched the back of hers as she slowed. Instead of following the circular drive toward the left and the enormous brick house with spotlights illuminating the front of it, she turned toward the right and a carriage house that stood in the dark. No lights glowed on it or within it.

He was especially glad he'd followed her. Even though there was a gate to keep out cars, the gates and fence had a scroll pattern with spaces wide enough for someone to squeeze through and wait in those very shadows for her. And when she left the garage to head toward the house, they could grab her and abduct her like little Henry and his grandmother had been abducted. Or they could hurt Blair or kill her right here on her own property.

Would that have happened at the gallery tonight if he and Milek hadn't arrived when they had? If that person with the crowbar had managed to get inside before they got there and scared him or her into running off?

The horrific thought chilled Ivan, and he quickly put his vehicle into Park and jumped out with the intention of checking those shadows. Even if she pulled inside the garage, she had to walk toward the house through that dark patch of the property. Ivan would suggest installing some security cameras here or at least extra lighting.

While he'd jumped out of his big, Payne Protection SUV, Blair sat in hers. But Angel barked and pawed at the glass of the window behind her. She'd harnessed him in so that he couldn't do anything other than touch the glass with his paws and then his big tongue.

Ivan chuckled. Angel was quite the character.

"Sure, you can laugh, you don't have to clean the window," Blair remarked.

And he realized she'd rolled down hers. "Do you have to clean it?" he asked. He gestured at the house behind him. "Don't you have servants for that?"

She snorted. "Servants?"

"You live in a mansion," he pointed out.

He once had, too, with his uncle, and he'd never been more miserable. And even though Uncle Viktor had had servants, Ivan had insisted on cleaning his own room. He hadn't wanted to owe his uncle anything. He'd hated even being with him, but nobody had believed him when he'd told them who'd killed his father. Of course, Uncle Viktor had paid someone for an alibi, and that person had been more believable than a traumatized eight-year-old child.

She stared at him through her open window, her brow furrowed as if she was confused. "That bothers you?"

He shook his head. "Not if *you* do." But he never wanted to live in one again. "That's your business."

"Yeah, which you and your boss and that damn insurance company are getting all up in," she said, her voice sharp with irritation.

He really couldn't blame her for being irritated with the situation. He didn't quite understand it himself. "I'm just trying to make sure you're safe," he said. "So I'll walk you up to the house."

"I don't live in the house," she said.

"What? Where do you live?"

She pointed toward the garage. "In there."

"You live in a garage?" he asked incredulously.

"In the apartment above it."

"But you said it has a security system."

She nodded. "It does. For the cars. Nobody can get in there." Angel whined from the back seat. "And if they do, my dog will slobber all over them."

Ivan glanced at the back window and chuckled again. "He sure will." As he smiled at the dog, he caught a reflection of something else in that back window, a glint of metal in the darkness on the other side of her vehicle. Realizing what that metal probably was, he tensed with fear and drew his Glock from its holster.

"What?" Blair asked.

"Get in the garage. Now!" He reached through her open window to hit the remote on the SUV visor. As the door wound up, he yelled, "Go. Go!"

His urgency must have penetrated because she pressed down on the accelerator and the SUV shot forward, and as it did, gunshots rang out. Bullets pinged off the metal of the other side of her vehicle.

"Go!" he shouted again. But once her SUV drove into the garage, he would have no cover. Nowhere to hide from the bullets. He could have followed her vehicle into the garage; he probably should have.

But he didn't want that son of a bitch to get away like he had in the alley. He wanted to catch him this time and stop him. But first, Ivan had to make sure he didn't get shot because then he would be leaving Blair with no protection at all.

The urgency in his voice compelled Blair to stomp on the accelerator. She drove so fast into the garage that she was barely able to stop before hitting one of the vintage vehicles inside it. That would get her evicted for sure if she damaged one of the collectibles.

But she wasn't worried about an eviction notice right now. She was worried about her life and Angel's and *his*.

What the hell had he been thinking? Why hadn't he come into the garage with her? Because once she drove away, she left him exposed to the bullets that had struck the passenger side of her SUV.

She'd gone through the gamut of emotions tonight. Annoyance. Fear. And then…

When he'd chuckled at Angel, she'd felt something else, something that burned low in her belly. He'd charmed her. And when he'd reached through that window to open the garage door, he might have saved her. If she shut it…

If she locked herself back inside…

But that left him out there. Alone.

And Blair knew all too well how it felt to be vulnerable and alone. But she also wasn't going to be able to help him if she got shot, too.

So she hit the garage door remote again and reached for her cell phone. Her landlord had probably already called the police. But she needed to make sure that help was coming. Because she had a feeling that Ivan was going to need it, and if that shooter got under the garage door before it closed, she was going to need it, too.

Just as the thought entered her mind, she caught sight of a shadow passing under that door. And Angel began to bark and growl, straining against the harness that held him against the back seat. Had the person gotten inside the door or had they just come up to it, trying to stop it from closing?

The door was closed now, but as big and shadowy as the garage was, with so many other vehicles parked in it, she had no way of knowing if the person was inside with her or outside with Ivan.

"Nine-one-one, what's your emergency?" The voice emanated from the Bluetooth speakers of her vehicle.

Angel barked louder.

Blair peered around the garage, but the light from the opener started to fade, leaving the space darker, casting more shadows. Anybody could have been hiding inside, crouched behind a vehicle, waiting to fire their gun at her.

"Nine-one-one, what's your emergency?" the operator asked again, louder, as if to be heard over the barking.

"I—I...want to report a shooting," Blair said, her voice cracking with fear.

"Is anyone injured?" the operator asked.

"I—I don't know..." But how could Ivan have avoided getting shot when she'd driven off and left him exposed?

He had to be hurt. Or he would be inside with her; he would have been the one who'd gotten under the door.

If anyone had…

She had no idea. It could have just been the shadow of someone standing close to the door as it had gone down. It might have been just a shadow and not a person. Because wouldn't the person have already started firing at her?

"Has the shooting stopped?" the operator asked.

Blair tilted her head to listen, but she could hear nothing but Angel's barks and growls. The dog was scared, more scared now than from the gunfire. The shooting must have stopped because surely she would have heard it even inside the garage, even with Angel carrying on.

But what did that mean? That the shooter was gone? Or that Ivan was?

"Please, send help right away," she pleaded. But she feared it might be too late for anyone to help Ivan.

He'd been more concerned about her safety and catching the shooter than he'd been about his own. What had his boss said? That he would willingly give up his life to protect someone else?

Had he done that tonight?

For her?

One down. One to go. They both had to die now; it would look less suspicious that way than targeting just one of them. The woman and the man had to die. That left more suspects, would make it harder to track the real murder back to them.

Just as that other murder had never been tracked…

Because no one knew about it.

And it had to stay that way. Killing these two would accomplish that. But in the distance sirens began to whine and then wail like that damn dog.

Someone had called the police, and they were on their way. Would there be time to finish her off, too?

Or would she get to live for a little while longer?

Chapter 5

Ivan dove so hard out of the line of fire that he nearly knocked himself out again when he struck a corner of the brick-and-stone carriage house. The oblivion of the concussion threatened again, trying to pull him back into the darkness. But he refused to go, just like he'd tried to refuse to go with his uncle all those years ago.

But he'd just been a kid then, so he hadn't won. He'd been helpless. And he hated that feeling so much that he desperately fought against it now, but several long moments passed with him struggling to clear his vision, to stay conscious.

And he had no idea where the shooter had gone. He'd stayed outside so that he could catch him but instead he'd lost him. And he might have lost Blair as well. Had the shooter managed to get inside the garage with her?

While Ivan had opened the overhead door, she would have had to shut it again. It was down now, but how long had it taken to completely close? Long enough for the shooter to get inside the garage with her?

Ivan had to get in there now, to make sure she was safe. He lurched to his feet and headed toward the side door. The handle didn't move, and he knew there was security. But he didn't care. He was the one who needed to keep Blair safe. And he wasn't sure if he'd already failed.

So he pointed his gun, which he'd managed to hang tightly to, toward the handle. And he fired until the handle snapped and the door crept open. An alarm blared. But he wasn't sure if he'd set it off or if the other shooter had.

"Blair!" he yelled.

Angel's barking echoed the alarm, and the dog frantically clawed at that back window now. But Ivan didn't see Blair in the driver's seat. He didn't see her at all.

Damn!

Was he already too late?

He noticed the glass broken on the front passenger's window. Had that happened outside the garage? Or since she'd pulled inside?

"Blair!" he shouted again.

And then shots rang out, pinging toward him from somewhere in the shadows of the garage. This time he managed to fire back, firing into the darkness, though.

The garage door hummed and shuddered as it went up. And then a shadow ducked under it and ran off toward those front gates, probably toward that vehicle that had followed him here. Ivan wanted to run after the person and keep shooting, but he first had to make sure that Blair was okay. She was the priority.

"Blair!" he shouted over the blaring alarm and Angel's frenzied barking. "Blair, are you alright?"

Dread and urgency shot through him, splitting him in two between wanting to stay and wanting to rush toward the car to make sure she was okay. But if he looked inside and she wasn't…

He couldn't imagine a woman as vital and independent and…beautiful being taken so soon from this world. "Blair…" he whispered now. And the whisper quieted Angel down some. Instead of barking, the big dog just whined.

"It's okay, boy," Ivan said softly as he began walking toward the vehicle.

But if Blair was hurt, it wasn't okay. Ivan had failed to protect.

He stepped closer to the driver's window that was still lowered from when she'd been talking to him outside the carriage house. But he couldn't see anyone in the front seat through the window.

"Blair?"

Was she lying down?

Hurt?

Or worse?

He stepped closer and crouched down to peer inside the window. But the driver's seat was empty. The only things in the front were glass fragments on the passenger's seat from that broken window.

"Blair!" he yelled.

Where the hell was she?

Had the shooter managed to drag her off somewhere?

Was Ivan so concussed that he'd missed the shooter pulling her through that garage door? He'd only seen one person. Or so he'd thought, but he hadn't been able to discern much more than a dark shadow. It could have been a man or a woman.

But if Blair hadn't been dragged off with the shooter, she had to be here somewhere. And he had to find her, to make sure that she wasn't hurt. But since she wasn't answering him, he was very afraid that she was.

"Blair..."

That was Ivan's voice. Without the sound of Angel's barking and gunshots reverberating in the garage and inside her head, Blair could hear more clearly now...even with the alarm still blaring. Maybe that was because the big service door was open now, and through it, the sirens she'd heard earlier were getting louder, too.

The police would be here soon.

But Ivan was here, and he was alive. Blair rolled out from underneath the vehicle, where she'd been hiding. "Are you alright?" she asked, feeling a twinge of guilt that she'd driven inside and left him exposed and alone.

But he was the bodyguard. And he must have been good at his job because she couldn't see any blood on him. Though he did look a bit unsteady when he turned toward her, as if he was slightly dizzy.

"What is it?" she asked. "Did you get hit?"

He shook his head and flinched. "No. I'm fine," he said. "What about you? What happened?"

"I saw something come under the garage door as it was closing, so I was going to crouch down and get out with Angel but the shot rang out..." She pointed toward the broken passenger window, and she was surprised to see how badly she was shaking. Earlier she'd had her doubts that she was in danger, or maybe she'd just been in denial. But now, she had to admit it was true. Someone wanted to hurt her, and she had no idea who or why.

"Are you okay?" he asked, and he stepped closer, putting his body between her and that open door as if afraid the shooter was still out there.

Were they?

"Blair? Are you okay?" he asked again, and this time he reached out, touching her face, sliding his fingers along her jaw.

She shivered as her nerve endings tingled with awareness. What was it about him? Why did he affect her so much? Or was it just the adrenaline from all the danger she'd faced since he'd come into her life?

And was he really protecting her from that danger? Or had he brought it to her? He was, after all, a Chekov. And maybe, like his uncle, he threatened people until they paid for his protection. But she wasn't paying him; she was paying the Payne Protection Agency. And she doubted they had to pressure anyone to hire them, especially Milek, whose art was in such high demand.

"Blair!" He repeated her name with a little more volume and a little more gruffness, like he didn't think she could hear him.

She could. But worse than that, she could feel him. As if his fingers, still on her jaw, were sliding over the rest of her body. She shook her head and stepped back, hoping to break whatever spell he was casting over her senses.

"You're not okay?" he asked with concern. "Where are you hurt?"

"I'm not hurt," she said, but her voice cracked. She cleared her throat. "I'm fine. I thought you were shot… when I pulled into the garage and left you out there…"

He touched his head. But there was no blood. "I think the shooter thought they got me, too. I dove for cover, though. I'm okay."

"Me, too," she said. But she couldn't stop shaking.

"Did you get a good look at them?" he asked. "Was it a man or woman?"

She shook her head and shrugged. "I don't know…"

"And you really have no idea who might be after you?"

Tears of frustration stung her eyes. "I don't know. Nobody from my past. But maybe…"

"What?"

"Your uncle?"

He sucked in a breath. "He's in prison."

"But maybe he has someone else doing his dirty work for him, making the threats," she suggested. And she stared hard at him, wondering if it was him. But he wasn't the one who'd shot out her SUV window, who'd shot at him as well. "I really don't know…" Her voice cracked with frustration and fear.

He moved his hand from her face to her shoulder and pulled her forward, against his chest, and that arm closed around her, holding her, comforting her.

It had been so long since anyone had held her. She wanted to step away, to be alone and independent, how she'd vowed to be after her dad died and Trevor had already left her and Angel. But now…

Now, she found herself looping an arm around his waist and stepping closer, so that her head touched his chest. Beneath her ear she could hear the beat of his heart, fast and loud and strong.

He was alright.

And so was she…thanks to him. If he hadn't sent her into the garage when he had, if he hadn't broken into that side door when he had…

Eventually the shooter would have found where she was hiding and would have killed her.

She'd thought earlier that someone was just trying to scare her. Maybe someone from his uncle's organization. And if that had been their goal, they'd succeeded; she was scared. But now she suspected they wanted to do more than scare her. They wanted to kill her. And if not for Ivan Chekov, they probably would have succeeded.

But why?

Why would anyone want to scare her, let alone kill her?

The gallery hadn't even opened yet. She had no valuables in it. All the money she'd had was already invested in the place, leaving her broke and with some big loans she'd managed to talk banks into giving her. She had nothing to give anyone, and no heirs but Angel to leave anything to, anyway.

"Why?" she whispered.

His hand rubbed her back, as if petting her like he'd petted Angel. "I don't know. But we'll figure it out…"

We.

She hadn't had anyone to include in a *we* in a long time, except for Angel. And the big rottweiler had never made her feel like Ivan Chekov did: scared and excited and somehow safe as well.

Nothing that had happened this evening made sense. Most of all, her reaction to him. Her attraction to him.

He must have felt it, too, because he moved his hand back to her face, glided his fingertips sensually along her jaw and tipped up her chin. And he stared down at her so intently. At her eyes and then her lips. Then his fingers trailed down her neck, over the pressure point where her pulse pounded fast and hard.

Was he going to kiss her?

Was she going to let him?

Then lights shone on the street, flashing red and blue, and the sirens grew so loud that they finally penetrated the fog she'd been in.

The shock.

That was all this was. Her inability to focus and her attraction. Just shock.

When someone in this neighborhood called the police, they expected more than a uniformed officer to show up. They expected to see the chief. So Woodrow Lynch had dragged himself out of his warm bed and left his warmer wife to make an appearance here.

But he hadn't done it due to politics because Woodrow had no interest in them. He'd done it because shootings in this neighborhood were rare. He'd also done it because the Payne Protection Agency was involved. Unfortunately, shootings involving them were not rare.

They happened all too often.

And the Payne Protection Agency was all family, even the branches like this one, that weren't run by his stepsons. The Kozminskis were as much family as the Paynes were.

"Chief," Officer Sheila Carlson greeted him at the gate, her voice as cool as the late-night spring breeze. "I'm not surprised to see you here." Then she blushed as she must have realized how disrespectful she sounded.

He was well aware that everyone in River City knew about his relationship with the Payne Protection Agencies. He and his wife cared about each bodyguard, not just the ones related to them by blood or marriage. Woodrow had an especially soft spot for this branch. Maybe he cared about them most because so few people ever had. One of them had spent five years in prison for something he hadn't done, and the others…

They all got raw deals but maybe no one more so than Ivan Chekov. While he had committed petty crimes in his youth, he'd had no choice. Now, someone was trying to kill him. But it wasn't the first time the man had had a hit out on him. He'd had one when he'd been just a kid.

But was that the real situation here?

Had he been the target or had the woman been?

"I am surprised to see you here, Officer Carlson," he said to the ambitious young woman. "I thought you were off tonight."

In the bright lights of the headlamps of his SUV, her face blushed an even deeper red. "I—I… Officer Brown had to leave for a family emergency, so I got called in…"

"Officer Brown is who took the report at the gallery earlier this evening," Woodrow said. Milek and Garek, who were standing on the other side of those gates with Ivan, had already filled in the chief when he'd called on his way to the scene.

Well, they'd filled him in as much as they were able. Someone had tried breaking into an empty gallery earlier this evening. But it hadn't actually been empty; the owner had been there. And the owner had been here, too.

So surely she had to be the target and not Ivan.

But why?

He searched the area for her and determined that she had to be the black-haired woman standing near Ivan Chekov. Or Ivan was standing near her, hovering, as if shielding her from danger.

Which put him in even more danger…

They both could have been killed tonight.

Suddenly a big dog bounded up and jumped, putting its paws on Woodrow's chest.

A gun cocked, the barrel pointed at the dog. Or at him?

"Put down your weapon, Officer Carlson," he said as he petted the dog. The rottweiler showed his appreciation with a big swipe of his tongue across Woodrow's chin. He chuckled. "He's harmless." Maybe he could talk Penny into getting a puppy. The grandkids would love one.

Officer Carlson hesitated a long moment before reholstering her service weapon. And he wondered if he'd really found all the corrupt officers within the department since taking down the biggest criminals in River City over the past few years. Or were there still a few who had worked with the crime bosses? With Luther Mills or with Viktor Chekov?

Sheila Carlson was young, but Luther had seemed to get to the young ones the easiest. He'd either intimidated them into giving their loyalty to him or he'd bought it. But Luther was dead now thanks to the man Woodrow wanted to succeed him as chief: Detective Spencer Dubridge.

But Viktor was alive. Behind bars. But alive…so still a threat. Since he was the one who'd put out that hit on his own nephew, the old man probably remained a danger to Ivan.

But as Woodrow noticed how Ivan looked at the woman standing beside him, he realized that Viktor might not be the only threat to the young bodyguard.

Chapter 6

Legally, Ivan was supposed to ignore the call coming in on his cell. Michigan had a hands-free cell-phone law, and his truck was too old for Bluetooth. So he could have just let it go to voice mail. Instead, since he was almost at his destination, he pulled onto the shoulder of the road, so that he could take it. Not that he wanted to. The call was from either Milek or Garek, or maybe they were making the call together. Yesterday, he'd been worried that they were going to fire him. Now, he was even more concerned.

He hadn't done a very damn effective job of protecting Blair Etheridge the night before, so it was good that the others had taken over her protection duty today while installing security in her gallery. While she hadn't been hurt last night, she could have been. She would have been had she not gotten out of her vehicle and hid like she had.

At the gallery she'd sworn that she could take care of herself, and she hadn't been exaggerating. She was smart and resourceful. And incredibly, incredibly beautiful…

If something happened to her…

He wouldn't forgive himself, especially if it happened because of him. So his bosses had been smart sending him home the night before. Garek had taken over security for her, and he'd hopefully helped smooth things over with her irate landlord, some millionaire named Lionel Sims.

Or she might be looking for a place to live.

And Ivan might be looking for a job if he didn't accept this call and maybe even if he did. He swiped his cell screen. "Hello."

"Are you alright?" Milek asked.

"Yes, I'm fine." He wasn't really, but he wasn't about to admit to a sleepless night and some new aches and pains from his mad scramble to avoid getting shot last night.

"Then where are you?"

Ivan peered through his windshield at the fence and gate ahead of him. These were not fancy wrought iron. This was a thick gauge chain-link, twenty feet high, with barbed wire rolled over the top of it. "Prison."

Milek's gasp rattled the phone. "Where?"

"The River City maximum security correctional facility," he explained.

"What the hell are you doing there?" Milek asked.

He released a ragged sigh. "I think you know..."

"You're visiting your uncle?" Milek asked. "I didn't think you did that."

They probably wouldn't have hired him if they'd thought he was still in contact with Viktor Chekov. "I don't," he said. "With the exception of seeing him in court for his sentencing a couple of years ago, this will be the first time I've seen him in years." Ever since Ivan, at sixteen, had escaped from his cruel guardian, he'd stayed away from him like his life depended on it, and it probably had.

"Why now, Ivan?" Milek asked.

"Because someone needs to talk to him to find out if he has anything to do with what happened last night."

"You think he's sent someone after you?" Milek asked. "After all this time?"

Ivan sucked in a breath then exhaled it in another ragged sigh. "No. I hadn't thought that..." But now, he wondered if he was the one putting Blair in danger instead of the other way around.

"And you shouldn't," Milek said. "Someone was already trying to break into the gallery before we got there last night."

But what if she was right and it had been just a homeless person and not the shooter who'd tried gunning them down later that night? What if two different perpetrators had been involved the night before and Viktor Chekov had sent one of them after *him*? Ivan wouldn't be able to protect anyone if he was the one actually putting them in danger.

If he'd put Blair in danger...

He wasn't sure how he would be able to make it up to her except to stay away from her. His stomach clenched like someone had punched him. He didn't want to stay away from her. He wished he was with her now, holding her, touching her like he had last night, his fingers gliding over her silky skin, as he'd tipped up her face to his. If the police cars hadn't pulled up when they had, he might have kissed her...if she'd wanted him to. And with the way she'd been leaning against him and staring up at him, her green eyes dark and intense, it had felt like she'd wanted him to.

He swallowed down the groan of frustration and desire that rose from his clenched stomach up the back of his throat. But he'd probably just imagined her reaction because earlier last night, when she'd heard his name, she'd looked at him the way that he'd looked at his uncle. With disgust and hatred and resentment.

This was probably a bad idea, coming here, trying to

get anything out of the old man. But he had to try. "I need to find out if he's involved with that gallery again like he was in the past," Ivan explained.

"You think Blair took up where her father left off with your uncle?" Milek asked.

"Not willingly," Ivan said. Clearly she hated Viktor Chekov. But a lot of people had hated his uncle and still done business with him. Like Ivan when he was a kid, when he'd had no choice. But if Viktor Chekov was the one threatening her like he'd threatened others, Ivan was going to be the one to stop him. This time.

"You should have told me where you were going," Milek said.

Ivan flinched. He should have, but he'd figured his boss would try to stop him.

"I would have gone with you," Milek said. "Or Garek would have."

"No. I don't want you two involved." Milek had a family, and Ivan had a feeling that Garek and Candace intended to start one soon. "I've got this."

"Ivan, be careful," Milek cautioned him. "He's a dangerous man no matter how old he is or where he is."

"I am well aware of that," Ivan said. "That's why I'm here. To make sure he's not trying to hurt anyone else."

"Blair Etheridge."

"Or me." But he hadn't considered that a possibility until Milek had mentioned it. His uncle had disowned him long ago and no longer considered him family, or he wouldn't have ordered the hit on him when Ivan was sixteen. Since another sixteen years had passed since then, Ivan figured the hit expired, especially since he hadn't been hiding that hard the past ten years. So when news of Viktor's arrest reached him, he'd considered it safe to come back.

Maybe he'd been wrong about that and about coming here. But he ignored the temptation to turn around, like he'd done the last few times he'd considered visiting his uncle, wondering if he'd needed closure or whatever. He'd already gone through the screening process. And Uncle Viktor had Ivan on his visitor list, like he'd expected him to turn up…maybe to gloat or something.

Because he'd been on that list and his uncle had expected him to come, Ivan had stubbornly stayed away. Maybe that was why he was so drawn to Blair Etheridge—because they had obstinacy in common among other things, like a connection to evil through Viktor Chekov.

Ivan went through the prison security process, the searches and questions, and finally sat at a table in the stark concrete visitation room. Because it was maximum security, tempered glass separated the visitor's side from the prisoner's side.

Ivan wasn't sure if that was for his protection or for the prisoner's at this point. There was a time, when he was much younger, that he'd wanted to kill his father's killer. An eye for an eye.

But every time he'd been tempted, he had remembered his father's last word to him: protect. His father had been such a good man that it would have destroyed him if Ivan had become a killer like his uncle. It was bad enough that Ivan had had to be a thief for a while, breaking into cars and houses and businesses on his uncle's orders.

A door on the other side of the glass opened, and first a guard, tall and muscular, stepped through. Then an old man shuffled through the open door, his feet not even leaving the ground, as if he didn't have the strength to lift them. His shoulders were rounded and stooped, and so thin that it looked like the bones protruded through his orange jumpsuit. The man's hair was white, and his face heavily lined.

They must have brought in the wrong prisoner. Ivan stood to tell them so, but then the man shuffled closer and Ivan recognized the sharp nose and the dark eyes of his uncle. His eyes had once been sharp, too, but they seemed cloudy and unfocused right now as if he'd just woken up from a deep sleep. Those eyes, once deep set, appeared to sit in hollowed-out sockets now. The man's once jowly face was also skeletal, like his thin body.

Was he sick?

Dying?

Ivan had spent most of his life hating this man, but actually felt a twinge of pity for him now. Viktor Chekov was wasting away.

Ivan's mother had died like that, slowly, painfully, from the cancer that had ravaged her body. "Is he sick?" Ivan asked the guard. Both sides of the glass had microphones and speakers, so they could hear each other without having to use telephone receivers.

"Sick? Who's sick?" the old man asked, his voice quavery as he stared around the room.

"Your nephew asked if you're sick," the guard said loudly, as if Viktor was hard of hearing.

Maybe he was. He was in his seventies now. But he looked even older than that and much older than he had at his sentencing hearing a few years ago. And he was nothing like the fearsome monster of a man he'd been when Ivan was a kid.

"His mother is sick," Viktor said. "Poor Maria…so very sick…"

Ivan's mother had been dead longer than his father had. "What are you talking about?" he asked.

The old man's head swiveled around again, as if he couldn't see him. Then finally, he shuffled closer and peered through the glass. "Ivan? What are you doing here? Why aren't you with Maria and your boy?"

Did Viktor really think that Ivan was his father, Ivan Senior? Or was this all some kind of sick game he was playing? "You really don't know who I am?" he asked.

The old man snorted. "I know my own damn brother."

"I'm not your brother, you killed him," Ivan said. "I'm his son."

"You are joking, Ivan, and it's not funny. You're my brother. I love you." He pressed one of his hands against the glass. It was bony, with veins protruding on the back of it. "I would never hurt you."

Ivan snorted now and shook his head. "You killed your brother right in front of his son," he said, his voice gruff with the hatred and resentment he'd carried for so long. No. He'd been right to never come here before. It wasn't bringing him closure. Instead it was bringing horrible feelings to the surface again.

Viktor shook his head, and the loose skin on his scrawny neck shook like a turkey's wattle. "No, no, no…never, never…"

Ivan sighed. "So you're still denying what I witnessed with my own damn eyes."

The guard cleared his throat. "He doesn't know what year it is or how old he is. He's not doing well, hasn't been since his daughter died."

"Tori?" Viktor whipped his head around to stare at the guard although his eyes didn't seem quite able to focus. "Tori isn't dead!"

The guard nodded. "Yes, she is, Mr. Chekov. She died a couple of years ago."

"No..." Then he began to sob, his skinny shoulders shaking as he wept like his heart was breaking.

Like he'd broken Ivan's all those years ago, and some of Ivan's hatred and resentment drained away at the sight of the broken old man.

Viktor Chekov wasn't behind whatever had happened last night. He wasn't mentally capable of having organized anything like that. So who had come after him and Blair? Or was just Blair in danger?

Last night had been a nightmare from which Blair had hoped to wake up and realize that none of it had actually happened. That nobody had tried to break into the gallery. That nobody had tried to shoot her or Ivan.

And Ivan...

He was so big, so broad, so damn handsome...that he didn't seem real. While his last name was Blair's worst nightmare, the man might be something else entirely for her. He had tried his best to protect her. And he'd realized she was in real danger even before she had. He was good at his job.

But now, aware of the threat, she could take care of herself and the gallery. She didn't need him to protect her, which was apparently good since he'd taken off last night and hadn't shown up yet today. She wasn't offended, though, because he didn't know her any better than she knew him. And she wasn't going to let him get to know her more or get any closer to her.

She was better off alone. Always had been and always would be. She'd learned long ago the only person she could count on was herself.

She wasn't alone right now, though. Garek Kozminski, who'd shown up last night, was directing a few other guys as well as some of her contractors on placement of cameras and motion sensors. Some of it was being installed now; some of it would have to wait until the remodel was complete. And the remodel needed to be completed quickly. The gallery had to be ready in time for the grand reopening celebration.

So, as she'd warned Garek Kozminski, this security install couldn't delay the contractors who'd already been working slower than she wanted. She'd been feeling anxious about the grand reopening, but now…

After last night, after the shooting…

She could no longer deny that she was in danger. But she refused to let someone scare her away from the dream she'd held for so long. Ever since her dad had sent her off to boarding school, she'd vowed to come back and make the gallery a success. Because his partner had gone to prison and his wife had taken off, her dad had struggled to run the gallery on his own. She needed to prove to herself and to him, even though he was gone, that she could make the Ethereal Gallery a success. With everything she had invested in it, both time and money, she couldn't back out now. She would be homeless like the people who'd been squatting in the empty building. But even though she was committed, she was also scared—of failure and especially of being physically hurt.

Her fingers shook so badly, she had to wrap them tight around her mug to still them so that she wouldn't drop the large coffee cup. Caffeine was probably the last thing she needed right now, but she hadn't slept the night before and this was the only way she was going to stay alert enough to keep everyone moving. And to keep moving herself.

She didn't dare return to her makeshift office in the back room, or she would probably curl up underneath the table with Angel. The dog was exhausted, too, and probably stressed over the night before, since he'd kept whimpering in his sleep. This was another reason she'd come out to the main showroom area.

And maybe because she'd been looking for *him*. But just to assure herself that he was okay after last night. That he hadn't been hurt worse than he'd admitted. That was the only reason she found herself staring out into the street again and again.

At Garek's recommendation, the front door had been replaced, along with the back door. While the door was still glass, it and the windows in the front were made of some special material that didn't break; it also had a reflective surface on the outside so no one could see in. And while she could see outside now, once it was dark, the interior side would be reflective as well. But right now she could see him jumping out of a vintage pickup truck and heading toward the front door.

His legs were long but muscular, once again straining the seams of his distressed jeans. He wore only a T-shirt despite the cool temperature of early spring, but he didn't look cold. And looking at him had heat flashing through her like it had last night, when he'd looked at her and when he'd touched her.

She'd wanted him to touch her everywhere. If the police hadn't shown up when they had, she probably would have kissed him. He'd been leaning toward her, and she would have had to only go up on tiptoe to reach his mouth with hers. Her lips tingled now as if they had touched his, and her pulse quickened. She wanted him. Or maybe she just wanted a release from all the tension and anxiety in her life. She certainly didn't want a relationship, now or ever.

But she wasn't sure if he would release her tension or

just add to it. Unfortunately, when he opened the front door, someone else tried walking inside with him. She hadn't even noticed the other man. All her attention had been focused on Ivan.

Ivan had noticed him, though, and he pinned the shorter man against the door, using his body to push it closed again. "What are you doing lurking around here?" he demanded.

"I wasn't lurking," he protested. "I was looking for Blair." He probably couldn't see her over Ivan's enormous shoulder, but he called out, "Blair! You need to tell this ox who he's messing with!"

Unfortunately, a very successful artist, Z, as he called himself, had started out painting graffiti on abandoned buildings but, seeing a market for his art, had turned to smaller surfaces, like car hoods and bus doors that could be sold out of galleries. And they sold for high prices.

"Ivan, let him go," she said. "Z has business with me." And she needed to remind the artist that business was all they had together.

Ivan waited a long second before he stepped back and let the thin young man slip around him. Z headed straight toward her and leaned in to kiss her cheek. Ivan's hands clenched into fists, as if he was going to punch the man, but then the door opened behind him again and he turned to confront the new visitor.

"Darling," Z said to her, "what is going on here?" He gestured around them. "You're actually installing security cameras? And what about all these blank walls?"

"I haven't received all my shipments yet." Any of her shipments, including the ones he'd promised to send, so she had to be nicer to him than she wanted, but not as nice as he wanted her to be.

"I meant the boring color." The contractor's painters

were layering white paint over the brick now. "Let me paint a mural for you, Blair. No charge." And he leaned in as if he was going to kiss her again and maybe not her cheek this time.

She leaned back to evade his lips. And a low growl rumbled. She glanced around to see if Angel had woken up. Her dog was nowhere in sight, but Ivan was. The growl must have emanated from him. The man next to him tensed as if concerned, but Z chuckled.

"Jean-Paul," she said, greeting the other man. "What are you doing here?"

Z snorted. "Still trying to convince her to display your work?" he taunted. "It's boring, JP, just like these walls." He glanced around again and shuddered. "It's not just the white, though. I don't understand the cameras."

"Of course, she wants to make sure the artwork is secure," Ivan replied with a condescending note in his deep voice.

Blair's lips nearly twitched into a smile. "That's why," she said. "I don't want anything happening to your work."

Jean-Paul St. James sniffed disparagingly. "What work? It's garbage."

"My garbage sells," Z said. "Yours collects dust."

Jean-Paul swung his arm as if trying to punch the other artist, but Ivan caught his fist and held tightly to it. "No fighting," he said. "Or I'll toss you both out."

Z held up his hands. "I'm not doing anything. And who the hell are you, anyway? Some rent-a-guard store-security cop?"

"He's my boyfriend," Blair blurted out. The last thing she wanted either artist to think was that she needed a bodyguard. If word got out, there would be no reason to rush to get ready for the grand reopening because nobody would come. And Z would never send that art he'd promised her because he wouldn't trust her with it.

"You told me you're not dating anyone," Z said, his blue eyes narrowed and cold as he turned back to her.

"I said I'm not dating artists." And that was true. After how her mother had treated her father and her, how easily she'd abandoned them, Blair would never risk a relationship with one. She wouldn't risk another one with anyone, though. She didn't have the time, and she didn't have the interest in having someone in her life who would just leave.

Ivan chuckled. "I'm definitely no artist. I can't even draw stick figures."

"Then what do you?" Jean-Paul asked, studying Ivan instead of her, almost as if he recognized him.

"I work for the family business," Ivan replied.

Blair shivered. His family business was crime. Was that how Jean-Paul knew him? She'd wondered sometimes about how Jean-Paul supported himself because his work didn't sell. Yet he drove a nice vehicle. Of course, he could have inherited family money, whereas Blair had just inherited family debt.

"Just like Blair," Ivan added with a smile at her, but there was something in his eyes, some speculation, as if he wondered what her family business really was. But her father had had nothing to do with his partner's mess. Blair Noto hadn't fought Viktor Chekov's involvement in the gallery like her dad had.

"What kind of business is your family's?" Jean-Paul asked Ivan.

Blair nearly shivered again. He had to know.

Ivan glanced around at his boss, who was hooking up a laptop to one of the cameras. "Securit—"

"Securities," Blair interjected. Although nothing about

the Chekovs had ever made anyone feel secure. But Ivan was different than his uncle. Or at least she hoped he was, because she was attracted to him. The artist was right, though; she had said she wasn't dating anyone right now. Not that she was considering actually dating Ivan. "But he was kind enough to come by today to help me get this place ready. You're going to have to excuse us, Z and Jean-Paul. We really need to get back to work."

And they needed to get the hell out of here.

"I just wanted a sneak peek at the place," Z said, but he was staring at her, not those boring walls. Then he glanced at Ivan. "But I guess there isn't much to see here." He turned and walked out.

Jean-Paul looked at Ivan again, too. Then he followed the other artist out onto the street. Ivan watched them, as if concerned that they might start fighting again. But they stopped outside the door and seemed to be in a quiet conversation.

Probably about her and this place.

"I doubt I'm going to get any of his work now," she said with a sigh. As if he'd felt her distress, Angel appeared and rubbed his head against her leg. He wasn't alone. Milek had come out from the back, too.

"You'll have some of mine," he said.

"I—I will?" she asked.

He nodded. "You and I can go over what pieces you'd like to have once the security system is completely installed."

Probably because he wanted to make sure his work would be safe. "Thank you for trusting me," she said. "It's been hard to get artists to give me a chance." And if they knew she was in danger, they definitely wouldn't.

"I think Z wants to give you more than that," Ivan said.

"Yes." She sighed. "That's why I told him what I did, you know..."

Not because she actually wanted Ivan to be her boyfriend. She didn't even really want him to be her bodyguard.

Garek had been watching the interaction between Ivan, the artists and Blair. Posing as her boyfriend might be the best way for Ivan to keep her safe, as he was clearly determined to do.

Other bodyguards had used that trick, going undercover as boyfriends to protect their clients or the person their client had hired them to protect.

Milek had finally arrived, hopefully to take over for Garek, so he could get some sleep. He walked over to join them just as Milek asked Ivan, "So how was prison?"

Blair Etheridge gasped. "What? You were in prison today?"

"Just visiting," Ivan replied.

"Who?" Garek asked, his heart beating fast.

"I wanted to see if my uncle had anything to do with what happened last night," Ivan admitted.

All the color drained from Blair's face. "Of course, he did. That's the only thing that makes sense because I have no enemies. Viktor Chekov is trying to scare me into doing what he had my father's partner doing for him."

Ivan shook his head. "He can't be behind this. He has dementia. He didn't even know who I was."

"He hasn't seen you in years?" Garek stated, but as somewhat of a question because he wasn't certain. The visitor logs showed he hadn't, but Garek knew there were ways around those if a prisoner had the right connections. And Viktor Chekov had once run all of River City.

"Other than his sentencing, he hasn't seen me since I ran

away as a teenager," Ivan said. "We both know that if he had tracked me down after I left, I wouldn't be here right now."

Blair Etheridge gasped again, and her eyes widened with shock.

"You were a skinny kid when you ran away, so, of course, he wouldn't recognize you now," Garek said. "He didn't even notice you that day in court."

"It wasn't that he didn't recognize me," Ivan said. "He thought I was my dad and that he and my mother were still alive. And he looks bad. He's wasting away physically and mentally."

While Ivan seemed to believe that and maybe even pitied his uncle a bit, Garek didn't buy it. He didn't trust Viktor Chekov, who was probably pulling an "oddfather" act like another famous mobster had pulled off for years to avoid prison. Garek would have to discover for himself if that was true or if the old godfather of River City was still a threat. "Just be careful," he advised Ivan.

The man had already suffered too much because of his uncle. And now…

Now, with the way Blair Etheridge kept looking at Ivan and the way that he kept looking at her, Garek was worried that the guy might wind up suffering even more.

He'd overheard their conversation about family business, too, when she'd told those artists that Ivan was her boyfriend. Her family business hadn't been just selling art. Her father and his partner had been laundering money for bad people.

Was she taking over that part of the business, too? Was that why someone had tried breaking into what was presumably an empty building?

There was nothing here to steal yet. There had only been her and her dog and then someone had tried to shoot her, too. The lady was obviously in trouble, but was she trouble as well? Milek claimed she hadn't reacted to Ivan's last name with anything but revulsion, but that didn't mean that she wasn't in business with his uncle. But with Ivan sticking close to her, he would discover the truth. Hopefully, he uncovered that before he got too close to her.

Chapter 7

Ivan had hated the way Blair had looked at him when he'd told her his last name. But the way she'd been looking at him while he'd talked to Garek just a short while ago had been almost as bad. He didn't want her pitying him any more than he wanted her hating him. But at least she didn't argue when Garek reassigned him as her personal bodyguard. Maybe because of that pity she'd felt for him, or maybe she had kind of backed herself into a corner with what she'd told the artists.

She was probably a bit embarrassed, because after that conversation he'd had with Garek, she headed to her back office instead of staying out front with the contractors and the crew Milek and Garek had left behind to install the cameras. The motion sensors had to wait until all the walls had been painted or rearranged, since apparently some had to be removed and some erected. When he followed her to the back, she didn't look at him; she was studying the architectural plans lying across the big old library table she used as a desk.

She really had a vision for what she wanted the space to be. But he had a feeling she hadn't envisioned the consequences of telling people that he was her boyfriend. Or at least she hadn't considered them until Garek had pointed out that it would be easiest for Ivan to protect her now, since he had a cover story for sticking close to her.

Ivan had no problem with sticking close to her; in fact, he would like to be as close as two people could be, especially with the way she leaned over that desk. He swallowed a groan at the thoughts flitting through his head of walking up behind her, pressing against her rounded backside, letting her feel exactly what she did to him, how damn hard she made him, his body aching for release. He wanted to be inside her, thrusting, moving, his hands holding her bare breasts. He nearly choked on the groan threatening to erupt from him.

He couldn't remember the last time he'd been this physically attracted to someone, and it had never happened with a client before. Before Garek and Milek had hired him for their new franchise of the Payne Protection Agency, Ivan had worked private security. He hadn't been the rent-a-mall-cop type of security like that arrogant artist had implied. Ivan had worked security for bigger artists than that guy. Like recording artists and actors, even some models.

Blair Etheridge could have been a model; with her long legs, she could easily strut down runways all over the world. And her face…was turned toward him again; she'd caught him staring at her.

"Why are you hovering?" she asked.

He was actually leaning against the jamb of the open door. Angel's heavy body was lying partially across one of Ivan's feet. The dog's enormous head rested on his enormous paws, his eyes closed, and his whole body relaxed. "Because your guard dog here isn't going to protect you."

She gestured beyond him. "There are other people here," she said. "I'm safe."

"You don't know if those other people are safe," he said.

Garek and Milek had Josh back at the office, running background checks on the contractors and every member of his crew. They had probably added those two artists to the list of people to check out.

"Your bosses and coworkers aren't safe?" she asked.

His bosses were, but he wasn't as certain about his coworkers. While he believed Josh Stafford hadn't done the crime for which he'd gone to prison, the other guys had. Blade Sparks had killed a man. And Viktor Lagransky had been named after Ivan's uncle because Viktor's dad had worked for Chekov. When they were younger, Ivan and Viktor Lagransky had worked together, stealing for Ivan's uncle. Yet Viktor and Blade had both stepped up to help Josh, and Viktor had helped Ivan when he'd gotten concussed protecting Josh's kid.

"I'm not concerned about my bosses and coworkers," he said. No matter what they'd done in their pasts, they were all good guys now. "You have a bunch of contractors working out there, too."

She sighed. "Not enough. They need to get working on the walls. I have installations planned for some of the pieces coming soon."

"Z's art?" he asked, irritation gnawing at him. He should have decked the guy when he'd tried to kiss her. Not that he was jealous or anything. He just didn't like arrogant people.

She nodded. "If he sends it…"

"You'll have Milek's pieces," he reminded her.

She smiled so brightly that her green eyes sparkled. And he sucked in a breath as his gut tightened. That irritation gnawed again that another man had made her so happy. But Milek was very happily married; he was no threat to Ivan. The only real threat was whoever had tried to hurt her last night, and Ivan needed to focus on just one thing: keeping her safe.

She tapped the plans. "Yes, and now I have to figure out where to place his work, too." She blinked and leaned closer to the papers, then rubbed her eyes. Dark circles rimmed them, appearing like bruises on her pale skin.

She looked exhausted but he remembered his father saying to never tell a woman that she looked tired; that was after Ivan had said that to his mother, who had been very tired as she'd fought the cancer ravaging her body.

"Maybe take a break and come back to the plans with fresh eyes," he suggested. "Have you had lunch?"

She shook her head. "It's late for lunch now."

"So how about an early dinner?" he suggested. "Or have you already made us plans for dinner?"

She turned back toward him with wide eyes. "What? Why would I have made plans for *us* for anything?"

Her disparagement stung a bit, so he decided to tease her. "I assumed we were going out since you just outed me as your boyfriend."

Color flushed her face, chasing away the pallor. But she just pursed her lips instead of responding.

So he nudged her. "What kind of relationship do we have?" he asked. "The kind where we go out so we can make the most of PDA, or one where we like to stay in with the dog and chill and stream movies and then all our displays of affection are private?" His pulse quickened at the thought of any display of affection with her.

Her green eyes narrowed in a glare, but her lips twitched as if she was struggling not to smile. Finally, she unpursed them and said, "The kind of relationship where we have nothing to do with each other."

"Sounds like some marriages I've witnessed," he remarked with a chuckle. Especially with the celebrities he'd protected over the years. They'd been so busy with their careers that their personal lives had suffered. And even though he hadn't been married, his personal life had suffered as well, because he hadn't had one.

"Witnessed or experienced?" she asked.

"I've never been married," he said. "You?"

She let out a sharp laugh. "God, no."

He chuckled again, and Angel lifted his head from his paws and glanced between them like they were tossing a ball back and forth.

"And I intend to keep it that way," she said.

"That's why you don't date artists?"

"I don't date anyone." She pointed at her dog. "Angel is the only companion I want."

"Well, unfortunately you're going to have to put up with me, too, now. And since you claimed me as your boyfriend in front of witnesses, we have to commit to my cover… unless you want to admit to having a bodyguard."

"I don't want to do that," she said. "I don't think artists will trust me with their pieces if they think I'm in danger."

"You really have no idea why you're in danger?" he asked.

She shook her head. "Your uncle is the only person who caused problems around here."

"What about those artists?" Ivan asked. "One seemed upset that you wouldn't show his art and the other seemed obsessed with you."

"Z is just a harmless flirt. And Jean-Paul is harmless, too."

Ivan wasn't so sure about that. Z seemed enthralled with her beauty, which Ivan understood all too well. And he would have to make certain that he didn't get as attached to her as her dog was. He just had to protect her. Not love her.

He wasn't sure if he could love anyone. After losing the people he'd loved the most, he'd kind of shut down. He'd closed himself off. He didn't want to risk his heart again.

Not that a woman like Blair Etheridge wanted it, or anything else about him. She was independent and focused on her gallery, and he had to make sure nothing threatened her success or her life.

But he was tempted to threaten her claim that she wouldn't date anyone. While he didn't want anything serious, either, he wanted her. "Angel can't do the things for you that I want to do," he said, and he stepped a little closer to her. He wanted to tempt her as much as she tempted him.

Her face flushed as her eyes widened. "You better be talking about just protecting me," she said.

He grinned. "Of course. What else do you want me to do for you?"

"Nothing."

Blair hadn't considered the consequences of her rash statement to Z. But with his questions about the security install, she hadn't wanted to admit she needed a bodyguard as well. Fortunately, no news crews had shown up the night before after the shooting, so maybe it wouldn't be made public. Her landlord would probably make sure that didn't happen. He was wealthy and private.

Lionel Sims was a former friend of her father's who'd offered her a place to stay for free when she'd returned to River City. But she'd insisted on paying him, and living in the apartment over the carriage house instead of in the big house. Because he hadn't wanted Angel in his mansion, he'd agreed to her staying in the garage, but he hadn't wanted to take her money. She wasn't even sure he'd been cashing the checks she left for him since he hadn't given her the option of paying him online.

But after last night, he probably would. He would also probably rescind his offer to loan her some of his private art collection, which her father had helped him curate. She needed that artwork to attract more guests to the gallery reopening. She also needed that money she'd been paying him. Because if he actually cashed those checks, she wasn't sure how she was going to pay for all the security the insurance company was requiring. Garek Kozminski had assured her that they had an installment plan that would work with her budget, though.

He had no idea how strained her budget was right now. She needed this gallery to open on time, and to be a success, or she would have to declare bankruptcy. While getting Milek's art was a coup, she also needed Z's. That was why she hadn't admitted to Ivan being her bodyguard, because she hadn't wanted Z to be worried about his pieces getting damaged.

But since calling Ivan her boyfriend, she'd started thinking about him like one. After hearing about his prison visit, she was also worrying about him like he was her boyfriend. She couldn't get what she'd heard out of her head enough to focus on those plans or anything else.

It didn't help that he just kept standing in the doorway, watching her, his dark eyes so intense and so damn hot. She felt hot, too, and drew in a shaky breath of stale air. "Okay, maybe you're right. Maybe we should grab an early dinner." Her cell dinged just as she said it, and she nearly groaned. When she read the text, she did groan. "Damn..."

"What is it?" Ivan asked, going from leaning against that doorjamb to tense and at her side in seconds, as if he had to physically protect her from that message.

"Just a shipment arriving earlier than expected," she said.

"Z's?" he asked.

She shook her head. "No. These pieces are on loan for display only for the event. I didn't need them this early, though. I'm really not ready for them."

"We'll make sure nothing happens to them," he assured her. He glanced around the back room. "We can keep them in here or out front, where there are cameras. We need some cameras in here, too."

She sighed, knowing it was inevitable. Garek had said the same.

"And you also need an assistant," he said. "I don't know how you're managing all of this on your own."

She tensed now. "I can manage on my own." She'd had to learn how to do that years ago.

"I have no doubt that you can," he said. "But you shouldn't have to."

She sighed again. "I interviewed some candidates and narrowed it down to a couple of possibilities. I just have to check their references and—"

"We need to do that," he said. "Working for you would be a great way for someone to get close to you."

He was standing so close that his arm brushed hers, and she gave him a pointed look. "Really?" she asked sarcastically. "Like what kind of person would try something like that?"

He chuckled. "Hey, you were the one who claimed I was your boyfriend."

"And I explained why I did that," she said. Because she'd been too tired to think of any other reason for his presence than that. She'd also been thinking of him entirely too often since meeting him just the night before. But he had saved her life, probably twice, because whoever had been trying to break in was likely also the person who'd shot at them.

"Did I even thank you last night?" she asked.

"Thank me for what?"

"For protecting me," she said.

He shrugged as if it was nothing. "Just doing my job."

She felt a twinge of regret that she was just a job to him. Of course, that was all she was. He didn't even know her; she was just an assignment to him.

And he was just a bodyguard to her no matter what she'd told Z or even the sympathy she'd felt for him when he'd talked about visiting the prison and the man who'd apparently wanted him dead: his own uncle.

But she didn't want to think about Viktor Chekov. He'd already affected too much of her life and, apparently, Ivan's as well. That sympathy rushed over her again, along with the gratitude she felt. While he had just been doing his job, he had still risked his life for hers.

"I want you to know that I really appreciate what you did last night," she said sincerely. As she stared up at him, she felt herself sinking into his gaze, into the intensity in his dark eyes. And she felt herself leaning closer to him like she had last night. Then he touched her face like he had last night while the direction of his gaze moved from her eyes to her lips, which tingled now in anticipation of the kiss she'd been denied the night before.

"I know how you can show your appreciation," he said, his voice that low sexy rumble in his muscular chest.

Her pulse quickened, and she licked her lips. "How—how's that?"

"You can take me out for an early bird dinner," he said.

She jerked back so sharply that she nearly stumbled and fell over Angel, who stood behind her now. As if she'd surprised the dog, he pushed back against her, sending her into Ivan's strong arms.

"Hey, are you throwing yourself at me?"

She'd been thinking about it, and heat rushed to her face. But instead of getting angry, she found herself laughing. "That was Angel's fault."

"I've heard about guys using their dogs to pick up women. Is that what you do with Angel?" He chuckled.

And she laughed. "I use Angel to scare guys away."

Ivan wound his arm around her back now and pulled her a little closer as he leaned down. Then he whispered, "I don't scare easily."

After what he'd been through as a teenager and just last night, she had to agree. She only wished that she could say the same but was suddenly very scared.

And it wasn't because someone had taken shots at her the night before. It was because of how damn much she wanted Ivan Chekov to actually kiss her. So much that she stretched up on tiptoe and pressed her mouth to his.

Just as his dark eyes and his light-colored hair were in sharp contrast, so was his mouth, which was hard, but his lips were soft. Silky. They moved across hers, and then he leaned closer and deepened the kiss, his hot breath mingling with hers as they opened their mouths.

He nibbled at her lips then swiped his tongue across the lower one as he pulled her closer. He was all hard muscle and sizzling heat.

Sensations shot through Blair, so intense and overwhelming that her head felt light, and a sound buzzed, softly at first and then louder in her ears. She pulled back from Ivan and blinked, dazed and going deaf, especially when Angel started barking and howling.

"They're testing the alarm," Ivan said, but he pulled his

weapon as he said it, as if he wasn't entirely convinced, as if worried that they might be in danger again.

Blair didn't have to wonder. She knew. She was definitely in danger, but the threat wasn't from whoever might have set off that alarm. The threat was from Ivan and all the things he made her feel.

The alarm rang out from that mirrored glass storefront of the Ethereal Gallery. It was back in business with an Etheridge running it.

That couldn't happen again.

The person standing in the shadows of an alley across the street from the gallery had been studying that storefront for quite a while, had been waiting for them to come out. The man and the woman. They should have died last night. It had seemed like they'd been hit, especially the man. But somehow, they had both managed to survive, unscathed.

That couldn't happen again, either.

Chapter 8

Ivan regretted what he'd done in the office just an hour ago. Not the kiss but the lie.

When he'd told Blair that he didn't scare easily, he'd been lying through his teeth. Because she'd scared him even before that kiss. And after…

If they'd not been testing the alarm, he wasn't sure that he would have stopped kissing her. He sure as hell hadn't wanted to stop.

And that scared him. He'd never had a kiss affect him like that. He'd come so close to completely losing control, to lying her down on her table, across the plans she'd been studying so intently, and taking her hard and fast. Even now, after that alarm should have brought him to his senses, his body ached for hers.

But he couldn't risk kissing her again. He couldn't lose control like that. Next time the alarm going off might not just be a test, but a real breach of security. And he had to be ready, not distracted.

Since they had to wait for the arrival of that shipment, they didn't leave the gallery for the early dinner he'd suggested. Instead, they ordered pizza delivered for the security crew and the contractor's crew. Ivan had thought he was hungry, too, but he was barely able to finish the one slice he'd snagged. His stomach was twisted in knots and ached like the rest of his body.

Maybe it was the kiss. Maybe it was the visit earlier that day with his uncle, but he felt on edge, like something was about to happen. And it wasn't going to be good, like that kiss had been.

Hell, that kiss hadn't been good. It had been exceptional. He couldn't remember the last time a kiss had ever affected him like that. Maybe one never had.

But that kiss wasn't the only reason he was on edge. He also had an odd sensation he was being watched. He'd had it since arriving at the gallery, which probably made sense given all the people milling around the place. The contractor's crew, the installation group from the Payne Protection Agency and then those artists. His bosses had left a while ago. And so had his other coworkers. Blade and Viktor had taken the rest of the pizza with them as the contractor's crew filed out, too, leaving them alone.

And yet he still had that sensation, that prickling of his skin like he was wet and cold. Vulnerable. Like he'd felt when his dad had died all those years ago and when, at sixteen, he'd run away from his uncle. But he wasn't a scared kid anymore. He was a man with a gun.

And he knew how to use it. But that gun wasn't going to protect him from Blair and his attraction to her. Now that they were alone, that attraction was even more intense, making him ache to finish what they'd started earlier. What she'd started earlier with that kiss.

"There it is!" she exclaimed, almost as if she was relieved.

Maybe she'd felt that tension, too, because her voice was a little sharp, and her hand shook as she reached out to open the door for the delivery person. Ivan stepped in front of her, shielding her with his body, as he opened the door.

He didn't like the size of the box or the size of the person delivering the package. "Where do you want it?" the deliveryman asked as he steered a dolly with the box on it through the doorway.

"Wait," Ivan said, with his hand on the box.

He didn't like this. Even with the cameras and the alarms on the doors, the gallery was going to be hard to secure with deliveries and contractors coming and going.

"It's just some paintings," Blair said, as if assuring him. "And Malcolm has delivered other things here before."

So she had guessed his suspicions. He smiled. "Okay, darling," he said, teasing her. The endearment rolled a little too easily off his tongue even though he wasn't the type to use endearments.

She blushed. "My…boyfriend is a little overprotective," she said.

"He has reason to be," Malcolm replied with a grin. "I would be, too," he added to Ivan. "Where do you want this? In the back?"

"There will be too many things in your way in the back," Ivan said.

"Angel?" Malcolm asked. "I've rolled around that big pussycat before."

Just as Ivan had suspected, nobody really bought that Angel was a guard dog despite the size of the rottweiler.

"No, just leave it here," Ivan said.

He still wanted to check out the box and to do it on camera. Somebody back at the Payne Protection Agency would be monitoring them and know if he needed help. There would be cameras in that back office soon, too, but he was the one who'd volunteered to put those up so that

Blade and Viktor could head back to the franchise headquarters, which were in the same old warehouse that had Milek's art studio and an apartment in it.

Malcolm looked at Blair, waiting for her acquiescence before he did what Ivan had requested with the box. He was a smart man because she was the boss. And when she gave a slight, reluctant nod, the deliveryman unclasped the belt holding the box onto his dolly, then dropped it onto the polished concrete floor.

Before he could leave, Blair pressed some money into his hand. "Thanks, Malcolm. You're always so careful with the packages."

"I don't understand art, Ms. Etheridge, but I do appreciate beauty." He was looking at her, though and gave her a big grin.

She was the beauty.

Once the guy left, Ivan sighed. "Is there any man who doesn't fawn over you?"

"Who fawns?" she asked.

He was tempted to, especially after that kiss. But he couldn't afford to be distracted again. "Z," he said. "And just about every member of your contractor's crew and that delivery person."

She smiled. "Jealous?"

It bothered him to think that he was, though he'd never considered himself capable of such an emotion before. He shook his head. "No. Frustrated."

Her eyes widened.

And heat rushed to his face. Yeah, he was frustrated that way, but that wasn't what he meant. "I'm talking about trying to keep you safe. It's going to be hard with people coming and going like they do here, and the place isn't even up and running yet."

"There's a lot to do to get it ready for business, but it has to open." Then she laughed but it sounded a little shaky. "And if your bosses are going to get paid, it has to be successful, too. I have to sell some stuff." She gestured at the box. "Not just take things to display."

"Then why did you take them?" he asked.

"For the draw," she said. "I need a crowd for the opening and the chance to see artwork like this from a private collection is a big draw."

He nodded. "Okay. I get it. So we better make sure these items stay safe, too."

"Yes," she said. "These items alone are probably why that insurance CEO pushed so hard for me to hire the Payne Protection Agency. Now that these pieces are in my care, custody and control, I will be responsible for them."

"But you won't be alone in that," he assured her.

Her eyes widened as if she was surprised.

"You did hire the Payne Protection Agency," he said. "We will help you."

She groaned.

"I thought you made peace with hiring us..." Especially after last night.

"No, look who's back," she said, gesturing toward the door that Ivan had left unlocked behind the deliveryman.

He turned to find one of those artists bursting back into the place. It wasn't the scrawny one, though. It was the taller, older one, the one with the phony-sounding name and accent.

"Jean-Paul," she said, greeting him with a cool tone. "Why are you back?"

"I want to show you one of my new canvases," he said. "It's not at all boring. Even Z said so when I showed it to him from my phone."

But he didn't have just his phone with him. He had a tube that probably contained that rolled-up canvas. He thrust it toward her. "Take a look, Blair," he encouraged her. "I know you got your fancy art degree and worked for museums and galleries in Europe, but you still haven't been doing this as long as—"

"I've been doing this all my life," she said. "I grew up in this gallery."

Jean-Paul shook his head. "I know your story, Blair. Your dad sent you away right after your mom left him."

She flinched but lifted her chin, either with pride or defensiveness. "For my education," she said. "He sent me to one of the premier boarding schools in Europe."

And another alarm went off for Ivan, but this one was only inside his head. If Elliot Etheridge had been able to finance that kind of fancy education, her dad must have been involved in the money laundering with his uncle, too.

Had Blair learned that business from her father, just like she'd learned the business of dealing art?

Blair was so damn tired from not being able to sleep after the shooting the night before that she didn't argue with Jean-Paul. And when she saw his work, she couldn't argue with him.

It was different than his other pieces…because it was eerily similar to Z's style. More graffiti artist than the formally trained artist that Jean-Paul claimed to be, just as he claimed that was his name but she wasn't entirely sure about that, either. She'd noticed that he and Z had been talking on the street together after they'd left earlier today. Had Z given him the canvas?

Not that he ever painted on anything as normal as canvas or that he would have done anything to help another artist or another person. He wasn't like Ivan, the man he'd disparaged as a rent-a-cop, who put his life on the line for other people. Was it the way that he'd addressed Ivan that had made her claim her bodyguard as her boyfriend?

Her *boyfriend* had been strangely quiet since Jean-Paul left moments ago. "You don't like the painting?" she asked.

He shrugged. "I don't know much about art even though my uncle had it all over his mansion."

Resentment surged through her. "Because he stole it from my father."

"Then how did your dad afford to send you to that fancy boarding school?" he asked.

She gasped like he'd punched her. "Are you saying my father took money from your uncle? That he was part of it?"

"His partner was part of it. He went to jail for it."

Since she'd been gone when all of that had happened, she'd never been sure what had happened exactly, and her father hadn't liked to talk about it. She'd understood. First, his wife had betrayed him and then his best friend had as well. "Don't you think my father would have gone to jail, too, if he'd been involved?"

He snorted. "Like Uncle Viktor should have gone to prison decades ago? Justice doesn't always get served."

She sighed. "I agree with you there. By the time your uncle went to prison, my father was broken. He had a stroke at fifty-five and closed the gallery. It was closed years before he died, and the building just sat empty."

"Because you were going to school in Europe?" he asked. "Is that why you didn't take it over before he died?"

She shook her head. "He didn't want me to have anything to do with it." She released a shaky sigh. "After my mother left us, I don't think he really wanted anything to do with me anymore, either. I reminded him too much of her."

"I'm sorry," he said, and he reached for her, closing his arms around her.

But she held herself stiff in his embrace. She was still annoyed and defensive. "I just want you to know that my father wasn't willingly involved with your uncle. Viktor Chekov terrorized him like he did everyone else in this town. He broke him. But he won't scare me away from this place, from making my dad's dreams of success for the gallery a reality."

He gently tightened his arms around her. "I don't think anyone was *willingly* involved with my uncle."

"Is that why you ran away from him?"

"I ran away from him because he killed my father."

"Oh, my God!" she exclaimed with horror. "He killed his own brother?"

Ivan nodded. "I was young when it happened. I think my father was going to turn over evidence that would have sent him to prison back then. My uncle found out, probably from some corrupt detective or district attorney. He had a lot of them on his payroll, which I found out the hard way."

"What do you mean?"

"I tried to report him for killing my father, but no one would believe me."

"You were a child," she said. "And how did you know?"

"Because I saw him do it," he said. "I was there." His throat moved as if he was struggling to contain sobs.

She wrapped her arms around him, trying to absorb his pain. "Oh, Ivan!" Her heart ached for him, for a young boy having to witness his father's murder at the hands of his own uncle. "That's horrible."

Ivan clasped her shoulders and held her back a bit. "I don't want your pity," he said. "That all happened a long time ago. And I dealt with it."

"But you went to see him today," she said. "That must have been horrific." She suspected he'd done that for her, to make sure his uncle wasn't trying to hurt her. She'd never had anyone make such a sacrifice for her…except for Ivan, the night before, when he'd urged her to safety while exposing himself to that barrage of bullets.

Ivan shrugged off her sympathy, or pity, as he seemed to see it. "It was kind of anticlimatic. Like I said, he's wasted away, physically and mentally."

"I might enjoy seeing him like that," she admitted. "I can still remember how my father and even my mother talked about him, with such fear. He was the monster in my closet and under my bed."

"Mine, too," Ivan said.

But for Ivan, Viktor Chekov hadn't been just figuratively there; he'd literally been in the same house with him. "No wonder you ran away."

"I had to," he said. "He was worried, after I got arrested for one of the petty thefts he made me do, that I would find a detective who might actually believe me. I was sixteen when he ordered one of his men to kill me."

She shuddered. "At least he didn't want to do that himself."

"I hadn't thought about that. Maybe he had some affection for me after all. I think he loved my father, too, but once he felt like someone betrayed him, they were dead to him."

"Literally," she said and shuddered again.

Ivan wrapped her even closer in his arms, offering her comfort when he was the one who needed it but had probably never had it. Like her, he'd had no one he could rely on but himself.

"You're alive," she said. "So you got away from the goon who was supposed to kill you?"

"He told me to run," Ivan said. "He had a son my age. A son he named after my uncle. And while Leo Lagransky worshipped Viktor Chekov, even the coldhearted hitman couldn't kill a kid for him. So Leo gave me some money and a head start."

She gasped again. "So you had to stay on the run, in hiding. How did you manage to survive?"

His lips, which had felt so electrifying against hers, curved into a slight grin. "Just lucky, I guess, like when you kissed me earlier today. Why did you do that?"

"Why do you think?"

"Pity," Ivan said. "That's what you're feeling for me now."

"I do feel sorry for what you've gone through," she said. "But I respect how strong you are to have survived it."

"I wasn't sure I was going to survive that kiss earlier," he said, his grin spreading and lighting up his deep, dark eyes with mischief and desire.

He was so damn good-looking. And while she'd been around good-looking men before, there was something else to Ivan. Something deeper. Maybe it was the pain he'd endured. "You're a survivor," she said.

He shook his head. "No, just lucky, like I said. But let's tempt fate, let's see if I can survive another kiss from you."

She knew he was deflecting. He didn't want to talk about himself anymore. She understood. She also wanted to kiss him again, to see if it was as amazing as she'd thought.

So she wound her arms around his shoulders and pulled his head down to hers. Their lips touched softly, sweetly, their breaths mingling. Then passion ignited, and Blair pressed her mouth harder against his, opening herself up to his passion. He kissed her deeply, hungrily, even growling low in his throat. Or groaning. His hands moved over her back, down to her hips. He pressed her against him, against the erection straining the fly of his jeans. He wanted her as desperately as she wanted him.

But then a sudden blast knocked them to the hard polished concrete floor. And smoke billowed around them.

Someone had just bombed the gallery.

Viktor Lagransky understood why Ivan had wanted to get back out in the field after his concussion. Watching the security camera footage was like watching paint dry sometimes, and at other times, it was like being a voyeur.

This time Viktor had wanted to watch the footage, though. Ivan had another close call the night before, so Viktor wanted to keep him safe this time. He felt like he'd failed him at Josh's soon-to-be in-laws' house that night a little over a week ago. He should have checked out the distraction the kidnapper had staged. Instead, Ivan had checked it out.

He was always willing to put his life on the line like he had last night for the woman who owned the Ethereal Gallery. She was beautiful, but Ivan didn't usually notice things like that. He'd obviously noticed Blair Etheridge, though.

Viktor hadn't wanted to listen to their private conversation, or see the kiss that had come after it, but he'd had an odd feeling after the big box had arrived and then the other guy shortly after it. Something wasn't right.

Then he overheard Ivan saying how Viktor's dad had let him go instead of following old man Chekov's order to kill him. "So he did actually do one good thing in his miserable life." Viktor had struggled to believe that, to believe Leo Lagransky had been anything but as evil as the man for whom he'd worked, for whom he'd named his own kid.

Viktor should have changed the name. He'd tried a few times, but when anyone had used the name he'd chosen, he hadn't known whom they were talking to. It hadn't felt right. Maybe carrying Chekov's first name was a good reminder to Viktor to be the exact opposite of his namesake and his own father. To be a good man.

Like Ivan…

Then Ivan disappeared into a cloud of smoke as the camera shook and a blast echoed from the speakers.

"What the hell was that?" Blade Sparks asked as he jumped up from his chair on the other side of the cubicle wall separating their desks.

Viktor had to clear his throat to answer, emotion choking him. "An explosion."

"Where?" Blade asked, and then his blue eyes widened. "At the gallery?"

Viktor nodded and the motion snapped him into action. "We have to call for help and get the hell over there." And hope that help wasn't going to come too late for Ivan this time. While he'd survived a hit on his life, he might not have survived that explosion.

Chapter 9

Ivan must have been lucky, like he'd claimed, because his body had shielded Blair's from the blast. The bits of debris from the box and the canvases struck his back, knocking him to the ground. On top of Blair.

She hit the concrete first. "Oh, God, Blair!" he exclaimed as he levered himself off her. Then he stared down at her pale face. His hand shook as he reached for her throat, to check for a pulse. The blast hadn't hurt her, but the force of his body knocking her into the concrete might have. What if she'd hit her head too hard?

He touched it now. Sometime during the day, she'd pinned up all that long hair to the back of her head. "Blair?"

She opened her eyes and blinked before staring up at him. Then she drew in a sharp breath, as if her lungs had been burning from lack of air. He'd probably knocked it out of her when he'd fallen on her.

"Are you okay?" he asked.

She blinked those long, thick lashes again and nodded. There was no flinch. No change of expression. Her head must not have been hurting, or she was in shock.

"Blair? Talk to me," he implored her.

She blew out the sharp breath she'd inhaled in a ragged sigh. "What happened?" she asked.

He hadn't done his job well enough. Again. But instead of admitting that, he found himself trying to tease a smile out of her. "That was one hell of a kiss. Literally knocked me on my ass. Or actually made me knock you on your ass. I hope it's alright."

Her eyes glistened. Maybe they were watering from the smoke, or maybe she was moved to tears. But then she laughed. "What is wrong with you?" she asked. "How can you joke around right now?"

He shrugged then flinched at a twinge of pain in his shoulder.

"You're hurt!" she exclaimed.

"I'm fine," he insisted. But he wasn't.

He was angry at whoever had rigged that bomb and angry at himself for being so distracted by Blair that he hadn't noticed it being snuck into the place. Had it been in the big box or in the tube that Jean-Paul had brought in with the painting? Hopefully the cameras had picked up something that could be used as evidence.

Blair wriggled out from beneath him and scrambled to her feet just as Angel slunk out from the back room. The dog whimpered and rubbed against her. She ran her hands over him. "I think he's okay, too."

Ivan leaned over and ran his hands over the soft fur, too. His fingers brushed against Blair's, and that spark ignited again, making the passion burn inside him. "He's fine," he said. Unlike Ivan, who couldn't focus. Maybe the blast, albeit small, had hit him harder than he'd realized. "Angel must have never left the back room."

"That's good," she said.

Ivan shook his head. "Not for his guard-dog status. He should have come out when the deliveryman and that artist showed up. Maybe he could have sniffed out the damn bomb."

"Bomb?" She gasped and then looked around. As much as she cared about her gallery, she'd worried about him and her dog first.

He felt a twinge of guilt now for even considering that she could have taken over the money laundering that had formerly operated out of this gallery. She was a good person, one who was really determined to do her father proud even though he was gone. He totally understood, since he was determined to do the same.

"How much damage—" She saw the big box that was reduced just to pieces now. And the painting, supposedly the best thing Jean-Paul had ever done, was also in tatters. "Oh, my God! That delivery was—"

Angel's sudden barking drowned out her words. Then the rottweiler howled, too, and finally Ivan heard what he had. Sirens.

The alarm must have gone off even though Ivan couldn't hear it. The authorities had been called. The Payne Protection Agency would show up, too. Hopefully they'd found something in the backgrounds of the contractor, his crew or in those artists' pasts that would link them to what was going on. Was one of them trying to kill Blair? Or him? Or destroy the gallery? And why?

Blair had worked so hard to talk the private owner into loaning that artwork to the gallery. It shouldn't have arrived this early, though. But after last night, she understood why he'd had it delivered sooner than planned. That private owner was also her landlord.

Maybe Lionel Sims thought the shooting was someone trying to steal that artwork, and he'd figured it would be safer here, especially after the Payne Protection Agency had sworn they would keep it safe.

That hadn't happened. And she should have been furious. But Ivan had kept her and Angel safe again, so she couldn't summon any anger toward him. At the moment he was talking to some of his coworkers. He'd already given his statement to the officer who'd shown up soon after the explosion, just as she'd shown up right after the shooting last night. His bosses and his coworkers had arrived right after Officer Carlson.

Blair turned to the Kozminskis and let some of her frustration out on them. "You promised you would keep this place secure. That's why you installed all this stuff today."

Then she noticed the man arguing his way past Officer Carlson. Tall with dark hair. And even though a few silver strands were sprinkled in with the black, his handsome face was unlined. He was young to be the chief executive officer of a company as big as Midwest Property and Casualty. They were the primary insurance company for Michigan and most of the Midwest, especially for commercial companies like the gallery and for high-value items.

If that blast had been bigger, her entire gallery might have become a casualty. "You!" she said, her anger bubbling over onto CEO Mason Hull. "You insisted on my using the Payne Protection Agency, and look what happened." She gestured at the destruction that crime-scene techs were processing. "Irreplaceable artwork has been destroyed."

Milek Kozminski snorted. He was standing as close to the crime-scene techs as the officer had allowed. "That's not irreplaceable."

"What do you mean?" Sure, art was subjective, but the value of those pieces was indisputable, as Mason Hull was probably well aware since he'd insured those works and now his company would have to pay out.

Hopefully he would hold off on canceling her policy until after the grand reopening. If she was able to open at all with everything happening.

"Since those canvases were obviously replicas and not the originals, they're easily replaceable," Milek said.

She tried to edge closer, too, but Officer Carlson stepped between her and the tech. "You need to stay clear of this area," the woman said. She was probably Blair's age, but she looked younger, maybe because of the freckles sprinkled across her nose. Her reddish-brown hair was pulled back into a thick braid that made her hat tip forward, shadowing her eyes, making it hard to read her expression.

"This is my place," Blair reminded her. "That property was in my care, custody and control." That was why she'd had to add the items to her policy.

Milek pointed toward the nearly melted canvases. "The material isn't that old to be the original," he said. "They're fake."

She whirled back toward the CEO then. "You had an appraiser look at them before adding them to my policy. How didn't they catch that these are forgeries?"

"We don't know for certain that Mr. Kozminski is right," Hull pointed out. "We'll leave it up to the crime-scene techs to determine if they are the property we insured. What we insured were the originals."

"Why would someone blow up forgeries then?" Blair asked. None of this made sense.

"To file an insurance claim," Hull replied.

Blair sucked in a breath. "Are you accusing me of setting this up?"

"It is a plausible theory," the officer replied. "You would be the one who would collect."

"No, not me. The owner..." She shook her head. "But he wouldn't do that."

"Who is the owner, Ms. Etheridge, if not you?" the officer asked.

"Lionel Sims."

"The property owner from last night's shooting?" the officer asked. "That's quite the coincidence."

"He's a family friend," Blair said defensively. "Lionel Sims has no reason to try to scam insurance." He was wealthy.

"Family friend?" Garek Kozminski asked. "A friend of your father's then?"

Tears of frustration stung her eyes. "I know what you all think, that my father was involved with Viktor Chekov. That's not true."

"His partner was," Garek said.

Those tears stung more as she willed them away. "Yes, but not my father." Ivan stood behind his boss and met her gaze, and the look in his dark eyes was the same one he must have seen and didn't like in hers: pity. Nobody believed her father was a good man. Nobody but her.

"So your father wasn't involved with Viktor Chekov," Officer Carlson repeated. "But aren't you involved with Ivan Chekov?"

Had word already spread of what she'd told Z earlier today? Or had the officer seen them nearly kissing in the garage when she'd pulled up last night?

Her face heated up as everyone stared at her, including Ivan. So she said, "He's just my bodyguard."

Despite those hot kisses they'd shared, that was all he really was. She wasn't looking for a relationship with anyone, especially not now, when her livelihood and her life were in danger.

So she was smart to deny any personal relationship with anyone. But she wasn't sure if she said it for her protection or for his. Because while his last name was Chekov, she was the one everyone was looking at with such suspicion.

Now, she knew how it felt to be judged because of who her family was and with whom they'd associated.

Milek didn't need the crime-scene techs to confirm he was right that the paintings had been forgeries and not even good ones.

"Maybe they were just used to get the bomb into the gallery," Ivan suggested. "Maybe it has nothing to do with an insurance claim."

"And nothing to do with Blair Etheridge?" Milek asked, raising one eyebrow.

Ivan glanced over to where Blair stood with Officer Carlson, answering more of her questions. "She's not trying to scam the insurance company."

"You better hope not," Garek said. "Because then she's scamming you, too."

"You heard her," Ivan said. "I'm just her bodyguard. Nothing else."

Viktor Lagransky snorted.

"What?" Garek asked.

Viktor shook his head. "Nothing."

But Ivan's eyes narrowed a bit as if he wondered what his coworker knew.

"It doesn't matter that she told the officer and Hull that," Garek said. "She told those artists, in front of the contractors' crew, that you're her boyfriend. It's still an effective cover if one of them is the person who planted this bomb."

Ivan nodded. "Yeah, that bomb might have been in the tube that Jean-Paul brought in. It might not have had anything to do with the box."

"We still need to find out what Lionel Sims knows about those forgeries," Milek said. He narrowed his eyes as he studied their employee's face. "Do you recognize that name?"

"From when I lived with my uncle?" Ivan asked.

Milek nodded.

Ivan shook his head. "No. I didn't recognize the place, either, last night, but Uncle Viktor didn't bring me everywhere he went."

"I would try to sell the boyfriend cover to Sims, too," Milek suggested.

"You want me to talk to him?" Ivan asked. He looked at Officer Carlson, who stood with Blair Etheridge, out of hearing range. "You're not trusting her to do it?"

"Absolutely not," Milek said. "She pulled her weapon on Josh just over a week ago. She was entirely too invested in what was going on with the jewelry thefts and now she's inserted herself in this investigation, too."

"You suspect her?" Garek asked, and he sounded surprised, probably because he was generally the more cynical one of the two of them.

"I don't trust her," Milek said.

"My uncle had a lot of police officers on his payroll," Ivan said.

"And while she's young, she could have been on the force already before he went to prison," Garek said and stared at her.

As if she'd felt their stares, she glanced over at them, and her face flushed slightly.

"It's late. I should get Blair and Angel back to her place,"

Ivan said. His focus was on the gallery owner and not the officer, but it was clear that he wanted to get Blair away from Sheila Carlson.

"If you get the chance, talk to Sims," Milek said. "Ask him about the forgeries."

Ivan nodded and then headed over to Blair. He stepped close to her, as if shielding her from the officer. Carlson wouldn't pull a gun here, in front of witnesses. She'd done that to Josh in a dark alley.

"You really don't trust her?" Garek asked with surprise.

"Are we talking about the officer or Ms. Etheridge?" Milek asked.

Garek sighed. "Maybe both."

"And what about him?" Milek asked. The CEO was lingering, too, near the officer and Blair, like he'd been eavesdropping on the interrogation. "There's something about him."

"I know," Garek said. "The fact that he hired us to protect valuables."

"Or to set us up?" Milek asked.

"The thought has crossed my mind," Garek admitted. "Maybe we're not the only ones he's setting up."

"Blair Etheridge, too," Milek said.

"I can't quite figure out if someone's trying to launder money through art, like Viktor did, or what the hell this is," Garek said, his voice gruff with frustration.

"Doesn't feel like organized crime," Milek pointed out. "It's too sporadic and messy."

"That doesn't mean Viktor Chekov isn't involved," Garek stubbornly insisted. "Like Ivan said, he's getting old. And maybe a little senile."

"You want it to be him," Milek said.

"Why would I want that?"

"So he won't get out of prison. Ever."

"You think that's the motive behind his dementia act?" Garek asked with genuine alarm.

"We don't know that it's an act," Milek said.

Garek released a ragged sigh. "You're right. This probably doesn't have anything to do with him because what would he have against Blair Etheridge? And she's clearly the target."

Milek looked again at the damaged paintings. "But were she and Ivan targeted tonight or was the art?" he wondered aloud.

"While this explosion wasn't very big, they could have died last night," Garek reminded him. "Someone was shooting at them."

They both turned to watch as their employee and their client walked out together with the dog. Somebody would follow them; they'd already determined that from now on Ivan would have backup.

But would it be enough to save them if someone tried again, like they had the night before?

Chapter 10

He's just my bodyguard...

The words reverberated inside Ivan's head, like the throbbing pain after his concussion. Blair saying that had struck him like a blow, and he wasn't sure why. He'd only just met her; of course, he wasn't really her boyfriend.

All they'd shared was a couple of ill-advised kisses and some close calls with death. But was the real danger whoever was after her, or what he was beginning to feel for her?

He had to push aside those feelings of attraction and jealousy and hurt because he needed to focus. Someone was following him back to her place again. But this time he knew who it was: Blade.

He wasn't offended that his bosses thought he needed backup; he was grateful for it. His wasn't the only life at stake; there was Blair's and Angel's. The dog was harnessed in the middle of the bench seat, between Ivan and Blair, in the front of Ivan's truck. Garek had driven Blair to the studio that morning since she had a broken front passenger window.

Ivan couldn't even see her around her dog. And Angel kept trying to lean across him to see out the window. Not that there was much to see, with as dark as it was now. Ivan gently pushed the dog back, so Angel's enormous head didn't block his vision. But then the dog whined and swiped his tongue across the side of Ivan's face.

"Once we get to your place, I'm going to need to shower off his slobber," Ivan remarked idly. He expected Blair to laugh but she just made some strange sound. "Are you okay?" he asked with concern. He hoped she wasn't crying, although he could understand if she was. She'd been through a hell of a lot the past couple of days. Actually, she'd been through a hell of a lot her whole life.

Like him.

Like a lot of the Payne Protection bosses and staff.

"Yeah," she said. "I'm just…"

When she trailed off and didn't continue, he filled in the blank with a guess. "Exhausted?"

"That, too."

"Upset," he added.

"That, too."

"I get it," he said. "You have a lot riding on the gallery opening—"

"Everything," she interjected. "I have everything riding on it opening. I'll go bankrupt if it doesn't open. I'll be completely broke."

And he suspected broken emotionally since she was so determined to make the place a success to honor her dead father.

She continued, "That's why it's preposterous that anyone would think I had something to do with that explosion."

"I didn't think that," he assured her.

"But you think my dad laundered money for your uncle," she said. "And I think you wondered if I was going to do the same thing out of the gallery."

He sighed and admitted, "Yes, I did. But I don't anymore. I can see how much it bothers you that people think your father did."

She released a shaky little breath.

He didn't know if she was relieved that he didn't believe her capable of complicity anymore. Or if she was just exhausted, as she'd admitted moments ago.

"You've had your doubts about me, too," he said. "About my character because of my uncle."

"Yes. Now I know how it feels to be judged by what someone else has done. I'm sorry."

He waved off her apology and Angel's big head. "I get it." He pulled up to the gate outside the mansion and the carriage house. "Now, I need the code to get in."

She unclasped her belt. "I'm not supposed to give that out to anyone."

"Didn't you give it out to the nine-one-one dispatcher last night?" he asked. "The gates opened when Officer Carlson's vehicle pulled up."

She leaned around Angel and shook her head. "I didn't give it out. Lionel must have called, too, and given it out or opened the gates for her."

"So it's okay for him to give it out?"

"It's his place," she said. "And after what happened today, I'm probably not going to be welcome here anymore. I'll have to find a new place to stay."

"That might be safer," he said. As well as Milek's studio, his bosses' franchise of the Payne Protection Agency had an apartment in the restored warehouse. He would have preferred to take her there, but Milek wanted him to talk to Sims with her. And Ivan sure as hell didn't want her doing that alone. He didn't want her going anywhere alone, not with the danger she was clearly in.

"Roll down your window," she said, and she edged between the dash and Angel and leaned over the steering wheel, which put her face very close to his.

A sudden urge to kiss her gripped him again. Hell, it wasn't sudden. It was constant, this urge to kiss her and more.

"You don't have power windows?" she asked.

And he realized he hadn't even reached for the crank. He did when she did, and their hands touched. That contact sent the same jolt through him their kisses had. That last kiss had sent more than a jolt; it had sent him to the ground…because of that damn explosion. He needed to stay focused, so he cleared his throat, and hopefully his head, and said, "I've got this."

She jerked her hand away, and he rolled down the window. Then she leaned over the steering wheel again to reach through the open window toward the security panel. But her hand fell short of the panel, and she wound up just about straddling his lap to reach it. The side of her body pressed against his chest. Heat radiated from her and seemed to scorch him because he got very hot.

After their last kiss ended with an explosion, he shouldn't have been so drawn to her. But it was as if his body had a mind of its own, and she was the only thing on that mind.

She entered the code then scrambled back to her seat as the gates began to open. "He didn't change the code."

Ivan wasn't sure if that was good or bad. If the gates hadn't opened for them, he would have been able to take her back to the Payne Protection apartment, where he knew she would have been safe. But Blade pulled through the gate behind them.

"Who's that?" she asked.

"Sparks," he said. "Blade Sparks. You met him at the gallery."

"I met a lot of people today."

People usually remembered meeting the former boxer. Ivan was happy that Blair didn't, though. That damn jealousy again…for which he had no right.

"Why is he here?" she asked.

"He's backup," Ivan said. "We're not risking a repeat of what happened last night and today." But just coming back here risked a repeat. Obviously, the shooter already knew where she lived.

Was that because he'd followed Ivan back here last night? Or was that because he lived here, too?

"We need to talk to Sims," he said, but dread curled in his stomach. At least Ivan was armed. But his backup, a former felon, wasn't allowed to carry a weapon. Fortunately, Blade was a weapon. In addition to boxing, he'd also won championships in mixed martial arts.

"*I* need to talk to Lionel," Blair said but sounded as if she dreaded it, too.

"You can't go in there alone."

"He's not going to let anyone but me inside the house," Blair said.

"But I'm your boyfriend," he reminded her. Instead of turning toward the carriage house, he followed the circular drive up to the double front doors of the mansion. While spotlights lit up the outside of the house, no lights shone in the many dark windows that faced the driveway. "Is he even here?"

"He travels a lot for his job," she said.

"What is his job?" Ivan asked. "Besides trying to pass off forgeries as original art?"

"I'm sure what he showed me was real. And the appraiser saw them, too."

"But that wasn't what was delivered to your gallery

today." Those forgeries and a bomb had showed up instead. And Ivan needed to find out what Lionel Sims knew about those.

Light suddenly illuminated the entire sky, like it was day instead of night. Like lightning had flashed. But it wasn't a flash. The light remained, and then the sound of chopper blades sliced through the night, too.

Sims had to be involved, and now he was trying to get away. Ivan wasn't going to let that happen. Not again.

One minute Ivan was behind the wheel of his jacked-up truck, and the next he was gone, the driver's door still open. Angel strained against the bench seat, trying to chase after him. Fortunately, he was harnessed in, but Blair wasn't. She threw open the passenger's door and jumped down.

The helicopter lit up the entire estate, spotlighting Ivan, glowing in his light hair and on his face, as he ran around toward where the machine was due to land in the backyard, behind the pool house. That was where Lionel's helicopter pad was.

Was he coming or going?

Either way, she wanted to catch him to tell him what had happened. But she didn't want to catch him as badly as Ivan seemed to. She ran, but she couldn't close the distance between them. Although she was tall, he was much taller, his legs much longer. He reached the backyard first, jumped over the clear glass fence that surrounded the inground pool and kept running.

He'd easily hurdled that fence whereas Blair slammed her body against the glass, unable to even grasp the top of it. She backed up and ran faster and then jumped, and even then she just managed to grasp the top of it. Her fingers burned, and her grip began to slip. She tried to get leverage with her legs and knees, but they slipped against the glass. She had to pull herself up. Panting with exertion, she finally managed to drag herself over the top. As she jumped down onto the concrete patio on the other side, another body joined hers, as the other bodyguard cleared it as easily as Ivan had.

Were he and Ivan bodyguards or supermen? Able to leap buildings, or at least high fences, in a single bound?

"Stay here," the man shouted, but he kept running in the same direction Ivan had.

And so did Blair.

They skirted around the pool house and came upon the brightly lit helicopter pad just as the machine started rising again.

As it rose, Ivan leaped for it, wrapping his arms around one of the landing skids as if he could pull the helicopter from the sky. But it kept going up, taking him with it, and his long body dangled from it.

The sound of the propellors drowned out the scream that tore from Blair's throat.

"Why haven't you questioned Lionel Sims yet?" Chief Woodrow Lynch demanded.

He'd had his doubts about Officer Carlson, especially given how quickly she'd shown up at the scene of the shooting last night and the explosion again tonight. So he'd called his best detective back early from his family leave, again, to take over the case. And to check out Sheila Carlson.

His predecessor, who'd been an FBI agent Woodrow had mentored, had served as an interim chief of the River City PD for a while to try to ferret out all the corruption. Woodrow had believed Nick Payne had done a good job until Luther Mills's rampage during his trial.

Woodrow had hoped that whoever was corrupt in the police department, district attorney's office and crime labs had been exposed then and there was no one left to worry about.

Then he could retire as planned, and hopefully turn over the reins to Spencer, so Woodrow could spend more time with his beautiful wife. Time that late-night visits and phone calls didn't interrupt like they did all too often now.

Spencer, who'd been pacing the wide front porch of the two-story yellow farmhouse where Woodrow lived with his bride, stopped and sighed. "He isn't a man you can reach without going through his lawyers first. They claim they will get back to me with a time that Sims is available to answer my questions."

"If he wants the insurance company to pay him out for that destroyed artwork, he's going to need to file a police report."

"He said he could do that through Officer Carlson," Dubridge said. "And I informed him that I was on the case now."

Woodrow cursed. "Too many people think they deserve preferential treatment from the police department," he said. "That they can pay them for what they want."

"Unfortunately, that happened a lot before Nick and you cleaned up the department," Dubridge admitted. "But not now."

"You don't think he's paying Carlson for that expedited police report?"

Dubridge shook his head. "I checked her out like you requested. I didn't find any red flags in her financials or in her human-resources records."

"I just don't like the coincidences of her showing up as quickly as she does to these crime scenes involving the Payne Protection Agency cases."

“Maybe it’s not a coincidence,” Dubridge conceded.

“Then what is it?”

“An ambitious young officer taking an initiative so that she can make detective fast,” he said. “I once worked with an officer like her, and now I’m married to her.” He glanced at his watch. “And I’d like to get home to her, too.”

“I’m sorry,” Woodrow said. “I know I keep bothering you while you should be taking care of your new daughter and your wife.”

“Keeli insisted I help out where I can,” Dubridge said. “She’s part of the Payne Protection family now as one of the bodyguards with Parker’s branch of the agency.”

“You’re a part of the Payne Protection family, too,” Penny said from where she was sitting in a swing on that wraparound porch.

Woodrow had been snuggling with her when Dubridge drove up a short while ago. Even though it was late, they hadn’t been able to sleep yet. Penny was on edge, and when she was on edge, Woodrow was, too. His wife had an uncanny and infamous ability to determine when someone was in danger. It was like her sixth sense or something. He knew it was because she was so empathetic and loving.

Woodrow wasn’t as empathetic and loving as she was, but he was pretty sure that someone was in danger, too. And he knew who that was.

Ivan Chekov.

He’d nearly been shot last night, and tonight he could have been blown up. He wasn’t certain what would happen to him next but knew something would.

Chapter 11

Just as he'd rounded the corner of the pool house, Ivan had seen the tall man in a suit jump into the back of the helicopter. He'd recognized Lionel Sims from the night before. While he hadn't spoken to him, he'd watched as first Officer Carlson and then Garek had. While the man was bald, he wasn't old, and probably not old enough to be the friend of her father's Blair claimed he was.

So what and who the hell was her benefactor really?

Wanting to know the answers to those questions, Ivan yelled at him to stop. But the sound of the helicopter drowned out his voice.

So he ran, closing the distance between himself and that helicopter just as it began to rise up into the sky. And he jumped and grabbed on to one of the landing skids. "Put it down!" he shouted. "Put it down."

The chopper's blades were so loud, whirring overhead, that he doubted they could hear him. The wind from those blades tore at his clothes, even made his skin move, as the helicopter continued to rise.

Then the pilot must have noticed him because the helicopter paused and hovered, still high enough above the ground that if Ivan fell, he was going to get hurt. Maybe badly. But if it kept going up, and he fell, he was going to die for certain. Did he let go now, while he might survive?

Ivan's whole life had been a battle to survive. And he wasn't about to give up now, so he fought. He wrapped his legs around the skid, too, and with them locked around the metal, he released one of his hands and reached for the door. He had to get inside the helicopter before it climbed any higher into the sky. His hand tapped the metal, but he couldn't reach the handle. So he pounded hard on the door, using his fist to pummel the metal until his knuckles hurt.

Finally the chopper started going back down. When it got closer to that landing pad, he released his grasp on the skid and dropped onto the ground. Then he curled up and rolled out of the way as the blades cut through the air.

Maybe the pilot was just dropping him off before flying away again. With Sims. And Ivan was going to miss his chance to question the man. But then the helicopter skids touched down, too.

He could see Sparks and Blair standing on the other side of the pad from him, their shoulders hunched up around their heads for protection as they ducked lower. Chopper blades had beheaded people before. They needed to get back. He shouted at them to do that, especially if Sims or his pilot were armed when those doors opened.

But then the chopper blades stopped and the engine cut out, leaving an eerie silence…until people started shouting. At him.

"What the hell were you thinking!"

"Who the hell are you?"

"You could've been killed!"

He couldn't differentiate the male voices but when Blair spoke, he recognized hers.

"Ivan…oh, my God…" Her voice shook with emotion.

He just wasn't sure what that emotion was. Anger or something else.

Wanting to comfort her, Ivan finally surged to his feet. And even though his legs were a little shaky, he started toward her, where she stood with Sparks, Sims and another man. Then a gun cocked, the barrel pointed at Ivan.

"Don't shoot him!" Blair screamed now. "He's my…boyfriend."

"What the hell was your boyfriend thinking?" Sims asked.

"I…we…have to tell you something," she began, her voice still shaking. Was it over his escapade with the helicopter, or what she had to tell her benefactor?

The older man sighed. And up closer now, Ivan could see the lines in his face. Sims was older than he'd thought, but still not as old as her father probably had been. "An officer and then a detective already called about what happened at your gallery, Blair."

"I'm sorry, Lione—"

"It's alright," he said, and he looped an arm around her shoulders to offer a comforting hug.

Why was it alright? Because he thought the insurance would cover them or because he knew the pieces were forgeries? Or because he had so much money he didn't care if he lost some?

"That delivery wasn't from me," he said. He gestured in the direction of his mansion. "The pieces I promised to loan you are still safely inside. I know the gallery isn't ready for them yet, especially after last night. And now…" He glanced from Ivan to Sparks. "What's going on, Blair?"

She blinked. "I wish I knew."

"I know you have big plans for your father's place, Blair,"

he said. "But maybe this was a bad idea. Maybe you should go back to Europe."

"Is that a threat?" Ivan asked, and despite the pilot still pointing the gun at him, he stepped closer to Blair.

"With everything that's happened to her over the past couple of days, it's just good advice," Sims said. The older man looked from him to Sparks again. "And Blair, I would also be careful about the company you're keeping."

Had Sims recognized him or Sparks? And from where?

Blair was almost giddy with relief, so much so that her knees were like jelly as she climbed the stairs to the carriage-house apartment over the garage. As if impatient with her slow ascent, Angel pushed past her to run up the rest of the way, probably to his food bowl. She slipped on a step as his stubby tail struck her, and she might have fallen but strong arms caught her, then wrapped around her.

"You are exhausted," Ivan murmured, his voice and his breath close to her ear. His chest pressed against her back.

Sensations raced through her. Relief, anger, desire…she felt all of that for him. And more…

Then he lifted her from her feet, carrying her up the last few steps and through the door of her apartment. She wriggled free of his embrace and whirled around to face him. "What were you thinking?" she asked.

He shrugged his broad shoulders. "That you were exhausted. I just wanted to make sure you got safely upstairs."

She shook her head. "Not that…"

Though she couldn't remember the last time anyone had carried her anywhere. Maybe her mother. Just as she did every time a memory of her mother crossed her mind, she pushed it away. Because every memory felt like a betrayal all over again—not just her mother's, but hers. Like just thinking about her mom, after how she'd hurt her dad, was betraying him.

She was dealing with too many emotions right now to add guilt to the mix. But she let anger whip through her. "What the hell were you thinking to grab on to a helicopter like that?" Blair demanded, her voice cracking as she remembered how terrified she'd been that he was going to fall. "You could have died."

"I'm fine," he said, his deep voice soft. "Not a scratch on me."

She shook her head, unable to say anything as tears threatened. She didn't know if they were tears of anger, frustration, or relief. But just like the memory of her mother, she suppressed them. There was one emotion she couldn't suppress any longer. Her desire for him.

And if something happened to him, which was likely with how much danger he willingly put himself in, she would regret never acting on that desire.

She cleared her throat and said, "Prove it."

His dark eyes widened. "What?"

"Prove it," she challenged him as she stepped out of her shoes. "Take off your clothes."

He sucked in a breath. "Blair…"

"Take off your clothes," she told him as she reached for the buttons on her own shirt and began sliding them through the holes until the silk fabric parted and exposed her lacy black bra.

He emitted something that sounded a lot more dangerous than Angel's growl. But Angel, exhausted from trying to get out of the harness in the truck, didn't even move from his big doggy bed in a corner of the living room.

Blair took a step backward, heading toward the open door to her bedroom. As she did, she unzipped her pants.

Ivan's throat moved as if he was struggling to swallow. Then he followed her, taking just one step, just as she had, as if they were dancing. His voice still a deep growl, he said, "Blair, this isn't a good idea."

"Neither was grabbing on to a helicopter as it was taking off."

He chuckled. "I can't argue with that."

"So you do dangerous things sometimes," she said. "What's stopping you now?"

"I'm supposed to be protecting you. I can't be distracted."

"You have backup outside, and Lionel said he would add some guards, too, if necessary." She was actually surprised he'd been so understanding. But that was probably because his artwork hadn't been damaged. She was so damn relieved about that, but not as relieved as she was that Ivan was alright. And that he was here, with her.

Finally, he unhooked his holster and slid it off. Then he lifted his shirt, dragging it up over his washboard abs and heavily muscled chest. The shirt dropped onto the floor with hers.

She unclasped her bra and let it drop.

He growled again. "You're driving me crazy."

"I know the feeling," she said. "You do the same to me." This was crazy, giving in to the passion burning between them. It was more likely to consume them than that bomb back at the gallery.

But she couldn't fight it and refused to. She just wanted him. She shimmied her hips until her pants slid down over them and then down her legs. She took another step back and stepped out of them.

Ivan took that step with her, toward her. His fingers jerked the button loose on his jeans, then dragged down the zipper already straining over the erection pushing against the fly.

He was big everywhere.

She emitted something like a growl now as her body began to throb with anticipation, with desire, with a burning need for release. "Come here..."

It seemed her words snapped an invisible leash he'd had reining him in because he shot forward like he had when he'd grabbed the landing skid of the helicopter. And he wrapped his arms around her the same way. Then his head started toward hers, but before their lips touched, he paused with just a breath between them and asked, "Are you sure?"

She reached out, gliding her fingertips over his chest and down the rippling muscles of his stomach to the waistband of his boxers. "Very, very sure..."

But even though she'd given consent—hell, she'd given him a green light to go as fast as he could—he held back, his mouth just above hers. "You just want to check me for scratches, right?"

She laughed hard. "Yeah, that's all I want to do..." With her fingers in the waistband of his boxers, she pulled him into her bedroom and back until her legs hit the side of her mattress. They tumbled onto the bed together.

But he rolled quickly, probably so he wouldn't crush her, and she tumbled across his chest, her naked breasts sliding over his muscles.

A moan escaped her lips, and he reached up and clasped her breasts, holding them in his big hands. Then he arched his head until their lips finally met. They kissed. Again and again, their mouths opening, mating, and he stroked his thumbs over her nipples.

Pleasure shot through her body from those sensitive points directly to her core where her panties were already wet. She wanted him so damn badly, more than she'd ever wanted anyone else. She straddled his body, which wasn't easy because he was arching up, dragging down his jeans and his briefs until he was lying totally naked beneath her.

Then he groaned again, as if he was in pain. Maybe he'd lied about not having even a scratch on him. She pushed her knees against the mattress and levered herself up. "What's wrong?"

"I don't have protection," he said.

Another laugh slipped through her lips. "Of course, you don't. You like living dangerously."

"Not with that," he assured her. "I never go without that kind of protection. But I haven't been in a relationship for a long time."

"Me, neither," she said. "I've been tested and I have an IUD. It's safe if you're safe."

"I've been tested, too," he said. "All clean."

But he wasn't safe. She knew that. He was destined to leave like other people she'd cared about had. But when he left, she wanted no regrets, and if they didn't do this, she would regret it.

He arched up again and rolled her over onto her back. Then he dragged her panties over her hips and down her legs, and settled between them. His tongue swiped over her once, twice, before dipping inside her. And his hands stretched up her body, cupping her breasts again. As his tongue swirled and his thumbs stroked her nipples, an orgasm gripped her. She bit her lip to hold in a scream as pleasure made her body convulse and shudder.

Then he moved up her body, kissing her stomach and her breasts. Her legs were still parted, and she felt his erection rubbing there. She reached between them and wrapped her fingers around him. He was so thick and long, and already pulsating within her grasp. The tension he'd released just seconds again gripped her again. She needed him inside her.

She guided him in as he levered most of his weight on his forearms. He used his hips, thrusting gently at first. Then she wrapped her legs around him, clutching him with her inner thighs.

He growled again like a dog fighting a leash.

Blair was beyond control. She writhed and thrust her hips and tried to take him as deep as she could, so that she didn't know where he ended and she began. She raked her nails down his back to his buttocks, which flexed beneath her grasp. The man was muscle everywhere.

Then he snapped his leash again and matched her frantic rhythm. The tension he'd built again with each thrust broke, and this time she couldn't contain her entire scream of passion, of release, as another orgasm gripped her with an intensity she'd never known. With a pleasure she'd never known.

It was almost too much. He was most definitely not safe. Not for her heart.

The explosion at the gallery had gone exactly as planned. Small and not too much damage. That had been part of the plan. But maybe a bigger explosion was in order now.

One that would take out both the woman and the man, as well as that other man who sat in his vehicle watching the carriage house. The bodyguard wasn't the only one watching them.

But the other person didn't want to protect them. They wanted to kill them.

Chapter 12

Another bomb had gone off, but just inside of Ivan. And it probably had done more damage than the one in the gallery the day before. He was shell-shocked by the intensity of the passion that had burned between him and Blair last night. He'd been so shell-shocked that even though he'd initially fallen asleep, like she had, wrapped up in each other's arms and tangled sheets, he'd awoken with a start and with a fear so intense that there had been no way for him to fall back to sleep.

Especially with Blair lying beside him, so beautiful with her naked skin still flushed from their passion. He couldn't sleep with her because that fear gripping him was both for her and of her.

He'd never felt pleasure so intense that it had been almost painful. And damn, he wanted to experience it again. But she'd made it clear at the gallery, after the real explosion, that he was just her bodyguard.

A bodyguard who wasn't doing a good job. While he'd managed to protect her, the best way to truly keep her safe was to find and stop whoever was behind these attacks on her.

He'd talked to Lionel Sims, but he wasn't sure he'd gotten honest answers or a story the older man had improvised after Officer Carlson had forewarned him about the forgeries. He'd been found out, so, of course, he would deny that they were his.

"What do you think?" he asked Angel, who'd abandoned his doggy bed to join Ivan on the couch. He rubbed his hand over the rottweiler's big head.

Angel just stared up at him. He didn't have any clue, either, what was going on, especially last night, when Ivan and Blair had dropped their clothes on a path from the stairs to the bedroom.

Ivan swallowed a groan as his body reacted to the memory of her undressing, teasing him, tempting him. She was a temptation he would never be able to resist. But he had to, so that he could stay focused on keeping her safe.

A creak on the stairs leading up from the garage forewarned Ivan of possible danger. He tensed and drew his gun from his holster. Angel lifted his head and peered at the door. The knob began to turn slowly, and a low growl emanated from the dog's throat and maybe from Ivan's as well. He moved quickly but quietly from the couch, making sure to keep his body between the door to the stairs and the door to Blair's bedroom. Fortunately, he'd put her clothes in it and shut the door after he'd left her bed. He was fully dressed now, too.

And awake and ready for whatever threat he faced.

What had happened to Blade?

He should have stopped anyone from getting inside the carriage house. Or maybe it was Blade. So while he flipped off the safety and trained his gun on the door, he only put his finger along the barrel, not on the trigger.

Not yet.

But he was ready. He would do whatever it took to keep Blair safe. Even take a life...or give up his.

* * *

The buzz of her cell reached Blair, pulling her from the depths of sleep, from the most delicious dream. She tried to resist because she would rather stay here, in Ivan's arms. But then she stretched her arms and felt only cold sheets. He was gone.

Had it been just a dream?

Had he not really kissed her or touched her or filled her up as he had?

But her lips felt slightly swollen from their hungry kisses. And her body ached from how tightly she'd grasped his, how desperately she'd clung to him as they'd driven each other to a release so intense it felt like madness.

And it had been.

What had she been thinking?

Her face heated with embarrassment and with passion. She wanted him again.

But those sheets were cold, so he'd left her bed a while ago. She opened her eyes, and she could see him nowhere in the light filtering through the blinds on the bedroom window. But she could see her phone lighting up as it continued to ring.

Maybe he was calling. She swiped to accept and breathlessly answered. "Hello?"

"Miss Etheridge?" That very feminine voice was definitely not Ivan's, but familiar. Unfortunately.

"Officer Carlson?"

"Yes, please open the gates for me. I have some follow-up questions for you."

"For me?" she asked. "Shouldn't you have those for Mr. Sims instead? Or did you already ask him everything when you contacted him last night?" Blair had been relieved that Lionel hadn't sent that delivery to the gallery yesterday, that the damaged artwork hadn't been his originals. But she'd seen the skepticism on Ivan's handsome face and on Blade Sparks's; the two bodyguards hadn't believed his story, especially when Ivan had requested to see the actual artwork and Lionel had refused. He'd claimed he was already late for an important meeting because of Ivan grabbing his helicopter.

Her heart fluttered with the fear she'd felt seeing him dangling so far above the ground. If he'd fallen, he would have been seriously injured or maybe killed instantly from the impact. That was why she'd wanted so badly to make love with him, to celebrate life after the past couple of days had brought them so close to death.

"Miss Etheridge, you need to open the gates," the officer said again.

"I already gave you my statement last night," Blair reminded her. "And I thought a detective was going to take over the investigation." Garek or Milek had mentioned that, too, and hadn't seemed to have a lot of faith in the ambitious young police officer.

Or was that trust?

There was something suspicious about her intensity to investigate while also speaking to Lionel Sims before anyone else. Like she'd warned him.

Or maybe Blair was just letting Ivan's suspicions cloud her judgment. She knew how hard it was sometimes for women to be taken seriously in their careers. She'd struggled to have people accept her as a business owner. She couldn't imagine the struggles against misogyny that the young officer had probably endured.

She sighed. "Give me a couple of minutes and I'll open the gate." First, she had to get dressed. Fortunately, the bathroom was off the bedroom, so she didn't have to walk out into the living room, where Ivan undoubtedly was. She cleaned up quickly and put on fresh clothes instead of the ones Ivan must have draped over a chair for her. Then she drew in a breath, bracing herself to face her lover before she opened the bedroom door.

Angel nearly fell into the room when she opened it; he must have been leaning against the door. While he was her furry companion, he seemed to have switched his affection to Ivan the past couple of days. So she didn't think he would have missed her if he'd had Ivan's attention.

But the man who glanced up when she stepped out was not Ivan. He was a big man, too, but it wasn't the former boxer, with his dark hair and crooked nose. It was the other big guy, who had sandy hair and hazel eyes and another name she didn't like. Viktor.

Viktor Lagransky. She glanced around to see if Ivan was somewhere else in the open living area. But he was gone; she should have known it because some of the energy seemed to have left the air. It felt stale and flat instead of tingling with invisible currents as it did whenever Ivan was in her vicinity.

Especially last night.

Last night had been like being electrocuted in some ways; all that passion and pleasure had shocked her entire system, especially her heart.

And her head. She knew better than to get involved with anyone. Especially when they left her like Ivan must have left. Pride stinging, she didn't ask where he was. Instead, she walked over to the security panel that operated the front gate as well as other alarms. "Officer Carlson wants to talk to me," she said.

"Good thing I made some coffee." Viktor gestured toward the pot on the counter in the kitchenette. It wasn't entirely full, but the man had no mug in his hand. "Ivan needed some, too, before he left to meet with our bosses."

So that was where he'd gone.

"Garek and Milek summoned him to report about Sims," Viktor continued, as if defending Ivan leaving her, like he knew how much it bothered her to wake up to find him gone. Like how she'd found her mom gone and how she'd found her bags packed for boarding school.

What had Ivan told him? Had he bragged about how she'd thrown herself at him last night?

She felt a twinge of guilt for even considering it because Ivan didn't seem the type to brag about anything. He'd spent too much of his life trying to hide from his uncle that she doubted he ever sought to draw attention to himself. Which was probably what made him such a good bodyguard.

But he was too good-looking and well-built to not attract attention, especially hers. That was probably why Viktor was explaining his whereabouts to her; he was probably used to clients falling for his coworker.

"At least he knows what they want to ask him about," she said. "I don't know what Officer Carlson wants. She already took my report last night."

Viktor stood and approached the door to the stairs. "And she's not even the one handling the case anymore. Detective Dubridge took over at the chief's request."

Despite being fully clothed now, Blair shivered. "There is something a little too intense about Officer Carlson," she admitted.

Viktor nodded. "Yeah. I figured it was just ambition."

But obviously, he had his doubts about her, too, which was understandable given how many people had been on the payroll of Viktor Chekov.

Footsteps sounded lightly on the stairs and Viktor

opened the door just as the officer appeared at it. "Hello, Officer Carlson," he greeted.

"I saw Josh Stafford outside," she said.

Did she have the bodyguards mixed up, or had Josh replaced Blade like Viktor had Ivan?

"Why are you here, too?" the officer asked Viktor.

"Because someone's trying to kill Ms. Etheridge, and we don't want that to happen, do we?"

As if the young officer would admit that she really did want Blair gone…

But what would be her motive for that? What would be anyone's motive for wanting to kill Blair? She didn't understand why anyone would come after her. Sure, Z wasn't happy she'd turned down his romantic advances, and Jean-Paul didn't understand why she wouldn't showcase his art, but neither was angry enough with her to try to kill her.

And what would that accomplish? She couldn't date Z if she was dead, and she couldn't showcase Jean-Paul's work if she was dead. If that had been his actual work yesterday, he certainly wouldn't have blown up the best thing he'd ever created.

"*I* don't want Ms. Etheridge getting hurt," Officer Carlson said. "That's why I'm here. I wanted to check up on you and make sure that everything was okay." The young woman peered around the place as if looking for someone, probably the same person Blair had been looking for when she'd stepped out of the bedroom moments ago.

Ivan definitely attracted attention and interest.

"Everything is not okay," Blair admitted.

The officer touched the gun strapped to her belt. "Do you need help?"

"I need you or that detective assigned to the case to

find out who's been doing these things and stop them," Blair said.

"I know you're afraid—"

"I'm pissed off," she interjected. "There is no reason for someone to be coming after me."

"It's quite a coincidence all this started just as Mason Hull insisted you hire the Payne Protection Agency," the officer mused.

Blair had thought the same thing herself, but to admit that now would feel like a betrayal. "Ivan Chekov risked his life to save mine," she said. "He isn't the one putting it in danger."

"He isn't the one who insisted you hire the Payne Protection Agency. What do you know about Mason Hull? And why is a CEO getting so involved with policy owners? The only person I talk to at my insurance company is the customer-service rep who takes my payments."

Viktor snorted but then almost begrudgingly nodded. "Same here."

"I have some valuable pieces that will be on loan and for sale in the gallery," she said. "My insurance policy, what they call an inland marine, for those items has a very high coverage amount for those valuables. That's what Mr. Hull wanted the Payne Protection Agency to protect."

"Specifically the branch that the sons of a former jewel thief own?" Officer Carlson persisted. "Isn't that like having the foxes guard the henhouse?"

"I am not a hen," Blair said. While she couldn't deny she needed protection, she resented the hell out of the fact that she did, that someone was trying to make her life as difficult as her father's had been.

"No, you're not," Officer Carlson agreed. "I was talking about the—"

"The fact that I'm a fox," Viktor Lagransky interjected. Then he flashed the officer a cocky grin.

The young woman blushed. "As in sneaky."

"Sexy," he repeated as if he'd misheard her.

"I didn't say—"

Viktor chuckled. "I see how you look at me, Officer Carlson."

"With suspicion," she said, then turned back to Blair. "And that's how you should be looking at them, Ms. Etheridge. You have to be careful of the company you're keeping."

Lionel Sims had given her the same warning the night before, and instead of heeding it, Blair was getting annoyed. "So you're rushing to judgment of people based on who their relatives were or what they might have had to do to survive in the past," Blair said. She wasn't just defending the Payne Protection Agency or even Ivan right now. She was defending herself.

"Good, honest people don't hang around criminal elements," the officer said.

She wasn't just ambitious; she was also idealistic.

"You did the same thing to me last night," Blair reminded her. "You're judging people based on associations and rumors. I was a child the last time I was ever around the gallery, so I don't know what all went on there. But I do know that my father wasn't part of it." At least not willingly, but as Ivan had pointed out, most of the people who'd been involved with his uncle hadn't done so willingly.

They'd had good reason to comply or they might have wound up dead, like Ivan's father. Like Ivan could have if his uncle's hit had been carried out. The thought of how many times he'd come close to death, especially last night, chilled her. Even just meeting with his bosses, he could be in danger.

How many times could he come close to dying before his luck gave out?

And then she would be alone again, just as she'd been when her mom left and her dad sent her away and then died. She couldn't put herself through another loss. She couldn't lose anyone else she cared about, so she had to get Ivan out of her life as soon as possible before she did something even stupider than having sex with him. Before she fell in love with him.

Garek narrowed his eyes and intensely studied the man sitting across from him. Was he still as evil as he'd always been? Of course, he was.

Even if this confused, old-man routine was real, that didn't make Viktor Chekov any less evil than he'd ever been. "Your nephew might have bought your act yesterday," Garek said. "But I don't."

"Patek?" Viktor asked, and he leaned closer to the glass separating them.

Just as he'd acted yesterday, like Ivan was his father, he was acting like he'd mistaken Garek for his. So his act wasn't even all that original, unless he was stuck somewhere in his dark and twisted past.

"If you weren't such a damn good thief," Viktor continued, his voice weak and thready instead of containing the booming strength it used to hold, "I think I'd have you killed just for being so pretty that you annoy me."

Garek laughed. "I think you'd have me killed for another reason than my looks."

"For what?" Viktor asked. "What have you done, Patek? Surely, you would never betray me. You have young children, probably more than you know you do."

Like Sylvie. His half sister, whom Garek had only previously suspected he had, recently came into his life. She was also Josh Stafford's half sister and now Garek's employee, too. Viktor had hinted at her existence before.

"Family means everything to you, Patek, just as it does to me," Viktor continued. "Unlike my brother…who did betray me, leaving his young son alone and helpless."

"Ivan isn't alone any longer," Garek said. "He has people around him who care about him, who will protect him. So you better not be coming after him or anyone else."

"As I said, Patek, as long as you don't betray me, you're safe."

Patek Kozminski had died a few years ago. He hadn't been safe. And Garek had a horrible feeling that nobody was.

Chapter 13

Getting called back to the agency in the middle of an assignment felt to Ivan like getting called to the principal's office. Like he'd done something wrong. Or worse, it reminded him of getting called to his uncle's office, but that had usually been because he hadn't done something wrong. He hadn't stolen enough stuff; he hadn't brought in enough money to pay for his food and board. When his uncle was appointed his guardian, it had come with a price Ivan had had to pay.

He'd probably have to pay for what he'd done last night, too. He'd crossed the line with a client…even before last night. When Viktor had shown up at the carriage house to take over his protection duty for him, he'd warned Ivan about the security footage from the gallery. That his kiss with Blair, just before that blast, was on the recording.

Not that he would have lied about what happened. Not that he even really regretted it.

Kissing Blair, making love with her, was the most pleasure he'd ever felt in his life. But he knew that it would probably lead to pain, too.

He just didn't want it to be hers. He wanted to get back to her as soon as possible. He wanted this meeting over with his bosses, but while he'd driven right away to the agency, Milek and Garek had yet to show up.

Hell, he'd been sitting at his desk alone in the office for over an hour. Finally, a door creaked and opened, the heavy metal banging back against the wall. He turned toward the sound, but the guy walking through the door had dark hair.

"Blade, why are you here?" What had the former boxer done wrong? Alarm shot through him. "You're supposed to be guarding the outside of the carriage house. Nothing happened, right? She's okay?"

Blade nodded. "Yeah, she's fine."

Maybe Blair was up, though, and already heading to the gallery. Reopening her father's livelihood and making a success of it mattered more than anything else to her. It meant to her what honoring his dead dad meant to him: everything.

He's just my bodyguard...

That was all he would ever be for her.

"Josh took my place," Blade said. "I got called back here to start a new assignment."

"A new assignment?" Dread clenched his stomach into knots. That better not be why he'd been called back here. "Blair is in serious danger. We should all be protecting *her* right now." That was definitely where he needed to be, at her side, keeping her safe.

"She's not the only one in danger," Blade said. "Apparently Mason Hull has another high-profile client in need of protection, and I'm getting assigned to be her bodyguard."

"What? Is there a life-insurance policy on her that he's worried about having to pay out?" Ivan asked. "I just don't get this guy. He takes way too much interest in his policyholders."

Blade shrugged. "I don't know much yet. Just that's she's

a very wealthy widow with a lot of valuable assets. Apparently there have been some attempted break-ins or something."

"So it's her stuff that's in danger, not her?" Then her assignment shouldn't take priority over Blair's.

Blade shrugged again. "Like I said, I don't know much yet. I'm here to get briefed. Why are you here?"

"I don't know," he said. But he could hazard a guess. His bosses had seen that security footage. Maybe that was why Milek and Garek weren't here yet; they were deciding what to do.

"It could be a few things," Blade said. "Like trying to tackle a helicopter or—"

"Kissing a client," Ivan said, finishing for him. "Viktor already warned me about the security footage catching that."

"What?" Blade asked, his blue eyes widening in surprise. "You and the gallery owner?"

Ivan nodded. "I thought you knew."

"No. Garek and Milek sent all that security footage over to the police department and to the Payne Protection Agency resident IT expert, Nikki Payne-Ecklund."

"A lot gets dumped on her," Ivan remarked.

"Yeah, I heard a rumor that she might be starting her own branch of the Payne Protection Agency focusing on cybersecurity," Blade said. "She's already hired a couple of people to help her with monitoring security footage. But enough about Nikki. Tell me about this kiss. Or don't you kiss and tell?"

Ivan shook his head. "It was nothing."

The lie burned the back of his throat. But that was what he needed his bosses and his coworkers to believe, so that he wouldn't be taken off this assignment for crossing the line with a client. He couldn't trust anyone else to protect her like he would. He would do whatever he had to in order to keep her from harm, even give up his own life for hers.

The door had opened again. Viktor Lagransky moved much more quietly than the former boxer. He moved with the stealth that his father, the assassin, had. But it wasn't just Viktor who'd walked into the office; Angel and Blair were with him.

From the look of pain on her beautiful face, he suspected she'd heard what he'd said about that kiss. That it was nothing. Instead of protecting her, Ivan had hurt her.

It was nothing.

Blair had overheard enough to know that Ivan and Blade Sparks were talking about a kiss. And she'd thought that he wasn't the type to brag. Had she been wrong about that? About him?

Was that how Ivan felt about last night, too?

That it was nothing?

She wished she felt that way. That she'd just been acting on the curiosity she'd felt about the attraction between them. Or she'd been using him as a distraction from the danger she was in and the stress she was under. But it had been so much more than that…to her.

To him, had it been nothing? She wanted to confront him, to demand to know if they'd been talking about her. But she was a professional woman, a business owner, and she needed to act mature and in control of her emotions. Her emotions were about the only thing she could control right now. Though she definitely hadn't been in control of them the night before…

And knowing that, knowing how much he affected her, she couldn't even let herself look at him. But Angel didn't ignore him like she was trying to; he rushed right over to him and licked his hand.

"What are you two doing here?" Blade asked. "Did the bosses call a big meeting?"

Viktor glanced at her, probably waiting for her to answer since coming here had been her idea, one she regretted now.

"If that's the case, where are they?" Ivan asked, his voice gruff with annoyance. "I've been waiting for them for over an hour."

At least Viktor had been telling Blair the truth about that; Ivan had been summoned here. He hadn't requested this meeting with his bosses to get reassigned because he'd been as shaken as she was about the passion they'd experienced the night before. After having to run for his life as a teenager, maybe that was how he reacted to fear. Not that she knew for certain he was as scared as she was. Maybe that meant nothing to him like the kiss had.

It had definitely not been nothing to her. The kiss or anything else. Even now, after overhearing his comment, she still wanted him. He wore the shirt he'd taken off last night, but his muscles had just about stretched the wrinkles out of it except for where it hung loosely over his washboard abs. His jeans were tight around his thighs, too, but she knew they hung loosely around his lean waist. And now, she also knew what he looked like without his clothes. She wanted to see him that way again. Last night should have satisfied her curiosity, her craving for him, but it had just made her want him more.

That wasn't why she'd had Viktor bring her here. It hadn't been to track down Ivan. "I need to talk to Garek and Milek," she said. "Does anyone know where they are?"

"They're supposed to be here," Blade said. "I was meeting them, too."

"I've been here," one of the Kozminskis said as he walked through a door that wasn't the one Viktor had had to enter a security code to open. The paint on his cheek and on his shirt identified him as Milek, and he'd been painting.

Apparently, his studio, as well as their offices, were within this huge warehouse that was located in the industrial area of River City. This building had a fresh coat of charcoal-colored paint over the metal and some accents of wood around that impressive steel door Viktor had opened.

"Garek was supposed to come and get me when he got here," Milek said. Angel ambled over to greet him, too. Milek rubbed his paint-stained hand over the dog's big head.

"Where is Garek?" Ivan asked, his voice a bit gruff as if he dreaded seeing the older of his two bosses. Or maybe he was just tired after last night.

She'd managed to sleep deeply for the first time since she'd started trying to get the gallery up and running again. There had been so much work to do, so many loans to apply for, so much to put into place. Ivan was right; she needed to hire at least one assistant, probably more.

But she wanted to make sure that whoever she hired would be safe, that there would be no more explosions in the gallery, no more threats to her life or anyone else's. They had to find out who was behind these horrible things. And they had to find out fast.

"Yes, where is Garek?" she asked.

"He was following up on some things this morning," Milek said. Then he pointed toward the door to the outside and smiled with obvious relief as his brother walked in. "There he is now."

"What things were you following up on?" Ivan asked his boss.

Garek shrugged, but his shoulders looked stiff, as if he

was carrying some kind of burden. "Following up leads about the delivery yesterday before the explosion and about Sims and—"

"My uncle," Ivan said, finishing for him. "You didn't believe me yesterday when I told you he has dementia."

"I believed you," Garek said. "I didn't believe *him*."

Maybe Viktor Chekov was still threatening the gallery, just like he'd threatened her father for years. Had her dad succumbed to the pressure along with his partner, or had he been as innocent as she wanted to believe he was?

And if Viktor Chekov really wanted her to launder money for him, why had no one approached her? Why had they only tried to kill her instead? She couldn't launder money if she was dead.

Blade watched as Garek shut the door to his office. He didn't need to look through the glass walls to see Ivan and the gallery owner were inside with the Kozminskis, and that dog, too, fortunately. The dog didn't seem to like him much even though it liked everyone else.

Viktor was the only one, besides Blade, who wasn't in the office, and was now standing next to him.

"So is he going to get in trouble?" Blade asked.

"For the kiss?"

"For crossing a line with a client."

Viktor smiled. "The Kozminskis have crossed some lines in their lifetimes, as we all have. They understand."

Blade nodded. "Yeah, they do understand." They'd given him a second chance that few other people would have. "But still, if she wants to talk to the Kozminskis to complain about Ivan, they might have to take him off the case." Blade would be happy to switch places with him. While Blair Etheridge was clearly in danger, he'd rather be dealing with that than bored out of his mind protecting some rich old widow and her baubles.

"You really think she's going to complain about him?" Viktor asked, and he grinned slightly.

Ivan was damn good-looking. Women noticed him even though he usually didn't notice them back. While Blade…

Women noticed him, and then they crossed to the other side of the street. That rich old widow was probably going to be in the Kozminskis' office next, asking to have someone else assigned to protect her, once she got a look at Blade.

"No," Blade said, as he remembered how she'd reacted last night when Ivan had dangled high above the ground from that helicopter. She'd been terrified for him. "He's doing everything he can to protect her, no matter how much danger it puts him in."

Viktor nodded. "Whoever gets close to her is in danger. Someone followed us back here. Josh saw them out there this morning."

Blade nodded. "I couldn't see them, but I felt them there last night."

Watching and waiting for the next opportunity to try to hurt Blair Etheridge again. While it might be more boring watching some old widow, it would definitely be safer. Blade wasn't going to be in the kind of danger that Ivan was.

Chapter 14

It wasn't nothing. The kiss and last night. It was everything.

Ivan wanted to tell her that, but he couldn't say the words in front of his bosses. He couldn't even tell her with his eyes because she wouldn't look at him. She hadn't since she'd walked into the building with Viktor, since she'd heard him lie to his coworker.

But maybe that was for the best. She wasn't looking for a relationship; she'd made that clear to Ivan after she'd lied to Z and claimed Ivan as her boyfriend. And if he gave any indication about how much last night had meant to him, she would probably have him removed immediately from her protection detail.

Or maybe that was why she wanted to talk to the Kozminskis. To stop her from asking for his removal, he spoke first, directing his question to Garek. "So what did you determine from your visit with my uncle?"

Garek hesitated a moment, and Blair must have wondered if it was because of her presence, because she said, "If you pulled Ivan in for a meeting about my case, then like I told Viktor, I should be here, too. This is about me and my gallery. So you better tell me what's going on and what progress you're making, if any."

As always, she impressed the hell out of Ivan. She was so strong and independent.

"She's right," Milek said before Ivan could. "This is her life."

That was what the gallery meant to her; it was more than a business to her. Opening up the gallery again and making it a success meant the same thing to her that *protect* meant to Ivan; it was a way to honor her father just as he wanted to honor his.

"He pulled the same thing on me that he did on you," Garek said. "Mistaking me for my father, or at least acting like he did."

"You think he is just pretending then?" Ivan asked, and his stomach churned. If his dementia wasn't real and his uncle was still a threat, Ivan could be in danger and endangering Blair. Maybe everything that had happened to them wasn't because of her. As if sensing his discomfort, Angel sidled closer to him and leaned against the side of his leg.

Garek shrugged. "I don't know."

"What do you know?" Blair asked. "Who else are you looking at besides Viktor Chekov?"

"We're running background checks on everyone around you. The artists, the contractor and his crew," Garek said. "We're looking at people who might've tried to buy up that building."

"It sat vacant for years with back taxes piling up on it," Blair said. "They had their opportunity to buy it. None of this makes sense." She closed her eyes and pressed her hand to her head, as if she was in pain from wracking her brain, from trying to figure this out. "I have a gallery to open soon. I need to hire employees, but I don't want to put them in danger."

She'd taken Ivan's advice to hire help instead of trying to

do everything on her own, which would have killed her as effectively as whoever kept coming after her. But she was still more concerned about the safety of those people than she was herself. So he was going to have to focus on keeping her safe, but he couldn't stop thinking about last night. Those thoughts had heat rushing through him.

"You are still determined to open up the gallery?" Garek asked, surprised.

Ivan's boss clearly had no idea how determined Blair Etheridge was.

"Of course," she said. "I have too much invested to back down now."

But this wasn't about money to her. Ivan knew that. Garek probably still suspected it was about money, though, about laundering money. But Ivan didn't believe Blair had anything to do with that. The insurance company CEO and Lionel Sims might, though. Ivan knew his bosses were checking them out as well as the other people Garek had listed off to her.

"What about the explosion?" Garek asked her. "Won't that set you back from reopening?"

"It was small," she said. "The damage can easily be cleaned up before the gallery reopening."

"It was mostly contained to that box," Ivan said, "that Sims claimed he didn't send. That those forgeries weren't his." He'd reported back to his bosses last night, before he'd gone upstairs with her in the carriage house, before he'd lost his perspective as her bodyguard.

Maybe he should confess to what he'd done; maybe he should have them take him off the case. Because with as much as she distracted them, he might not be able to protect her or himself. And if his uncle wasn't senile, he might be coming after Ivan, adding to the danger Blair was already in.

He cleared his throat and began, "Something else happened last night that I didn't tell you about. Something that I shouldn't have done..."

Blair gasped—clearly, she suspected what he was about to confess to...

"Don't," Blair whispered, her face flushing with embarrassment and with anger. What happened last night had been more her fault than his; she'd thrown herself at him. But it wasn't out of pride that she didn't want him to talk about last night. She didn't want him to confess to how they'd crossed the line because she didn't want him removed from her case.

She trusted him.

Even if what had happened between them didn't mean anything to him, she still wanted him as her bodyguard. Maybe she wanted him even more because of that, because then he wasn't going to fall in love with her. He wasn't going to ask for more from her than she was capable of giving, like her heart. She wasn't going to entrust that to anyone.

But her life...

Ivan Chekov had already proved he would do anything to keep her alive. He looked at her now, his dark eyes narrowed, his brow furrowed as if he was trying to decide whether to listen to her or go on with his confession. Kind of like when she caught Angel chewing on one of her shoes, and when she said, "Don't," he stopped but didn't drop the shoe, as if trying to determine whether to listen or ignore her.

"Don't," she said again, like she usually had to with the rottweiler.

"Don't what?" Garek asked the question, one of his blond eyebrows arched over a silvery blue eye. "Don't tell me about hanging from a helicopter?"

"Blade told you?" Ivan asked, and she could hear the hurt in his voice. He thought his coworker had betrayed him.

"No. Lionel Sims did," Garek said.

"You talked to Lionel?" Blair asked.

"Yes, and he was actually impressed by the lengths Ivan went to in order to talk to him," Garek said. "He wants to hire us. He's figured out that he can use some extra security."

"That's good," Ivan said. "Then he'll have to show us his pieces of art and Milek can verify that they're the originals he claims they are."

Blair needed to know if they were real because she'd already advertised that they would be on display at the gallery reopening ceremony and also because her father was supposed to have curated the artwork for him. She didn't want to believe her father had had anything to do with forgeries or money laundering. As if sensing she needed his support, Angel came over to her and bumped her leg with his big head.

"He swears that when he returns from Milan, he'll show them to us. I also talked to the delivery person who admitted to picking up the box from a shipping dock and not from Sims's house."

Blair let out a slight breath. She wanted to trust Lionel. Not only was he her landlord, but he was also supposed to be her father's friend.

"You have been busy," Ivan said to his boss.

"I haven't been grabbing helicopters out of the sky," Garek said, "but I have been working."

"And visiting prisoners," Ivan remarked.

"Yeah, that process, of getting through security, took longer than I remembered," Garek admitted. "That was why I was late."

"Longer than you remember?" Blair asked. "You've visited other prisoners?"

"Until just a few years ago, our dad was one," Milek said. "He was a jewel thief, although that isn't what he was sent to prison for."

"I was in jail once, too," Garek said.

"So Officer Carlson was right? Mason Hull hired the foxes to watch the henhouse?" Blair asked.

Garek snorted. "I didn't hear her say that last night."

"Neither did I," Ivan said.

Blair glanced at him. "She paid me a visit after you left this morning."

"Why?"

"She claimed to have questions, but it seemed like she had more warnings than questions."

"Seems like she needs to be checked out more thoroughly," Ivan commented.

"The chief is already looking into her," Garek said.

Blair shivered at the thought of an officer being behind the horrible things that had been happening.

"She didn't make you reconsider having the Payne Protection Agency for your security, did she?" Milek asked.

She suspected if she did fire them, her insurance policies would be canceled and Milek would withdraw his offer for her to sell some of his art in her gallery.

She shook her head. "I feel like I don't have much of a choice. But I do want your assurances that my gallery and the people working in it will be safe." She'd already had a call from the contractor this morning, threatening to quit. Maybe that was because he knew the Payne Protection

Agency was checking him out or maybe it was because of the explosion.

"I think it's a mistake to push forward right now," Garek said. "I wish you would reconsider your grand reopening being a little less than two weeks out and give us more time to catch whoever is behind everything that's been happening."

"I don't have time to give you," she said. "I've already been marketing the reopening." The only mistake she'd made had been last night, thinking that having sex with Ivan would get him out of her system and let her focus again. She needed to stay focused on the gallery, on making it the success it would have been if not for her father's former partner and Viktor Chekov turning it into something else.

Her father had opened the place to showcase his wife's art, to keep her happy and devoted to him. But she'd left him and Blair, anyway, crushing her father's dream and his heart. Blair had never been able to fix his heart, but she was determined to make his dream a reality.

Even if it killed her…

Milek felt just a twinge of guilt for all the work Garek had done without him. Candace had helped him, as always, while Milek had been distracted. As he showed Blair Etheridge around his studio, that guilt evaporated.

"Oh, my God…" she murmured with awe.

Even Ivan, who was glued to her side lately like that big dog of hers, looked impressed. "I saw the portrait you did for Josh of his son and how you added in him and Natalie, too. But this…" He trailed off into a sharp whistle, as if he couldn't find the words to describe what he was seeing.

Milek had canvases leaning against every wall, some of

them several stacks deep. Whenever he had a burst of creativity, his wife, Amber, encouraged him to go with it, to create as much as he could while the creativity was flowing.

His art dealer, on the other hand, told him to ration the pieces he put out in the market. Less available made them worth more, so he wanted Milek to produce less. Milek liked being prolific, though.

"There is so much variety here," Blair said, "so that every piece is very original."

"Unlike your friend Jean-Paul or even Z," Ivan remarked.

She nodded. "True. Jean-Paul seems to mimic others, and Z mimics himself. While you, Milek, you are always different."

"'Evolving,' a critic once said." He wasn't sure that he liked that description.

"I've seen some of your earliest work," she said. "And the maturity was already there. You're not evolving into something else or even a better version of yourself. Every painting you create shows a different facet of your talent, a different mood, a different energy and a different take. I am sure painting like this keeps things more interesting for you, making each one more of a challenge to express yourself. Since you did this painting this way—" she lifted one canvas away from the wall "—with these colors, how would it have looked if you'd taken another route…" And she crossed the room, the dog plodding behind her, to pull out another canvas. "And then it would look like this…"

He whistled now. "You have a great eye."

She smiled.

"And an even sharper understanding of artists."

Her smile slipped away. "My mother was one."

"I'm sorry," he said. "She passed away?"

She shook her head. "Ran away. I haven't seen her since I was a child."

"Would you like us to find her for you?" Milek asked. "In addition to protecting things, we are very good at finding things and especially people, even if they don't want to be found."

Her brow furrowed. "I'm sure she doesn't care if anyone finds her or not. She didn't care enough about us to stay." Her face flushed with color and embarrassment. "I'm sorry."

Ivan reached for her, as if to slide his arms around her shoulders and comfort her. But she quickly stepped away to avoid his touch.

"I'm sorry I mentioned anything but these brilliant pieces," she said. "I would love to show as many of these in the gallery as I can find space for, if you and your agent are agreeable."

He didn't care what his agent recommended. He liked Blair Etheridge. With her eye for art and understanding, her gallery could be very successful if she survived. Ivan clearly was determined to make sure she did.

The younger man's brow furrowed as he studied the canvases. "Your pieces are all original," Ivan said. "But you easily recognized those forgeries last night even with as damaged as they were."

Milek nodded. "Yes, it was probably easier to tell because they were damaged. The paper and paint reacted differently to the heat than they would have had they been as old as they were supposed to be. What I could see of the art looked close to the original depictions. They wouldn't have fooled an honest appraiser, though."

"Sims said they weren't his," Ivan said. "But he could have been lying, and if he was, then the insurance-company appraiser authenticated forgeries."

"Forged artwork is a lucrative and a dangerous business," Milek said. He knew, because he'd been coerced into doing some of that himself once.

By Viktor Chekov.

Was his brother right about the old godfather? Was the whole dementia thing just an act? Was Viktor Chekov still in the game?

Or had someone else taken it over now that he was in prison? And to take over the reins from Viktor Chekov, this person would have to be just as smart and dangerous as the old man had been.

Chapter 15

Ivan still wasn't certain what had happened at the Payne Protection office. Why had his bosses called him in? To reprimand him for his stunt with the helicopter, or for that kiss they must have seen on the security footage?

Or just to bring him up to speed on what they'd learned? So the delivery person hadn't picked up the box from Sims's estate but from a shipping dock. That didn't prove that it wasn't his box. And even if he had the originals still in his possession, that didn't prove that the forgeries hadn't been his as well. He could have planned to defraud the insurance company, maybe even with the insurance company's help.

While those thoughts kept running through his head, he didn't express any of them to Blair. Instead, the minute he slammed the truck's driver's side door shut, he turned to her and confessed, "I lied."

Angel sat on the seat between them, so he couldn't see her face around the dog's big head. He only heard her gasp.

"What did you lie about?" she asked.

"That kiss," he said. Just saying it made him want to kiss her again, deeply, passionately…like they'd kissed last night. But he knew that like last night, he wouldn't stop at a kiss. "It wasn't nothing. I was just saying that to Blade to…"

"Save face?" she asked when he trailed off.

"To make sure I didn't get removed from this assignment."

"Why do you want to stay?"

He still couldn't see her around the dog; it was almost as if she was hiding behind the animal now. And Ivan didn't mind hiding behind him, too. "Because I don't want anything happening to you," he said.

"I hope you didn't read more into last night than I intended. I'm still not looking for a relationship."

"I know," he assured her. "You're focused on getting the gallery opened, on making it a success to honor your father's memory."

She made another strange sound, like a gasp. "You understand that?"

"Yes. More than you know..."

"I know you're a bodyguard to honor your father," she said. "Because you couldn't protect him from his own brother, you want to protect other people from harm."

He sucked in a breath. She did understand him, better than anyone ever had. "That's why I want to protect you," he said.

"You don't trust your coworkers to do it?"

"It's hard for me to trust anyone," he admitted. "But I do think Garek and Milek were right to give them second chances. I think Viktor and Blade and especially Josh deserve them."

He wasn't as sure about their most recent hire, though. Josh's half sister was the reason he'd gone to prison for a crime he hadn't committed, and now she was the newest employee of the Payne Protection Agency. Fortunately, she was in training right now because Ivan wouldn't have trusted her anywhere near Blair and her art gallery.

But maybe Sylvie would be able to figure out what was going on with the forgeries. She still seemed to be part of the dark world that he and the others had left behind. But she wasn't an artist like Milek, who had so easily recognized the forgeries.

"You don't think everybody deserves a second chance?" she asked.

He shrugged. "Depends on what they've done. What about you? What do you think?"

"Depends," she agreed. "I offered to give Jean-Paul a second chance last night, and then the piece he brought me to consider for a showing was destroyed. I really need to let him know."

"He was probably contacted last night. Either Officer Carlson would have reached out to him like she did Lionel Sims, or Garek or Milek followed up with him." He'd voiced his suspicion last night about Jean-Paul's timing and that tube he'd left behind. Officer Carlson had assured him the crime techs would go over everything, but everybody else had seemed to focus on the big box instead of that little tube. The stuff inside that big box might not have been the only forgeries, either.

"You didn't seem entirely convinced that painting was his, that it looked more like something Z would have painted," he reminded her.

"Exactly," she said.

She shared his suspicions about Jean-Paul. "What do you think? He forged it for you to show or to use it as a ruse to get some explosive device inside the gallery?"

"That's what you think," she said.

He nodded. "We reacted to the blast instinctively and fell down, but I'm not sure it would have knocked us down. It really didn't do much damage except to that box. But why would Jean-Paul have wanted to blow up that box?

Or maybe he'd thought the bomb would do more damage than it did..."

"To us or the gallery?" she asked. "Maybe he was madder about me refusing to show his work than I thought."

"Why didn't you want to? Is he really that bad?"

"He's just not original."

"Maybe he is responsible for the forgeries," Ivan said. "We need to find out if anyone has interviewed him about last night." He was sure that they had; the Payne Protection Agency was thorough. He reached for his cell phone.

"We need to interview him," Blair said. "I can use our visit as an excuse to tell him about last night and to offer to find something else in his studio that I would be willing to show."

"It's a good plan," Ivan agreed, "except for one thing."

"What's that?"

"It's too dangerous." His job was to protect her, not bring her around possible suspects.

"An artist isn't going to destroy his own studio or home," she said. "And Jean-Paul works out of his apartment, which is between here and the gallery. We can stop on our way."

She made sense, but still Ivan hesitated. "I don't think it's a good idea..." Because there had already been too many close calls with her life.

"We'll be safe," she said. "It's broad daylight in a higher end area of town." She gave him the address, and when Ivan neared the apartment complex, he had to agree.

"This is a really nice area of River City."

"He has one of the penthouses in this building," she said.

Ivan's suspicions grew. "Is someone else showing his work and selling it?"

She shrugged. "I don't know."

"He's making money somehow."

"I think he's a trust-fund kid," she said.

Ivan had some questions for the young and not-so-struggling artist. Even though the area was as safe as Blair had claimed, Ivan had reservations about letting her go inside the building with him.

"I'm still going to call in the agency and make sure they know where we are, and maybe wait for backup to arrive," he said.

Josh was already at the gallery, waiting for them, as well as checking to make sure it was safe before her arrival. Hopefully, Viktor was available or Garek or Milek for backup because for some reason Ivan had a feeling he was going to need it.

This situation wasn't safe for Blair because if Jean-Paul was a forger, or worse, he might be so desperate he would do whatever he had to protect himself.

Even kill.

Blair was impatient, locked up in the truck with Ivan and Angel, waiting for backup. The clock ticking away in the cab wasn't driving her crazy although it should have. She didn't have any time to spare. Her deadline for being ready for the grand reopening celebration was tight, and with each incident at the gallery or to her, it kept getting tighter. Maybe Garek Kozminski was right; maybe she should postpone it. But that felt like a failure, like her father had been right all along about her. That she was no more help than her mother had been.

All the online buzz she had going about the pieces she'd be displaying, about the food and music, would die down if the celebration didn't happen. If her guests had to wait, they might decide not to come at a later date.

She had to make sure she opened. She probably should've

had Ivan bring her to the gallery instead of Jean-Paul's apartment. But she'd figured this would be a quick visit to question the man. Not this interminable wait, locked inside this small pickup cab with the man she'd had sex with the night before. The man she'd had incredible sex with...

Even the soft sound of his breathing was driving her crazy. And the way his chest rose and fell with those shallow breaths drove her crazy, too. His muscles pushed against the thin material of his T-shirt, and she wanted to peel it off him. She wanted to peel all his clothes off him again.

The man's body was a work of art, like it was sculpted of marble or mahogany, hard and smooth and all so damn beautiful. And so tempting...

If not for Angel wedged between them on the front seat, she might have succumbed to her desires again. She might have climbed over the bench seat to climb all over him again.

She was glad he'd admitted that kiss hadn't been nothing. But maybe it would have been better if it had been, then he wouldn't be such a distraction. Such a temptation... so intense that it was almost impossible for her to not act on it, to not reach for him...

"This is stupid," she remarked, annoyed with herself as well as the situation.

"We can leave for the gallery," Ivan offered. "And let the others talk to him." But he sounded as reluctant to leave as she was.

"Nobody talked to him?" she asked.

"Just Officer Carlson," Ivan said, which was a repeat of what he'd already told her.

When he'd called for backup, he'd talked to Garek about Jean-Paul. Officer Carlson had spoken to him last night at his apartment, and according to her report to the chief of police, she had no reason to suspect his involvement with the bombing or the forgeries. So Garek and Milek hadn't delved deeper than their initial background check on him. Milek was following up with his art-circle contacts right now.

"All we have to do is talk to him," she said. "Then we can go onto the gallery."

"You'll know if he's involved just from a conversation?" he asked, one of his blond eyebrows arching with skepticism.

She shrugged. "I'll know more from talking to him than sitting in this truck with you and Angel."

"Angel and I are hurt," he said with a chuckle as he petted the dog's big head. "You're not enjoying our company."

She wanted to enjoy Ivan's company like she had last night. And that was a distraction, he was a distraction, she couldn't afford right now or ever.

"I'm not enjoying wasting my time." She reached for the door handle. "I'm going in with or without you." And she threw open the door.

"Blair, this is a bad idea," Ivan reiterated, but he pushed open his door as well.

Before he could come around to her side, she jumped down. Unfortunately, she'd worn heels today, and even though there was a running board, the wedge sole slipped off. She fell to the pavement, hitting it with one knee. Fortunately, she had worn jeans, so the denim held against the asphalt. But she cursed at the jab of pain.

"Blair!" Ivan exclaimed.

She didn't know if he was alarmed that she'd fallen or if he noticed the shooter just as gunfire rang out.

Their showing up here was an opportunity that the killer hadn't expected but was fully going to take advantage of to finally get rid of both of them.

The woman and the man had to die. So the killer pressed their gloved finger against the trigger, firing shot after shot and knowing that eventually one of them would hit its target. Or maybe all of them would…

Chapter 16

When Blair disappeared as she stepped out of the truck, Ivan hadn't immediately realized why. And then, when the gunfire rang out…

He'd been so damn scared she'd been hit. Maybe it was because she'd fallen that she hadn't been. He was not nearly as lucky. The bullets came too close to his head and shoulders as he leaned over her, using his body to shield hers. He drew his weapon, too, and peered around, trying to see from which direction the shots were coming.

The apartment complex.

He'd been right to have suspicions about Jean-Paul and to want to wait for backup. The man was clearly as desperate and complicit as Ivan had been afraid he was.

But where the hell was the backup now?

Ivan drew his weapon, intent on returning fire, and hopefully hitting the bastard and putting an end to the danger Blair was in.

He had to get her out of the line of fire, to safety. "You have to get in the truck with Angel," he said. The dog was whining from inside the cab but was harnessed to the seat and hopefully safe. The old truck was made of thick, heavy metal that had withstood other bullets in the past. It should withstand these, too. Not that he wanted her to stick around.

He pressed the keys into her hand before he levered himself up and opened the passenger's side door.

Bullets pinged off the metal of the door as he pulled it open. Then, using the door as a shield, he lifted her into the cab. "Get out of here!" he told her.

To protect her and the dog from any more bullets, he started firing. He'd seen the flash, the burst of gunpowder, from the weapon being fired off that balcony of the penthouse she'd indicated was Jean-Paul's. So Ivan returned fire until the shooting stopped.

Had he hit him?

Or had the guy seen that Ivan's backup had arrived? Two Payne Protection black SUVs pulled into the lot, tires and brakes squealing.

Knowing that they were there, that Blair would be safe, Ivan rushed toward the building. It was a high-security building, with a doorman, but the doorman had already opened the door, probably trying to determine where the gunfire was coming from. His eyes widened when he saw Ivan, but he didn't move fast enough to stop him from rushing through the open door. Ivan headed toward the elevator. He might have taken the stairs, if it wasn't so tall of a building.

And he didn't want the son of a bitch to get away, like he had the last time he'd taken shots at him and Blair. This time he was going to make sure that Blair would be safe from this guy forever.

He'd done it again. He'd used his body to shield hers. And he'd wanted her to drive off again and leave him alone to face the gunfire. But Blair was damn well not going to leave him again.

She was the one who'd insisted on coming here; she

was the one who'd put him in danger. And if she'd waited for backup and not stepped out of the truck, they probably would have stayed safe.

But just like last night, when they'd made love, Ivan had only been able to hold on to his control for so long. He'd been able to patiently wait for his bosses or coworkers until she had, once again, escalated the situation, and then he'd lost his cool. Instead of taking cover with her, he was running headlong into danger.

Blair had to stop him. She dropped the keys he'd pressed into her hand on the floorboard, and then pushed open her door again and jumped out. A twinge of pain passed through her ankle when her feet hit the ground. But she ignored it. She also ignored the guys jumping out of the black SUVs that had just pulled into the parking lot. They were too late.

Ivan was already going in alone. She raced toward the building, where the doorman leaned against the open door, staring out at all the vehicles that had pulled into the parking lot. His face was pale, as pale as hers probably was, and he looked like he was in shock.

"Are you alright?" she asked him.

He just stared blankly at her.

"Blair!" someone yelled from behind her.

Knowing they would stop her if they caught up with her, she ignored the shout and rushed past the doorman. One of the elevators dinged as it came down to the lobby. She braced herself, wondering if the shooter had come down.

Jean-Paul?

Could he really be the one who'd been shooting at them? She'd had her suspicions about his involvement in the forgeries. But shooting?

That didn't seem like his style. If he was behind it, he

might have hired someone to do it. The elevator was empty, though, as if someone else had pressed that button before her, but hadn't stuck around for it to come.

Had Ivan taken the stairs to the penthouse? She wouldn't have put it past the man who would grab a helicopter out of the sky. With her ankle already aching, she was not going to make it up all those flights.

She jumped into the empty elevator. Just as someone called her name again, she pressed the button to close the doors and bring her to the penthouse. That should have required a security code or something to get her up there, but it seemed it had already been accessed by someone, which allowed her to ride right up to the apartment.

The doors dinged and then opened directly into Jean-Paul's living room. She had been there once, a few weeks prior, to look over his pieces. Unlike Milek Kozminski, Jean-Paul hadn't had many pieces to show her. And he hadn't even allowed her into the room that was his studio. He'd just set up a few easels in his living room with the pieces he'd considered his best work.

It had all reminded Blair of art shows in hotel lobbies with bland canvases of bland scenes that were used for commercial decorating or boring interior designs. He'd had better pieces on the walls; originals, she'd thought at the time, adding to her belief that he had family money. But what if those hadn't been originals?

The elevator doors began to close on her, and she shoved her arm between them and stepped out. If the shooter was here, he wasn't shooting anymore.

And neither was Ivan.

The place was eerily quiet, so much so that she didn't dare break the silence and call out for him. Because what if the shooter was just waiting…

And it was too late for Ivan to hear her, anyway.

The thought stabbed her heart like the sharp blade of a knife. Even though she'd only known him a few days, she couldn't imagine a world, her world, without Ivan in it. He was so vital, so giving…

So giving that he might have given up his life to stop the person trying to hurt her. But why would Jean-Paul want to hurt her?

Was his ego that fragile?

Or was it about the forgeries?

As she moved quietly through the living room, she glanced at the dark wood walls. Some areas were darker, where paintings had once hung, but they were gone now except for one. Only *Woman with a Parasol* by Claude Monet had been left behind. One of her favorites. Every time she was in DC, she visited the National Gallery of Art to see it, and this wasn't it. It was good, but it wasn't quite right, just as Milek had noticed last night at her gallery. Maybe it was the canvas or the oils. Maybe it was just that Jean-Paul wasn't as good at copying talent as he'd thought.

Finally, she heard something, the rustling of the curtains over the open patio door. She held her breath, waiting for that shooter to appear. This had to be where he'd been firing the shots from. Was the shooter still out there? Or was Ivan?

She froze, uncertain of what she should do. Go out onto that balcony or turn and run…

Turning and running would be the smart thing to do, the safe thing. Instead of running in after Ivan, like she had.

But she'd done that because she was worried about him. And because she was worried about him, she stepped closer to those curtains. Pushing them aside, she peered out through the open patio door at that big balcony…and the body lying on the concrete floor of it, blood pooling beneath it.

And a scream of horror clawed up the back of her throat, struggling for release.

The only elevator that went to the penthouse was already on that floor, leaving Viktor, Blade and the Kozminskis to take the stairs. Blade was faster than Viktor, but Viktor made certain to be faster than his bosses. He didn't want either of them stepping into the line of fire; he owed them too much.

Blade beat him to the door to the penthouse. And the former boxer stepped back as if he thought he needed to kick the thing in, but Viktor could see that it wasn't even closed tightly. Someone had come out this way or gone in…like maybe Ivan.

He held up his hand to stop Blade, and then he reached for the door, pulling it all the way open just as a scream rang out. Blair Etheridge's.

Were they too late to save her or Ivan?

Chapter 17

Blair's scream startled Ivan, and he jumped back from the body he'd been standing over. Her sudden appearance snapped him out of the shock he'd be in, the memory where he'd been stuck.

"What are you doing here?" he asked. "You were supposed to get in the truck and drive away." He'd thought she was safe or he never would have left her. She was definitely not safe here. He moved closer until he stood between her and those fluttering curtains. "I didn't even secure the entire apartment yet."

The shooter could have been inside, could have taken her out while he'd been standing on the balcony in a stupor. He'd gone there first because it was where the shots were being fired from. He'd wanted to stop the shooter, so that he could protect Blair. But here she was…

Staring down in shock at the artist's body just as he'd been. All around Jean-Paul's body lay spent shells, some rolling across the concrete toward him. This was definitely where the shooter had been; Ivan just wasn't sure that Jean-Paul had been the shooter.

"Was it him?" she asked. "Did he shoot himself or did you…?"

"Kill him?" he asked, finishing for her.

He'd checked his pulse, had seen if there was anything he could do for the guy, but there was so much blood, like there'd been when his dad had died all those years ago. And for a moment, Ivan had slipped into that nightmare of his past, and he'd been trapped there, as a child helpless to save his father. Blair's scream had snapped him back to the present. He hadn't been able to do anything for Jean-Paul, either. The artist's eyes were open and glazed, with no pulse in his body.

"I aimed some shots up here from below," Ivan said, "to draw his fire away from you, but..." He heard a noise within the penthouse and pointed his gun toward those fluttering curtains while making sure that Blair stayed behind him, out of the line of fire in case the shooter had returned or had never left.

But Viktor and Blade pushed aside the curtains and stared out onto the balcony. "It looks like he's been dead for a while," Viktor said. He gestured at the pool of blood. "It's dark and already congealed."

Ivan released a breath he hadn't realized he'd been holding. "So I didn't kill him..." He wanted Blair to be safe, but he would rather catch the person who was terrorizing her and send them to jail than kill them.

"I don't think he killed himself, either," Blade said. "Where's the gun?"

"Where's the art, too?" Blair asked. She gestured toward the penthouse. "There were several pieces missing that I remember from when I was here last."

"You shouldn't be here now," Ivan said again as he considered what might have happened to her. "The place isn't even secure yet," he warned the other bodyguards. "We need to check it."

"I have a feeling the shooter got away," Viktor said.

"The stairwell door was partially open, unless you came up that way..."

Ivan shook his head. "I took the elevator."

"Me, too," Blair said. "It was already programmed to come up to this floor, as if someone had put the passcode to the penthouse in it."

Ivan nodded. "That's right. We need to talk to the doorman."

"I think we're going to need to talk to her first," Viktor said, and he pointed toward the police vehicle that was racing into the lot with lights flashing and siren blaring.

The rest of them would probably get away with just talking to Officer Carlson or the detective who'd taken over the case. But Ivan had no doubt that he would be interrogated and probably have his weapon confiscated. He couldn't be unarmed right now, though, not with a killer on the loose.

They took Ivan away, leaving Blair afraid but not alone. She feared for him right now, that he might be accused of something he hadn't done. Like she'd accused him.

Although if he had shot Jean-Paul, it would have been self-defense or in defense of *her* life. She knew he wouldn't have killed someone in cold blood, like Jean-Paul had been gunned down on his own balcony. She shivered with revulsion over how he had looked lying there, his blood pooled beneath him.

Like Viktor had pointed out, that blood had already congealed. He'd been dead before they'd arrived at the apartment complex. But his killer hadn't left right after killing him.

Blair knew why; they'd been stealing the forgeries Jean-Paul had painted. But they hadn't managed to take them all before she and Ivan had arrived. As well as the fake

Monet in the living room, some other *classic* paintings had been left behind in his studio, which was where she and Milek were with Detective Dubridge. They were the only ones he'd allowed to remain in the penthouse, along with the coroner and the crime-scene technicians and Officer Sheila Carlson.

"So these are all fakes?" Dubridge asked.

"Not all," Milek said.

"These are his work," Blair said, pointing toward the artist's too-long signature on the canvases. The signature was the most interesting thing about the boring pastoral scenes. She'd seen more original art at bachelorette parties, where the attendants all painted the same scene while drinking.

"But he was definitely a forger," Milek said. "All the tools of the trade are here. The old oils, the vintage canvases..." He pointed toward supplies stacked in one corner of the big studio.

"Should I ask how you know?" Dubridge asked.

Milek chuckled. "I think you know how I know."

"Is this recent knowledge?" Dubridge asked. "Or something from the past?"

"The past," Milek assured him.

"Milek's originals are worth more than these forgeries," Blair said in the brilliant artist's defense.

Milek chuckled again. "More than forgeries, yes, but if these were the originals..."

"True," Blair conceded.

"So we need to be on the lookout for some forgeries flooding the market," Dubridge said to Carlson, who was taking down notes on a tablet.

She nodded.

"We need to be on the lookout for a killer," Blair said, still shaken from the earlier shooting.

"I think we have him," Officer Carlson said. "He should be getting booked right now."

"No!" Blair exclaimed in his defense. "Ivan did not kill Jean-Paul."

"How do you know?" Carlson asked. "Coroner determines time of death was two hours ago, probably just shortly after I talked to you at the carriage house on Lionel Sims's estate. Ivan Chekov wasn't with you then."

"His bosses had called him down to the Payne Protection office," Blair said. "Viktor told you that."

"Can his bosses verify that he was there then?" Dubridge asked Milek.

The artist pushed a hand through his overly long hair. "I was in my studio."

"And Garek?"

"He was late."

"So you can't verify that Chekov was there," Dubridge said.

Blair shook her head. "It doesn't matter. Ivan was with me when someone was shooting at us earlier. He was by the truck, saving my life, when someone was firing those shots at us from up here, from that balcony."

"St. James was already dead then," Officer Carlson said, "according to the coroner's preliminary time of death."

"He wasn't shooting at us," Blair said. "Whoever was is who also shot him, and that is not Ivan."

"She's right," Milek confirmed.

"We'll run a gunshot residue on his hands—"

"He fired his gun," Blair said. "To defend us."

"Well, then we'll have to see if ballistics from his weapon match the slugs that the coroner takes out of our victim," Dubridge said.

"And until you do that, you have no reason to hold him," Milek said, taking the words out of Blair's mouth.

Not that she would have been as diplomatic. She was about to lose her temper.

"He's a person of interest," Dubridge said.

Blair couldn't deny that; Ivan was a person of interest, to her. Of interest and attraction. And she couldn't imagine him spending any time behind bars for something he hadn't done. It wouldn't be fair, not after everything he'd already been through. She remembered the look on his face as he stared down at Jean-Paul's body. He'd been so horrified and almost frightened.

It had probably brought back memories of witnessing his father's murder, of being there when he'd bled out from his gunshot wound like Jean-Paul had.

"We can verify the time Ivan entered our building and there's an outside camera," Milek said. "We can prove he was at the office."

"Until you do, we will be holding him," Dubridge said.

"You need to talk to the chief," she said to Milek. "He will listen to you and make sure that Ivan is released from their custody."

Officer Carlson leaned closer to the detective and whispered, "The chief does have a soft spot for the Payne Protection Agency, even the Kozminskis' land-of-misfit-toys franchise of it."

Dubridge chuckled and so did Milek, surprisingly.

She was offended. "Ivan is not a misfit, and he is not a killer. He is not the reason Jean-Paul is dead. You need to find who really did this to him and took those forgeries."

"She's right," Dubridge admitted. "Now, we need to clear this area, too, and let the techs do their job." He guided

Milek out while Officer Carlson took Blair's arm as if she needed to be dragged out.

Blair couldn't wait to get out of the penthouse. But when Milek and Detective Dubridge continued on toward the elevator, Officer Carlson held Blair back.

"You don't think Ivan Chekov is a misfit?" she asked.

"Of course not," Blair said. "He's a good man who's risked his life to save mine several times now."

The officer smiled slightly. "So you're in love with him?"

Panic pressed on her lungs for a moment. "Of course not."

"So you're just toying with him?" Carlson asked.

"He's my bodyguard," Blair said.

"Yeah, right…he's more than that," the officer insisted. "How much more. Your enforcer? Everything comes back to you and your gallery, Ms. Etheridge. What kind of art do you intend to sell there? These forgeries that conveniently disappeared before the police arrived?"

Blair had to hang on to her temper now, so that she didn't get taken into custody with Ivan, for assaulting an officer. "I would not sell forgeries," she insisted. "I would not sell any of Jean-Paul's work."

"I guess we'll see about that," the young woman said, "if your gallery ever opens."

She waited for another rush of panic, and it came but wasn't quite as intense as the one she'd felt earlier when she was getting shot at, or that she'd felt seconds ago when Officer Carlson had suggested Blair had fallen for Ivan.

Maybe she wasn't panicked, though, because she was determined. "My gallery will open," she said.

"But how many more might have to die before that happens?" the officer mused, and finally she released her grasp on Blair's arm.

As Blair walked toward the elevator, where Milek and Dubridge were holding the doors for her, the officer's words went through her mind again and again. And Blair couldn't help but wonder if that was an idle question or a threat.

"It is about the forgeries," Milek said to his brother, "just as I've been telling you."

Garek shrugged but then noticed a look of annoyance that flashed across his brother's face. "It's not like I doubt your opinion. I also think forgery has something to do with this, but I'm not sure that's all it's about."

But maybe after his visit to see his old tormentor, Viktor Chekov, in prison, and a trip now to the River City police lock-up, Garek wasn't thinking clearly. Or maybe he hadn't been thinking since finding out that Candace was pregnant, that he was going to be a father. He'd had responsibilities before, at too young an age, he'd become responsible for the safety and well-being of his younger siblings. But he felt like he'd failed them. He didn't want to fail his child.

"You still think Viktor Chekov has something to do with this?" Milek asked.

"I checked his visitor logs, his correspondence, and I can't find any way that he could be contacting someone on the outside and still running his business. But…" He shrugged again. "I don't know for sure."

It was the not knowing that was tormenting him now. Was the old man faking? Or was he really not a threat anymore?

Garek wished to hell he knew. But Viktor Chekov was a master manipulator. He couldn't be trusted. He could be the one manipulating this whole situation right now.

Or maybe someone else was just as good a manipulator…or maybe even better.

"This whole assignment, not just the gallery, but all the other cases, too, for Mason Hull feel really suspect right now," he said.

"You don't trust the guy."

"Do you?" Garek asked.

Milek sighed. "I don't know."

"You don't think it's weird he hired our branch of the Payne Protection Agency?"

"We advertise ourselves as experts at keeping your valuables safe," Milek said. "Why wouldn't he hire us?"

"Because we're us," Garek said.

His brother chuckled. "The franchise compared to the land of misfit toys."

"What?"

"That's what Officer Carlson called us," Milek said, but smiled. "Blair took great exception to Ivan being called a misfit."

But she hadn't insisted on coming down to the jail with them. She'd wanted to go to her gallery instead, so Garek had had Viktor take her and her dog there. When Ivan was shown out of the holding cell area, he looked around, as if looking for her. Then, even though he'd been released without charges, he looked disappointed, his broad shoulders bowing slightly.

Maybe he was just exhausted. He'd been through a hell of a lot lately. And it wasn't over yet.

"We need to investigate Hull," Garek said. "And I have a plan to do that..."

It was going to take some time to have someone get close enough to the guy to figure out what and who he really was. In the meantime, they had to stop this person messing with the gallery and Blair Etheridge before another life was taken. Like Ivan's...

Chapter 18

She hadn't come to bail him out. Not that Ivan had needed to be bailed out. No charges had been pressed because he'd had nothing to do with the death of Jean-Paul St. James.

Who had? It had to be the same person who'd shot at him and Blair. She had to see now how much danger she was in; that person wasn't just someone trying to scare her away from the gallery. That person was a killer.

The police could have held Ivan longer, had they wanted to, but according to a disgruntled Detective Dubridge, the chief had ordered his release. Ivan wasn't used to having support from law enforcement.

When he'd been a kid, desperate for justice for his father's murder, no law-enforcement officers had listened to him or wanted to help him. That was probably because they'd been paid to look the other way.

Away from the real guilty person. His uncle.

Garek doubted that the old man really had dementia, but Ivan believed it, maybe just because he wanted to believe it. He wanted the monster he'd feared for so long to no longer be a threat. But even if his uncle wasn't a threat, someone else was. A threat to Blair. And whatever happened to Blair would affect Ivan, too. More than he wanted it to.

After losing his mom and then his dad, Ivan hadn't let

himself get close to anyone. He hadn't wanted to love someone only to lose them, too. Because it was a real possibility he might lose Blair, he couldn't let himself fall for her even though he was so damn close.

Maybe it was good that the Kozminskis had forced him to take the rest of yesterday off. They'd pointed out that he would be of no use to anyone with as exhausted as he was. That it was safer for Blair to have someone else protect her, someone who wouldn't be so distracted.

Obviously, they knew about the kiss and, with as savvy as they both were, they probably knew that there had been more than a kiss between him and Blair. They had to be well aware that he'd lost his objectivity when it came to her. So he was almost surprised when, after a day of rest, they'd authorized him to resume his protection detail.

Even though not twenty-four hours had passed since he'd seen her last, Ivan felt like it had been days. Weeks, even. He'd missed her so damn much. But when he pushed open the door to the gallery, she didn't even look over from where she was talking to some of the contractor's crew.

Angel, on the other hand, ran over and jumped on him with so much exuberance he almost knocked him down. Ivan chuckled and petted the rottweiler's big head. "I missed you, too, big guy."

"First time I've seen that dog move that fast," Viktor said. "Usually he's sleeping. Did you get caught up on your beauty rest?"

He shrugged, knowing the dark circles under his eyes probably gave away the truth. He hadn't been able to sleep that well worrying about the monsters, not in his closet, but in Blair's, threatening her peace and her very existence.

"At least you weren't locked up," Viktor said.

"Thanks to the chief and his connection to the Payne Protection Agency."

"Penny Payne-Lynch," Viktor said. "Yeah, I think we all owe her a lot."

"Who's Penny Payne-Lynch?" Blair asked as she joined them. She'd been close enough to overhear.

"The matriarch of the Payne clan," Viktor said. "And a real sweetheart."

"The Kozminskis owe a lot to her," Ivan said. "And I probably do, too." He wasn't sure that the chief would have ordered him released if his wife hadn't been whispering in his ear.

Blair shrugged. "I haven't met her."

"You should," Ivan said. "Make sure she's on the guest list for the gallery grand reopening."

She nodded and gazed around at the crew, who seemed to be working extra hard. A young woman was also running around with a cell phone pressed to her ear.

"The new assistant?" he asked. A lot had happened since he'd seen her last. The damage from the small explosion had all been cleaned up.

"Yes—Melanie," Blair said. "She's worked at galleries in New York and Chicago."

"And she wants to be in River City?" he asked, already suspicious of the young woman's motives.

"She just had a baby and her family is here to help her," Blair said.

"Melanie passed all the background checks Nikki ran on her," Viktor assured him.

So Melanie was not a threat.

"I was still nervous about hiring her," Blair admitted. "I didn't want her in danger. So I have her mostly working from home. She just stopped in to let me know about her progress on some things." The woman waved at her now as she headed out the door.

"You made progress here," Ivan said, gesturing at the work. The debris had been cleaned off the floor, so that the polished concrete was shiny again. And a couple of short walls were being constructed, probably for more space to hang things.

"I added a couple of walls since Milek has so many pieces to show," she said. Her face was flushed, probably with excitement for the opening.

She'd worked so hard for this and wanted it so badly to be a success. They had to find out who was trying to prevent that from happening. Ivan didn't want her just to be safe; he wanted her to be happy, too.

Hell, he just wanted her even more now than he had before. But he couldn't afford to get distracted again. Neither of them could with a killer on the loose.

Blair had missed him so much. But having him back as her bodyguard was a distraction she didn't need, though she tried hard to ignore him. But a man like Ivan, that big, that good-looking, was impossible to ignore. She did her best to focus on work instead.

And there was still so much to do before the opening. Melanie was an asset and was taking over the marketing and publicity, which were the things Blair hated the most. She wanted to focus on the art and the artists, and the business end of things, on how to make the gallery money.

Her father had always claimed it hadn't. But he had sent her to that fancy boarding school for a while. It was after his partner had gone to prison, though, so maybe he'd been able to run the gallery like he'd wanted, without Blair Noto and Viktor Chekov's interference. But that money hadn't lasted long. Blair had had to pay her own way through college and grad school.

Not that she'd minded. She'd learned a lot from juggling school and work, like how to work hard under pressure to meet deadlines. Those deadlines had never been literal until now. As had kept happening since yesterday, Jean-Paul's face flitted through her mind, his eyes open and staring up at her.

She shivered.

"Are you cold?" Ivan asked. "Do you need to turn up the heat?"

She shook her head. "No. The crew likes it cool in here to work."

"The crew is gone," he said softly. "I let them all out an hour ago and locked up. It's nearly eight o'clock at night, Blair."

A sense of panic rushed over her. "I needed them to stay late today," she said. "I needed them to get more done."

"You've accomplished a lot in just the day that I've been gone," he said.

"Was it just a day?" she asked, the question slipping out, along with the angst she'd felt the past twenty-four hours. It had felt like so much longer.

"Did you miss me?" he asked.

God, she'd missed him so much, but she struggled to admit that to even herself. But as she'd fallen asleep the night before, he'd been on her mind, and in her dreams, he'd been in her body, taking her like he had the night before. She couldn't get attached to him, though. She couldn't get attached to anyone because they always left her alone. But she couldn't deny that she'd ached for him. To be with him. To see him. To touch him…

Now, they were alone in that back room. Angel had

fallen asleep out front despite all the pounding and sawing and sanding that had been going on earlier. How had she not noticed how quiet it had gotten? Was it because her heart was beating so loud that it seemed to throb in her ears, like other parts of her throbbed, for him?

"I missed you," he said. "I thought you might even show up to spring me from jail."

"They had no reason to hold you," she said. "Milek and Garek promised they would get you released."

"They kept their promise," he said.

"But you didn't come here once you were free," she said, and her voice broke slightly. She'd been hurt he hadn't shown up. Had he been angry with her?

She was the one who'd insisted on going by Jean-Paul's apartment to talk to him. It was her fault he'd been taken into custody at all. It was her fault they'd been shot at, so she wouldn't have blamed him if he'd asked to be taken off her assignment.

"My bosses had one condition on going to bat to get me released," he said. "That I had to get some rest."

She'd already noticed the dark circles beneath his dark eyes. She had some, too, but she'd been able to conceal hers with makeup.

"How did that work out for you?" she asked with a smile.

"I think you can tell," he said.

Realizing why he might not have been able to sleep, she let her smile slip away. "I'm sorry. That must have been so hard for you yesterday, finding Jean-Paul like that…"

He shrugged. "I know that's a possible hazard of this job," he said. "But usually protecting people has meant that nobody dies."

"I'm sorry," she said again.

"None of that was your fault. Jean-Paul was obviously associating with the wrong people."

She smiled. "That's what people keep telling me I'm doing with you and your coworkers."

"Officer Carlson and Lionel Sims," he said.

She nodded. "She called your branch of the agency the land of misfit toys."

He chuckled. "That's actually funny."

"I didn't like it. You're not a misfit. You've just had some misfortunes."

He nodded. "Haven't we all?"

She shrugged. "I'm sure there are some people who've lived a charmed life."

His lips curved into a slight grin. "Yeah, they're probably really boring, though."

He was definitely not boring.

Just this conversation, being in the same room with him, had her pulse racing. "Boring might be nice," she teased him.

"Nice might be boring," he said.

"You're nice," she said. "You put other people before yourself."

"I'm just doing my job."

"That's all I am to you?"

"Isn't that all you want to be to me?" he asked.

She sighed. "It is. Or it should be…"

He stepped closer to where she stood over the table with the plans for the gallery on it. "It's not?" he asked, his voice gruff as his eyes got even darker.

She shook her head. "I also want you to be as attracted to me as I am to you." She reached out then and trailed her fingers down his chest. His heart pounded fast and hard beneath her touch.

"I'm not," he said.

"You're not attracted to me?" she asked, and she dropped her gaze to where his erection strained against the fly of his jeans.

He chuckled. "I'm not as attracted to you," he said. "I'm much more attracted to you."

Now, her heart was beating fast and hard. "Oh…" She shot him a challenging smile. "Prove it."

"I've had so damn many fantasies about bending you over this table or laying you down on top of it," he said. "Of undressing you or just lifting your skirt…"

"I'm not wearing a skirt," she pointed out.

"In my fantasies you are."

She laughed. "And now I wish I was."

"You can just undress for me like you did that night," he suggested.

She had been brazen that night, and she'd loved it, had loved watching him watch her. It was better than the feeling she'd recently had of someone else watching her, someone who didn't like her.

Viktor or Blade or Josh? They'd all taken a shift to protect her, but none of them had seemed to dislike her. But none of them had looked at her like Ivan was looking at her…with such heat and…

Affection?

What was it that he felt for her?

Not that she wanted to define his feelings any more than she wanted to define or even acknowledge what she felt for him. She wanted to focus only on the desire now. The passion. So, knowing there were still no cameras in this back room, she was brazen again. She unsnapped and unzipped her pants and let them slide down her legs, revealing her white thong. "Does this fit your fantasy?" she asked as she twirled for him.

He groaned. Then he moved closer, sliding his hands around her waist. And he leaned down to kiss her, just briefly, his teeth nipping gently and tugging on her bottom lip, before he pulled away. Then he inched up her lightweight cashmere sweater, gliding his fingertips up her stomach and over the lacy cups of her bra. He dragged the sweater over her head, tangling her hair around her face and bare shoulders.

Her nipples pressed against the white lace, begging for more of his touch. And he obliged, stroking them through the lace as he kissed her again, sliding his tongue into her mouth.

She nipped at it lightly, teasing him as he was teasing her. Then she reached between them and stroked her fingers over his fly.

He groaned again.

She tugged on the button, pulling it free, and the zipper seemed to slide down on its own, his erection forcing the denim to part. She pushed down his jeans and his boxers to free him.

And he set his holster aside and pulled off his shirt, revealing all those rippling muscles.

Her heart beat in her core now, throbbing, pulsating. She wanted him so damn bad. She dropped to her knees to kiss his erection, to close her lips around it. But he tugged her back up.

"I have to be inside you," he said with yet another groan.

He moved his hand down her body and pushed aside her panties. He stroked her core until heat and passion overtook her. And she came, crying out softly at the shock of pleasure.

Then he turned her around until she leaned across that table and her plans and slid his erection between her legs. She reached between their bodies, guiding him inside her vagina. She was so ready for him that she nearly came again, especially when he pushed down the cups of her lacy bra to caress her breasts. He gently tugged on her nipples while he thrust in and out of her.

Then he slid one hand down between her and the table and stroked the most sensitive part of her. And she came again, crying out at the intensity of the pleasure. He thrust harder and faster, driving her up again and again, and the next orgasm shook her. Then his body shook as he came, too. And he wrapped his arms around her, holding her against him as he leaned over and kissed her cheek.

She turned her head and he kissed her mouth. And she could feel him stir inside her again.

But then an alarm sounded, and they jerked apart before cursing.

"It's probably Angel," she said. "He set off the alarm yesterday." But Viktor had adjusted the sensors, so that wouldn't happen again. "Or Melanie came back." She scrambled around to grab her clothes and get dressed.

But Ivan was faster. He was already in his clothes with his gun drawn. He obviously didn't think that alarm going off was an accident.

Somebody was out there, and they didn't know the code, like Melanie did. It could have been a member of the contractor's crew, but they would have called out when it went off. Anybody who had a reason to be there would have either shut off the alarm or called out for her to shut it off.

Ivan pointed at her to stay in the room, and then he started off alone with that gun drawn, once again putting himself between her and danger, risking his life for hers.

But if he lost his life because of her, she wasn't sure she would be able to live with that guilt or without him.

Sylvie Combs appreciated that the half brothers she'd only just recently met had offered her a job. She even appreciated that they were training her first before putting her out in the field as a bodyguard or security expert, whatever she was supposed to be.

But she would rather be out in the field than watching security-footage feed with some of the other newbies from another branch of the Payne Protection Agency. But then, when an alarm went off at the Ethereal Gallery, she was glad she was there and hadn't fallen asleep. Because she was able to call the others and warn them that Ivan Chekov and the woman who owned the gallery were in danger. While she wasn't there with her gun to step in and help him, at least she could send help to him.

She could do some good instead of just harm for once.

Chapter 19

The second Ivan stepped out into the front room of the gallery, Angel slunk up and cowered behind him, as if scared of whoever had entered the building. Or maybe he was scared of the blare of the alarm and the flashing lights that illuminated the area like strobes or paparazzi flash bulbs. The light irritated Ivan, too, so he snapped on the regular ones that dispelled the alternating shadows. And he turned his barrel on a man, slinking like Angel, into those shadows.

"Put your hands up!" Ivan shouted. "The police are on their way." Or they would be if he didn't shut off the alarm.

The man, probably in his late fifties or early sixties from the silver in his black hair and the lines on his face, raised his hands above his head. "Don't shoot. And you can shut off the alarm. I have every right to be here."

Ivan gritted his teeth. He was probably another damn artist. "Who the hell are you? And why do you think you can just walk in here?"

The man was a little bit shorter than him, but somehow managed to stare down his nose at Ivan like he was the hired help. Even though that was pretty much all he was, Ivan still bristled at the attitude.

"Because I own the place," the man remarked.

Ivan snorted just as the alarm shut off. He glanced over his shoulder at Blair, who'd disarmed the system. "No, you don't." He waited for her to say it, but she just stood there, pale and shaky, almost leaning against the wall. "Blair owns it."

The older man snorted now. "You haven't told your boyfriend much about yourself yet, have you, Blair?"

Ivan waited almost hopefully for her to say something. To either deny him as her boyfriend or claim him as such, to even admit he was her bodyguard. But she said nothing, just stood there, with Angel nuzzling against her side as if he felt her discomfort, too.

"Blair?" Ivan called out to her. He was always so careful to stand between her and danger, but somehow, this time, it had slipped right past him without him realizing it. Because clearly, she was hurt or at least in shock.

Who the hell was this guy? Because her dad was dead; she'd said so several times. But the way she was staring at the guy was how someone would stare at a ghost, like they couldn't believe their eyes…

Blair's stomach churned, and she was damn glad she'd been too busy to eat much that day or she would have lost it. She felt like she was losing it now, her grasp on reality and her control.

"You're not going to tell your boyfriend who I am, Blair?" the man taunted her. "That you actually got your name from me?"

"Blair Noto," Ivan said, his dark eyes widening in surprise. "I thought you were in prison."

"I actually did very little time there," the man remarked with pride. He lowered his arms and adjusted the sleeves of his tailored suit.

"You were laundering money," Ivan said. "You were brought up on racketeering charges."

He shook his head then reached up to smooth back his thick black-and-silver hair. He didn't look any older than he had when Blair had seen him last, whereas her father had aged so much. He'd died at sixty, the same age as his former best friend and business partner, but he'd looked like he was eighty. "Those charges were all reduced."

He was so damn smug that Blair's shock and resentment turned to anger. "What are you doing here? You have no interest in the gallery anymore. You signed off your shares to my father years ago."

Noto shrugged. "I did that to save the gallery for your dad, to keep it out of the hands of the government and Viktor Chekov. But your father and I had a deal, Blair. I was still his partner."

She shook her head. "No. The estate passed through probate with no legal claims against it. I am the clear and only owner of Ethereal Gallery."

He shook his head. "I am disappointed in you, Blair. I thought you would honor a promise. That you would respect your father's wishes."

"I am," she said. "That's why I'm reopening the gallery."

"If that's what your father wanted, he never would have closed it."

She felt a twinge of unease then, but she shook her head. "He closed it because he couldn't afford to run it anymore. He was broke." And broken. So very broken. "And unhealthy—he had that stroke, but yet he hung onto this building. He could have sold it to pay off his debts."

The estate lawyer had suggested she do the same, but her father keeping it had told her what he'd really wanted. He'd wanted the gallery open again.

"He couldn't sell it without me," Noto persisted. "We had an agreement."

She shook her head. "No, you nearly destroyed him and his business. He had no allegiance to you after that."

"What are you doing here?" Ivan interjected. "Like Blair said, you have no claim to anything, not now that it's all passed through probate."

"I expect my namesake to do the right thing."

Blair glared at him. "Like you did? You put my father and his livelihood at risk when you did business with Viktor Chekov and his associates."

Noto grinned that slimy grin he'd always thought was so charming but had repulsed Blair even as a child. How had her father been his friend? How hadn't he seen how selfish and lazy this man was? But they'd been friends for a long time, so maybe he'd just been so used to Noto's selfish behavior that he hadn't noticed anymore.

"You should still be in prison," she insisted. She'd hoped that was where he was.

He shook his head. "No. As I said, the charges were reduced."

"You gave the prosecutor something. You cut some kind of deal," Ivan said. "What did you give them?"

"Something they didn't use," he said. "Something against Viktor Chekov." He glanced at Ivan again and narrowed his eyes. "But that wasn't my fault. After doing that, I needed to lay low for a while. Now that Viktor is finally in prison and losing what was left of his wicked mind, I'm back."

"None of that has anything to do with me," Blair said, but she glanced at Ivan, too. She hoped Viktor Chekov did have dementia, so he'd forgotten the hit he'd put out on his own nephew. So Ivan would be safe.

"I could have turned evidence against your father, too, Blair, but I didn't," Noto said.

"Because there was no evidence against him," she said. "If there had been, he would have been prosecuted just like you were."

"I protected him," Noto insisted. "I took all the blame for the money laundering."

She shook her head. "No." She glared at him. "You wouldn't do something like that." He would never be that selfless.

"I had nothing to lose whereas he was the one with a kid who had no mother anymore," Noto said, and he looked at her the way Ivan hated being looked at—with pity.

Her stomach churned again, and she shook her head, willing him to stop. To just go away like he had all those years ago, like her mother had, and never return.

"He couldn't go to jail, or you would have gone into foster care," Noto persisted, "and not that fancy prep school. So you owe me, Blair, even more than he did."

She kept shaking her head. "No. You're the one who got involved with Chekov."

Noto sighed. "Nobody chooses to get involved with Chekov. He was putting the pressure on us to launder his money through the gallery. I kept resisting, but your father is the one who caved. Again, he was the one with a wife, then, and a child. And his wife, especially, wanted nice things. Wanted this gallery to be successful so that her art would be successful. Because of that, your father is the one who made the deal with the godfather of River City."

"You're lying." He had to be lying because her father had been an honest man.

"You don't remember your father as who he actually

was, Blair," Noto said. "You remember him as who you wanted him to be."

She wanted to argue with him, but she'd been a child when her father had sent her away. And when she'd come back, he'd been so broken and sad that she struggled to remember him as anything but that. Her mother had broken him and Blair Noto had and Viktor Chekov.

Noto turned back toward Ivan and narrowed his dark eyes as he stared at him. "You look so familiar to me. What is your name?"

Ivan opened his mouth as if he intended to answer him and she stepped between them. "Get out!" she yelled at her father's old friend and betrayer. "You have no right to be here!"

"Blair, you know I'm telling the truth," he persisted, "about everything."

She shook her head. "Prove it because the only way you can set foot in this gallery again is with a lawyer."

"I might just do that," he said. Then he walked out, setting off the alarm again as he pushed open the door.

Ivan cursed and rushed to disarm it. Then he cursed again. "What the hell was that?"

She shrugged. "I don't know." But she refused to accept it was the truth and that man had any claim on her business.

"I'm not talking about just him, Blair," Ivan said. "You wouldn't let me tell him who I am. Are you ashamed of that?"

Heat rushed to her face. "That wasn't why…" But it kind of was. She hadn't wanted Ivan to admit that he was a Chekov, not to Blair Noto.

Ivan shrugged as if it didn't matter. "Whatever. I guess I am just your bodyguard."

She hadn't said that this time; she hadn't denied that

he was her boyfriend. She just hadn't wanted to bring up the Chekov connection when she blamed Noto and Viktor Chekov for what had happened to her father, to how he'd died an early death because of those men and her own mother. She knew Ivan's only connection to his uncle was his last name, but she hadn't wanted Blair Noto to call her any more of a hypocrite than he already had.

How could she blame him for associating with a Chekov when she was doing the same thing? But she was doing more than that—she was falling for him. Hard.

And that scared her more anything else. Because she remembered how her mother had broken not just her father's heart, but his very soul. She couldn't let that happen to herself; she couldn't let herself depend on anyone, even someone as amazing as Ivan.

She had to count on only herself, as she always had. It was the only way for her to really stay safe and strong and independent. She had to protect her heart as much as she had to protect her life right now.

Someone had put in the passcode and shut off the alarm in the gallery, so Sheila Carlson had had no reason to show up at the scene. But she'd wanted to check it out. She wanted to keep an eye on everything to do with this new branch of the Payne Protection Agency. While Chief Lynch had a soft spot for them, she didn't understand why anyone would trust them with anything of value let alone their lives.

But she found just Blair Etheridge and Ivan Chekov in the gallery, and she couldn't help feeling that something wasn't right. "I'd like to speak to Ms. Etheridge alone for a moment," she said, following the protocol for dealing with potential domestic-violence situations.

But in this case, Blair didn't look like the wounded one.

It was the brawny bodyguard who looked hurt. "Is everything alright?" she asked the gallery owner.

The dark-haired woman nodded. "Yes, I had an unexpected visitor who set off the alarm."

Better an alarm than a bomb, like had happened before.

"You're alright?" she persisted.

The woman nodded. "I'm fine. I just would like for all of this to be over..." And she spoke loudly enough that the man heard her and flinched.

Sheila felt a pang of pity for him. Clearly, he was more emotionally invested in his bodyguard assignment than he should have been. That was a mistake Sheila would not make. She wanted to focus only on her career, like Blair Etheridge seemed intent on doing.

But was Blair's career just owning and operating an art gallery? Or was she reopening the money-laundering business again?

And what about the art forgeries?

And the murder?

There was so much going on that involved the gallery and the Payne Protection Agency, and even that insurance company. Even though a detective had been assigned to the case, Sheila wasn't going to stop investigating. She wanted to find out the truth and make sure nobody else wound up dead.

Chapter 20

For the past week, since her father's business partner's visit, Blair had been keeping Ivan at arm's length. At first, he'd been angry with her, so he hadn't minded. But now, he wasn't sure what was wrong.

Was his last name that big an issue for her? Or was it the intensity of the attraction that burned between them?

Even though she was ignoring him, Ivan couldn't ignore her. She was too beautiful. She was as stubborn and strong as she was beautiful, though. And she was determined to reopen the gallery despite the danger, despite Noto's claims, which Garek and Milek had already investigated. Even despite the contractors not removing the walls she wanted down.

She walked around the space after the crew had left, with the architectural plans stretched between her hands. "Why is it so hard to get competent workers…?" she muttered.

"Are you talking about the contractor or the Payne Protection Agency?" Ivan asked. She had to be as frustrated as he was, if not more, that they'd come no closer to finding out who had killed Jean-Paul and who had been trying to kill her. But the stalled investigation wasn't the only reason he was frustrated.

He was frustrated because that night, when her father's

ex-partner had shown up, was the last time he'd touched her. She hadn't actually told the man that Ivan wasn't her boyfriend, but since that night, she had made it clear to Ivan that he wasn't. That he was just her bodyguard again. And maybe not a very good one at that.

Nothing else had happened since then, but there was this feeling he hadn't been able to shake, this sense of being watched, and of impending danger. Like whoever it was that was after her was just out there, waiting for an opportunity to strike. And he had a pretty good idea when that would be.

She'd ignored his question just like she'd been ignoring him for the past several days, but he forged ahead, determined to make her hear him. "This grand reopening celebration is not a good idea."

There would be too many people there and even with handheld metal detectors and other things in place for her protection and the protection of her guests, it was going to be hard to keep her safe.

"While I can't keep everything according to plan," she said as she wadded up the architectural designs, "I can keep to my schedule. The celebration is going to happen."

"But will it be a celebration?" he asked. Because she didn't seem too happy although he could understand why. He wasn't happy, either, right now. He wanted whoever was responsible for those attempts on her life behind bars for good. Not the relatively short number of years that Blair Noto had spent behind bars.

The Payne Protection Agency had thoroughly checked him out. But just as Blair had said, her father's former partner had signed off his rights to the gallery. He had no claim on it, which was probably why he hadn't returned with a lawyer. Fortunately, he hadn't returned on his own, either.

But ever since he'd been here, Blair had been even more

preoccupied and determined to make the gallery a success. For her father more so than for herself, he suspected.

"What do you mean?" she asked.

"You're putting everything you have and everything that you are into this business, but I can't see that it's making you happy, Blair." But he could make her happy, if she'd let him.

He understood her not wanting to get close to anyone because he'd felt the same way for so long. But she'd gotten past his defenses, and he'd fallen for her. She hadn't let him get close to her again, even though he was still protecting her.

"Well, as you pointed out, this hasn't been easy for me," she said. "What with someone trying to shoot me and blow up the gallery before I had a chance to open it. Of course, I'm not happy."

"Is it because of that or because of what Noto said about your dad?"

She gasped. Maybe she was surprised that he'd finally brought it up.

Officer Carlson had shown up to investigate the alarm before he'd been able to comfort her or even talk to her that night. Then, ever since, anytime he'd tried to broach the subject, she'd shut him down.

And she used the same line now that she had then. "I have too much on my mind in the present to think about the past. I'm not going to talk about any of that anymore."

"You don't want to talk about your dad or his partner?"

She shook her head. "I won't let Blair Noto get to me. He was lying to manipulate and upset me because he wants a part of the business again. I won't let him win."

"But if he's the one behind everything that's been happening—"

"What is he going to gain by killing me?" she asked.

"He's not my heir. He's not going to get the gallery back if I'm dead."

"Who is your heir?"

She shook her head. "I don't have one. And with all the debt on this place, it would probably go back to being an abandoned building with homeless people living in it if something happens to me."

A pang struck his heart at the thought of something, anything, happening to her. While she'd been able to shut off whatever she'd felt for him, even if it had just been attraction, he hadn't been able to shut off his feelings. In fact, watching how hard she'd worked the past week, how creative and determined she was, he'd fallen even more for her.

"I don't want anything to happen to you," he said.

"Then find out who's behind those attempts," she said. "Find out who killed Jean-Paul and stop trying to prevent me from making my dream a reality."

"But is it your dream? Or is it your dad's?"

She gasped again, but then she drew in an even deeper breath. "Why can't it be both?" she asked. "And what about you…aren't you trying to honor your father, too? You're keeping his name and trying to make it stand for something else, something not criminal…"

"Protect," he murmured.

"What?"

"That was his last word," Ivan said. "The thing he said with his dying breath."

"Protect what or who?" she asked.

He shrugged. "I never knew…"

"That's why you're a bodyguard," she said. "For your father, so don't begrudge me what I'm doing. I'm opening this gallery up. I'm having that celebration for it, and I will celebrate."

She wouldn't be able to do that if she was dead, though. Ivan had to make sure that didn't happen. But while she could focus only on her job, he wasn't quite there yet. "I understand why you don't want to talk about the past," he acknowledged. It was painful for him, too, to talk about his dad, and his had been gone longer than hers had been. Her pain was fresher. "But what about us?"

"Us?" she repeated, as if she didn't understand the word. "There is no *us*."

The jab of pain that struck his heart was so sharp that it took his breath away for a moment. Then he forced himself to nod in acceptance. "Okay, I understand that, too."

That whatever they'd had meant nothing to her. He meant nothing to her. That wouldn't stop him from doing his job. Hell, it might even make it easier for him, make him more objective and less distracted. Now, he wouldn't have to worry about getting hurt because he already was.

As Blair lay in bed staring up at her ceiling, she felt guilty for how she'd treated Ivan, and not just earlier today but the entire week, ever since Blair Noto had shown up at the gallery. The reason she'd been keeping her emotional and physical distance from him as much as possible had nothing to do with her father's former partner, though. It was just about Ivan and how much she'd already started to fall for him.

She hadn't wanted to fall the rest of the way. With the dangers of his job, his luck was eventually going to run out. And then she'd be as devastated as her father had been when her mother left. At least with her mom there had been the chance, the hope, that she would return.

If Ivan was dead, he was gone forever. And that would destroy her...if she let herself love him even more than she was already beginning to. So even though she hadn't requested that he be replaced as her bodyguard, she'd insisted that he stay out in the living room, sleeping on the couch that was probably too small for him. Angel had chosen to stay out there with him, probably making that couch seem even smaller. And she slept alone in her room, in her bed, and ached for him.

She'd been called stubborn before and had taken pride in the adjective. To her it was a compliment, meant she stuck to her decisions, her principles, just as she'd believed her dad had stuck to his. Blair Noto hadn't made her doubt her father. She didn't believe his lies.

But after seeing how hurt Ivan had looked when she'd told him today that there was no *us*, she was beginning to think that maybe she wasn't being stubborn now. Maybe she was being stupid. Ivan was a great guy, no matter what his last name was, and making love with him had brought her the most pleasure and happiness she'd ever felt before.

And to deny herself that…

That did seem stupid, albeit probably safer than letting him any closer than he already was. But she ached for him, to touch him, to feel him inside her again. To be with him, as close as two people could be…

But she'd pushed him away so hard that she didn't know if he would give her a second chance. But she wouldn't know if she didn't ask.

She tossed back her blankets and crawled out of her cold, lonely bed. She considered seducing him again, like she had that first time and maybe their second, but first she wanted to talk to him. To apologize.

She put a robe on over her nightgown. Then she drew in a deep breath and opened the bedroom door. The lights were off, so she could only make out the big shadow lying on the couch. There were no deep breaths, no rising and falling of his chest.

As if tense, he seemed to be holding his breath, as she was holding hers. She released hers in a shaky sigh and whispered, "I'm sorry."

He didn't reply.

Maybe her apology was too late.

Or maybe he was sleeping very quietly. She raised her voice and called out, "Ivan?"

"He's gone," a deep voice replied.

She gasped even though she recognized Viktor's voice in the darkness. What he'd said and his tone made her think for a moment that Ivan wasn't just gone, that he was dead. And the thought of that, of losing him forever, was almost too painful to bear.

But that wasn't what his coworker meant, or he wouldn't have said it so calmly. No. Ivan was fine; he probably just didn't want to protect her any longer. And she could hardly blame him.

She just hoped he protected himself because after Viktor said that, she couldn't help but think of something horrible happening to him. Of him being gone forever.

And then she wouldn't ever get to apologize to him. To make it up to him for how she'd treated him, like he didn't matter, when the only reason she'd started pushing him away was because he'd begun to matter too much to her.

"Where is he?" she asked, because she had a sudden urgency to see him and make sure he was safe.

"He was going down to the gallery. A couple of your shipments are due to arrive."

"Yeah, tomorrow," she said. Sims's shipment that he swore were the originals he'd promised her for display purposes. Nobody had seen them yet because he hadn't been back in the country. Milek was also sending over his work, too.

"No, the deliveries got moved up," Viktor said.

"That would have gone through me," she insisted. "I would know that."

"Ivan didn't want you there when they came in," Viktor said. "He didn't want a repeat of last time, of the bomb."

So once again, he was putting her safety before his. He'd already done that earlier when some of Z's work had arrived. He'd opened those boxes, too.

Just as he intended to open these. Nothing had happened with Z's work. It was fine. As brilliant and strange and beautiful as it was. And she'd struggled to find open space for it.

If only that damn contractor had carried out her orders to take down the wall, she would have had more floor space available for the dumpster that Z had painted on every side, and even the plastic lid.

But she was worried less about that now, about the gallery, than she was Ivan. The last time they'd received a shipment from Sims, it had exploded.

He hadn't been hurt then. But this time…

She wasn't sure that he would be that lucky if it happened again.

The man had to die; it was the only way to get to the woman and put an end to everything. But the guy always had backup when he was with her. Except for now…

He'd left her place and had returned to the gallery alone. He was more worried about her, clearly, than he was himself. And that was going to be his downfall and his demise.

Chapter 21

Ivan had been at the gallery late before, but never without Blair. The place felt different without her presence—empty, even though more art had arrived over the past few days. He'd managed to get to those deliveries before her, and had opened and inspected them. He didn't want any more explosions, big or small.

She'd worked hard to get the gallery open and had invested so much of her time and herself. He felt like a fool for suggesting she had done it for her father and not herself.

Clearly, she loved art and it made her happy. Even the literal dumpster that Z had had delivered. Ivan had to admit that it was kind of cool. Every time he looked at it, he noticed something else about it, something he hadn't noticed before.

So he was glad she hadn't put in the alley like he'd suggested. But with limitations on space, she'd placed it in the back room, which also meant she'd gotten rid of the big table she'd used as a desk. He should have been relieved since every time he'd looked at it, he'd thought about what they'd done on it, or, actually, against it. But he'd liked thinking about that even though his body ached from wanting her again.

He'd never been as into anyone as he was her. But the

feeling wasn't mutual, and he would just have to accept that. And focus on his job, like she focused on hers.

And his was keeping her safe. So he'd made certain that Sims's delivery was picked up early and brought to the gallery when she would be sleeping. But he hadn't done that just to check for explosives. He'd done it to check for forgeries.

"What do you think?" he asked his boss.

"I love the dumpster," Milek remarked.

Ivan shook his head but chuckled. "What about Sims's stuff. Is it the real deal or more fakes?"

Milek lifted one of the canvases from the box that they had already inspected and determined did not contain any explosive device, like either the previous box or the tube Jean-Paul had used to carry his painting to the gallery had. If the River City PD had discovered which one had contained the explosive, they hadn't shared their results with the Payne Protection Agency yet.

Ivan suspected that Detective Dubridge didn't hold any higher opinion of them than Officer Carlson did. He probably wasn't going to share anything with them about his investigation.

Milek studied a canvas. "I don't know. If it's a fake, it's a really good one."

"Not like the others?"

"Jean-Paul created forgeries that would only fool *some* appraisers."

"Like appraisers that were bribed to look the other way?" Ivan asked.

His boss nodded. "I've been telling Garek this is about the art…"

"About forgeries and insurance fraud," Ivan said, finishing for him.

Milek gently slid the canvas back into the box. "Yes, we will have to bring in a real expert to determine the authenticity of these paintings. But at least Blair is not offering them for sale."

"Her insurance policy is still covering them while they're in her possession, though," Ivan said. "And if she displays them as originals, it could hurt her reputation and ruin the gallery."

Milek whistled. "You understand the art world very well, Ivan."

He shook his head. "No." But he understood Blair and how much Ethereal Gallery being a success meant to her. "You and Blair are the experts. I'm just the bodyguard."

But he'd left her with Viktor in the carriage house to protect her and Josh guarding the perimeter of the building. Even though he trusted his coworkers now, a shiver of unease raced down his spine, chilling him.

"What is it?" Milek asked. "What's wrong?"

"I'm just worried about Blair," he said. And he hoped like hell the others were keeping her safe. "We need to find out who's been trying to hurt her."

"They haven't tried lately," Milek said.

Ivan shivered again. "I wish you hadn't said that," he remarked with a groan.

Milek chuckled. "You're superstitious."

"Not usually, but I've had this feeling lately..."

"Uh-oh," Milek murmured. "Penny Payne-Lynch gets these feelings when someone close to her is in danger."

"Now, who's superstitious?" Ivan teased. "You believe in psychic abilities?"

"I believe in empathy," Milek said. "And when we're close to someone, we are very attuned to them. That was why I knew that my wife and son weren't dead years ago even though the news claimed they were."

Ivan hadn't been living in River City then, but he remembered the story. "They were in witness protection."

Milek nodded. "And my insistence on finding them put them in danger again."

"That ended well," Ivan reminded him.

Milek smiled. "Yes, it did. Very well. For me. But I still recommend that you be careful with your feelings."

His boss's advice came too late. Ivan had already been hurt. But he didn't care about himself.

"Well, I doubt this is any supernatural connection or empathy or anything like that," Ivan said. "I'm not that close to Blair." Not anymore. She'd made certain of that. "It's just making me uneasy, knowing that person is still out there who wants to hurt her."

"We'll figure it out," Milek said. "Or Detective Dubridge will. He's good at his job. He's the one who brought down Luther Mills."

Mills had been just as dangerous and murderous a criminal as Ivan's uncle used to be and maybe still was.

"Do you think Garek is right about my uncle?" Ivan asked. "That he's faking the dementia?"

"I don't know if my brother really believes that," Milek said. "I just think he can't trust anything about Viktor Chekov."

Ivan shivered again, but this had nothing to do with a premonition, or whatever, of danger to come. It was with revulsion over the danger of his past.

Misfortunes, Blair had once called them. They'd been a hell of a lot worse than that…for both of them. She deserved happiness, and despite what he'd said about the place, he believed it would make her happy if she could make it the success her father never had.

Or had he?

"Did you reach out to people from the past?" Ivan asked. "Did you learn more about Blair's father?"

"Was he innocent like she believes or guilty like his former partner claims?" Milek reiterated. He shrugged. "I think a lot of the people who might know that are gone or biased. As she said, there is no proof, or he would have gone to prison, too."

"My uncle didn't," Ivan reminded him. "Until Garek got him to plead guilty in order to save his daughter from prison and get placed in a psychiatric facility instead."

Milek sighed. "True. Evidence and eyewitnesses against your uncle and Luther Mills tended to go missing."

Forever.

But Ivan had returned. And so had Noto. The timing roused Ivan's suspicions. But like Blair had pointed out, killing her wouldn't benefit him at all.

He sighed. "None of this makes sense."

"It's late. You need some rest," Milek said. "And so do I."

"I won't rest until this is all over." And Blair was safe.

But then the door to the alley rattled in the jamb as the knob began to turn. And it brought him back to that night he'd met Blair. That night he and Milek had been in the alley, and she and Angel had been inside when someone had been trying to get in, to get to her.

Blair opened the door to stare into the barrel of a gun directed at her. Two barrels actually. Milek held one, too. But it was Ivan's that she stared down, or actually up toward his handsome face, which went pale as he quickly lowered his weapon.

"What are you doing here?" he asked, but he didn't give her time to answer before he turned his attention to Viktor, who was standing behind her. "Why did you bring her here?"

"Because he can't hold me prisoner in my own apartment," Blair said.

She'd had to point out to Viktor that could be construed as kidnapping. Or at least holding her against her will. Her will was to be here, in the gallery, with Ivan.

But now that she was here, she was furious with him. "And you can't just come and go in my gallery as you please," she told Ivan and Milek Kozminski. "Without my permission, even though you have the passcodes, that could be construed as unlawful entry."

"You know a lot about the law," Ivan said, and his brown eyes sparkled with amusement, like he was teasing her.

Her pulse quickened. "I dated a lawyer once or an almost lawyer." Angel's original owner. "I'm not sure he passed the bar, but he left his study flash cards all around the apartment." Just like he'd left her and his dog. Just like everyone else had left her.

Even Ivan. He'd left her tonight, but had it only been to come here?

"And moving my deliveries around..." She wasn't sure what crime that was, but she was pissed about it, anyway.

Ivan arched an eyebrow, as if waiting for her to cite the law. And her lips twitched with the urge to smile. God, she'd missed him, and not just for the hours he'd been gone tonight, but for the past week that she'd pushed him away.

What a fool she'd been. But getting in any deeper with him would be foolish, too, especially when he could go behind her back like this.

"I don't know what the law is," she admitted. "It doesn't

matter. All that matters is that this is my business." And only hers, no matter what Blair Noto had claimed. "And nobody should be making decisions about it but me."

"You're right," Milek said. "Ivan just wanted to make sure that there were no explosives hidden inside these deliveries."

"And he managed to do that over the past few days, with me present, with everything else I received." Even the catalogs and brochures she'd had printed up for the opening had been inspected.

"This was Sims's delivery," he said. "I wanted Milek to see if they were forgeries."

"You didn't think I could tell?"

"I can't," Milek said. "If they are, they're good ones. We'll need an expert to weigh in."

She could have taken offense that he was saying she wasn't one, but she was more an expert on contemporary art than classic pieces. Z's stuff, like that crazy dumpster, were much more to her liking. And Milek's bursts of brilliance in color and composition always awed and inspired her.

She'd wanted to open the gallery to honor her father, but also because she loved art. Maybe that was because of her mother. She closed her eyes on that thought and closed her mind to anymore. Her mother had probably hurt her father more than Viktor Chekov or Noto ever had. Because her mother was supposed to love him, her betrayal had probably hurt him the most.

"It's late, and you're tired," Ivan said, his deep voice a bit gruff but gentle. "There were no explosives in that box, so we can all leave, get some rest and go over everything tomorrow."

She wasn't sure what he wanted to go over. All the stupid things she'd said to him? Or how she'd shut him out?

She wasn't about to ask for clarification in front of the others, so she just nodded. "Okay. I left Angel back at the carriage house." And he didn't do well alone for very long. He would start howling forlornly when he got lonely. The rottweiler was really a big baby.

She turned to step out the back door they'd left open, but Ivan rushed forward, stepping in front of her, just as the gunshots rang out, echoing off the brick walls of the alley. Her scream echoed those shots.

A scream shattered the quiet of the night and Woodrow's sleep. He jerked upright next to his wife, who'd already done the same as her scream hung in the air between them. He slid his arm around her shaking shoulders. "Are you alright?" he asked with alarm. And he peered into the shadows.

Had someone broken into the farmhouse? Had she heard or seen something he'd slept through?

"Not me," she murmured. "In the dream..."

He exhaled a ragged breath. "It was just a dream..." But even as he said it, he remembered that all too often these things that awoke his wife, or unsettled her when she was awake, were not just dreams.

His cell began to vibrate on the nightstand, and he knew this was the case once again. He reached for the cell with his free arm as he kept his other one around her. But he didn't know if he was offering her comfort yet or seeking it himself.

"Chief Lynch," he answered. Then he closed his eyes as the dispatcher brought him up to speed. And he wished like hell he could go back to sleep and that it had all just been a dream.

"What is it?" Penny asked when his call was done.

"There was a shooting at the Ethereal Gallery."

"Ivan," she whispered. That was what had awakened her; she'd dreamed something had happened to the young bodyguard. And her dream might have come true.

Chapter 22

Ivan's head pounded, the sound of gunshots ringing in his ears. Thank God none of them had struck anything more than the brick walls of the building and the metal door he'd managed to slam shut after stumbling back inside. So nobody had been hit…except him.

And that had just been with a shard of brick that scratched his chin. A paramedic applied a liquid bandage and a butterfly patch to it. "You should really go to the hospital for stitches," the young woman said.

He shook his head. "This is fine."

"But it would be a shame for you to get a scar from this," she said, then blushed.

"He said it's fine," Officer Carlson said. "And I need to take his statement."

"Through with me so soon, Officer?" Viktor asked her. "That was kind of a drive-by, too."

"You didn't see anything," the officer reminded Viktor.

"But you," Viktor said. "We really need to stop meeting like this, Sheila."

Now the officer's face flushed, but hers was with anger and annoyance. "I wouldn't have anything to do in this city if the Payne Protection Agency left the area."

"So you have us to thank for your job security?" Viktor asked.

Ivan chuckled. "Let her do her job," he told his coworker.

"I think she thinks her job is to harass us," Viktor persisted, which surprised Ivan because the man was usually pretty mild-mannered.

"My job is to serve and protect," Officer Carlson said. "I thought yours was, too, but the Payne Protection Agency doesn't seem to be doing a very good job."

"Nobody got hurt," Viktor said defensively.

Officer Carlson pointed at Ivan.

"He's gotten worse cuts shaving," his friend said.

"He got a concussion just a few weeks ago," the officer remarked. "Weren't you supposed to be his backup then, too?"

"Ding, ding, separate corners, you two," Blade Sparks said as he ducked under the crime-scene tape at the end of the alley and walked up to where Ivan was sitting in the back of the ambulance.

"No!" Carlson said. "No one else can contaminate this crime scene. Out."

"Sheesh," Blade said. "I'm checking to make sure my friend is alright."

Ivan wasn't sure which one of them the former boxer was referring to, him or Viktor. But Blade looked at him and nodded. "Vik's right. He has gotten worse cuts shaving."

"He could have been killed," Officer Carlson said with the sharp tone of a teacher whose patience had run out. "Blair Etheridge could have been killed. Milek Kozminski could have been killed." And she turned back to Viktor. "And you could have been killed. This is no joke."

"No kidding," Viktor replied. "We know how serious this is, Officer. That's why we don't have time to waste standing around giving you statements about the obvious."

"What's obvious?"

"That someone is trying to kill Blair Etheridge."

"Of course, and I want to find that person," she said.

"I hope that's true," Ivan said.

"What do you mean by that?" the officer asked.

He shrugged. "Let's just say there have been some officers on the River City PD who were getting paid to do something other than their jobs."

She gasped. "I'm not one of them."

"Prove it," Viktor Lagransky challenged her.

The officer started sputtering again as the two continued to argue. Ivan was tired of it; hell, he was just tired. So he got up and walked over to where Blair, Milek and Detective Dubridge stood a few yards away.

"You're the last one to give your statement," Dubridge said to him. "I hope you saw more than anyone else since the shots came closest to you."

Ivan shook his head. "I didn't take the time to look around." He wished he had. "I just wanted to get the door shut and keep the bullets out."

Spencer Dubridge touched his own chin. "Looks like you came close to getting your head blown off, anyway."

Ivan's stomach pitched while Blair's face got pale. She stumbled a bit, as if she'd taken a step. And he and Milek automatically reached out to steady her. "Josh was right. You really got to work on that bedside manner, Detective."

Dubridge sighed. "I'm sorry. I didn't mean to upset anyone."

"Then let us leave," Ivan said. "It's late. We're all exhausted." Viktor and Blade looked pretty well rested, though, and they were sticking close to him, along with the female cop. "If we think of anything else, we'll call you."

"Well, should I call you, Officer Carlson?" Viktor Lagransky asked her. "Or should I nudge you?"

Dubridge shook his head. "Keep talking to her like that and you'll be getting shot next, Lagransky," the detective warned the bodyguard.

Viktor just chuckled.

Ivan ignored them all to focus on Blair, who still looked too pale and shaky. "Let's get you home," he said. "Back to Angel."

She nodded.

"Before you leave," Dubridge said, "let me ask again the same damn thing I've been asking all of you for the past week and a half. Can anyone think of any reason these things have been happening? Any known enemies? Any reason for these attempts on your lives?"

Viktor and Blade snorted. Even Carlson might have.

"Like we haven't all been wondering what the motive is for whoever is behind this," Milek remarked, softly stating what they were all probably thinking.

Ivan had been giving some serious consideration to the motive for a while now. "It feels like someone is trying to scare Blair away from the gallery, like they're trying to warn her away from it, and if she won't heed that warning, they're willing to kill to stop her from opening."

Dubridge nodded. "That actually makes more sense than some things. But what about Jean-Paul and the forgeries?"

Ivan shrugged. "I don't know? Unrelated? Or somebody was using him to get that bomb in here and then considered him a liability after the fact?"

"Possible," Dubridge acknowledged. "All good theories, Chekov. You might have a future in this."

Since he'd been doing private security for a while, even before the Kozminskis had hired him, he just sighed.

"If that is the reason," Blair said, "it's not going to work, just like the messages the homeless left on the walls didn't work."

"What exactly did these messages say and how are you sure the homeless left them?" Ivan asked what he should have asked when she'd first mentioned them.

She shrugged. "It had to be the squatters…they kept breaking in and leaving messages on the walls, telling me to go away that kind of thing."

"You didn't report it," Officer Carlson said.

She shook her head. "I didn't take it seriously then," she said.

"What exactly did these messages say?" Ivan asked again.

She cleared her throat. "The last one said 'leave or die.'"

"So this is about you going away, leaving the building," Ivan said. But he knew that nothing was going to stop her from reopening the gallery.

"That's not going to happen. Nobody is going to scare me off," Blair said.

That would leave whoever was behind this only one option: to kill her. The thought struck him sharper than that brick shard had his chin. He had to make sure that didn't happen. He had to do whatever was necessary to protect her: even give up his own life for hers.

She was lying.

Ivan had scared her off. Or at least the feelings Blair had been having for him scared her. Tonight, she'd briefly considered putting aside those fears, but then the shooting had happened. And he'd been hit. Like the detective had bluntly put it, he'd come close to having his head blown off.

Blair couldn't get that thought out of her mind, that he could have died. And even though he hadn't, he still could, protecting her or protecting whoever else he would be hired to protect after her. His job constantly put his life in danger. There was always the chance that something bad was going to happen to him, that he could die.

Blair didn't think she could live knowing that every time he went to work, he might not come back to her. That he might leave her, like so many other people in her life had.

While she had no problem risking her own life to fulfill her dream of reopening the gallery, she wouldn't risk her heart on a man who regularly risked his own life.

Sheila was furious. "We shouldn't just let them all leave," she said.

"They gave their statements," Dubridge replied. "Unless you want to arrest Lagransky for harassing you."

She wasn't sure if he'd been harassing her or flirting with her. But she didn't care. She would never trust anyone from this particular branch of the Payne Protection Agency. They were all former thieves and thugs. And she suspected some of them might still be.

"I want to arrest the person who murdered that artist and has been going after Ms. Etheridge," she said. "I want to close my case."

"My case," Dubridge said, but he didn't sound like he was reprimanding her for claiming it. Instead of being suspicious of her, like the chief and the Payne Protection Agency seemed to be, Detective Dubridge seemed to understand and recognize her ambition.

She wanted to make detective before she was thirty. She wanted to crack the big cases, make the big arrests. And most of all she wanted to prove that River City PD didn't need the Payne Protection Agency to help them maintain law and order.

Right now, the security company seemed to be putting more people in danger than keeping them safe. There had been no fatalities tonight, but eventually their luck was going to run out. And the next fatality might be one of their own, one of the bodyguards.

Chapter 23

Ivan wasn't surprised that she hadn't postponed the grand reopening celebration. She had too much riding on it. The invitations and the press releases had gone out long ago. The catalog and brochures had been printed. And finally, the gallery was done. Or as done as she'd had time to get it before the celebration.

The party was in full swing now. The building full of patrons of the arts, artists and, fortunately, bodyguards as well. Only Angel was missing; he was spending the night at a doggy day care Blair used for him whenever she had to travel.

Blair hadn't wanted any of the bodyguards to stick out, so they were all dressed in formal attire, like she was. She wore a long red dress. While the neck was high, the back was virtually nonexistent, displaying her silky skin and the sexy curve of her spine.

Since Ivan was playing the part of her boyfriend for the party, he was able to rest his hand against that exposed skin, at the small of her back. But touching her was like touching an open flame. Hot and certain to burn him.

Ivan had played with fire before, but he couldn't stop himself from playing again, from stroking his fingers over her skin.

She shivered and jerked away from him. "What are you doing?"

"Playing my role," he said. "You were the one who claimed I'm your boyfriend."

"Only to Z..."

"I heard my name," the artist said, and he swooped in like he was about to kiss her.

But Ivan wrapped his arm around Blair's waist, pulling her closer to his side. And he glared at the younger man. Z must not have read his invitation, or he'd ignored the black-tie requirement. He was wearing black, though, but jeans and a hoodie instead of the tuxedo that Ivan and his bosses and coworkers wore.

Dark jeans and a dark hoodie with the hood pulled tight was what the person with the crowbar had been wearing that first night Ivan had come to the gallery. But why would Z have wanted to break into an empty building?

Not that it had been entirely empty. Blair had been there that night, working late and alone, but for Angel. But anyone who knew Blair would know that her big dog was no protection for her.

But Ivan was.

Z's face flushed when he met his glare. He knew that Ivan was warning him off. If only he knew for certain that Z was the one trying to hurt her...

But if the artist was as besotted with her as he seemed, why would he want to harm her? Why would anyone, though?

Or the gallery...

That had been Ivan's guess days ago when Dubridge had asked for their conjecture for motives. But it made sense; Blair had had no issues with anyone until she'd started trying to open the gallery.

And it hadn't been just the attempts on her life; there had been so many other things that had gone wrong during the remodel. Like that wall…

He should have just taken it down for her, but the contractor claimed there was plumbing and electrical in it they would have had to reroute, tearing up the concrete floors and potentially other walls. So she'd conceded that it could stay.

It had given her more wall space for the extra pieces Milek had offered to show and sell. He was definitely the busiest of all the artists, but maybe that was just because so many Payne family and work associates had shown up for him.

Blair had no family, and after being gone for so many years, she had few friends, too. She was alone. Like he'd felt for so many years.

His arm tightened around her again, and it had nothing to do with Z or even with whoever was after her. He just wanted her to know that he was here for her. Not just as a bodyguard…but as a friend, too.

Blair was all nerves, and not just because of the grand reopening celebration. She was tingling from Ivan's constant touch, his fingertips stroking over the bare skin of her back. His muscular thigh pressed against hers, the heat of his body, the closeness of it. If he was just playing up his undercover role, he could win an Academy Award for his acting ability. And if he'd wanted her to want him again, he hadn't had to do anything at all.

She'd never stopped wanting him. Even with the last-minute things she'd had to accomplish for the opening, she hadn't been able to get him off her mind, hadn't been able to stop thinking about his kisses and his touch.

But then she would also remember all the times he'd risked his life, all the times he could have died doing his job. And she couldn't…

She couldn't imagine losing him like that. Couldn't imagine being that alone again. Because the past several days, there had always been someone with her, protecting her. Usually Ivan. And the constant companionship, the protection, had made her realize how alone she'd been the past several years. Even when she'd been in a relationship with someone, whether romantic or just friendship, she'd kept a distance between her and the other person to protect herself.

She'd tried that with Ivan, but she still felt closer to him than she had anyone else. Ever.

Except maybe her mother. She could remember her fleetingly, when she let herself, of her hugs and her smile and her laugh. And sometimes, when she laughed, she heard her mother's. They didn't just look alike; they sounded the same, too.

Ivan was the only one who'd made her laugh lately. The only one who made her aware of how alone she'd been. She'd managed to slip away from him, with the excuse of using the bathroom, to be alone for a moment in the back room with that colorful dumpster of Z's.

"I caught you without your bodyguard for once," Z said as he stepped out from behind the dumpster.

She jumped at his sudden appearance and his words. "Uh, bodyguard," she nearly stammered. How had he figured it out? Was it because of all the Payne Protection Agency bodyguards and family that were present? But they probably attended every showing of Milek's. "Uh, Ivan is my boyfriend."

Z snorted. "Yeah, I can tell. The man can't keep his

hands off you. Not that I blame him. If you were mine, I wouldn't be able to stop touching you, either."

She'd always known the young artist was arrogant, but she hadn't realized he was misogynistic as well. "I don't belong to anyone."

"An independent woman," he said with a smirk. "That's what I've always liked about you, Blair, although I have wondered about your relationship with Lionel Sims. Is that how you were able to get this place up and running so quickly?"

She laughed. "Quickly?" It took years. First her father's estate had had to go through probate and then she'd had to apply for loans and draw up her architectural plans. "And how do you know Lionel Sims?"

He shrugged. "I've done some murals on some of the buildings he owns in the city."

Was that all he'd done for him? It felt as if he was leaving something unsaid, as if he wondered how much she knew.

"Lionel was friends with my father."

"Your father helped him build his *art* collection," Z said, again with that tone, like he was fishing to find out how much she knew.

"Yes, he did," she agreed. "That was all he did."

"What else would he have done, Blair?"

She shook her head. "Nothing. And I need to get back to my guests and my boyfriend."

"You didn't look too happy with him earlier," Z said. "Trouble in paradise?"

Paradise. She'd never believed such a place existed despite all the places she'd traveled and lived. But paradise might not be a place but a person. Being in Ivan's arms, as close to him as two people could get, had been paradise. And instead of going back there, she'd run away from what they'd had because she'd been afraid she wouldn't be able to survive if she lost him. "No," she said. "No trouble."

At least for the past few days. There had been no more shootings, no more explosions…just the chaos of trying to get ready for tonight.

"You're in a bit of trouble with me," he said. "Hiding my favorite piece away back here. You might as well have put it in the alley."

She fought against the urge to smile as she remembered that was exactly where Ivan had wanted to put it. "The contractors weren't able to get rid of all the walls I wanted gone. But after the celebration tonight, I will make sure that gets done." Even if she had to do it herself. "And I'll have a better place to display it. But I am making sure that everyone sees it."

Just as she said that, a throng of people spilled into the room from the hall. "Please, take your time looking over this piece," she said. "You will find something new every time you look at it. And here is the brilliant artist, Z, to answer all your questions."

She left him there, basking in the praise of his admirers, and headed back into the hall, where Ivan was leaning against one of the walls. "You were watching me," she said.

"It's my job."

She stepped closer to him and whispered, "I thought your job was to protect me."

"It is."

"Then don't you have to watch for danger?"

"That's why I'm watching you," he said, and his lips curved into a slight grin.

He was so handsome, and in that tuxedo, he looked like a Bond hero, or villain maybe. The scratch he'd gotten the other night had begun to heal, but it might scar, which would only make him sexier.

"I'm no danger," she said.

"You are to me," he whispered.

He was the danger, to her heart, to the independence she valued so damn much. But she went up on tiptoe and pressed her lips to his. His big hand touched her back again, fingertips trailing over her bare skin. She wanted to arch against him and purr like a cat. And she wanted him to take her against the wall like he'd taken her against her desk that day. But more people were coming down the hallway to see Z's damn dumpster. So she stepped back, but her legs were a little wobbly, her head a little light.

He was definitely the danger. Because she was beginning to care more about him than anything else, even the gallery. Tonight was a success, and she was happy about that, but a hollowness was inside her. An emptiness that only Ivan had filled with first the desire she'd felt for him, and now the love. She was falling for her bodyguard.

Even though Milek was staring at the wall in front of him, he was aware of Ivan walking up beside him.

"Admiring your own art?" the bodyguard asked him.

Milek chuckled. "No, no…" Whenever he looked at a piece of his after he'd done it, he considered how he might have done it differently. Instead of redoing that painting, he would just recreate his alternative universe of it. And he couldn't leave for his studio now, not during the middle of a gallery showing, and not with their current assignment unresolved.

"Did you tell her about the man you turned away?" Milek asked.

Ivan released a ragged sigh. "No."

"You don't think she has a right to know that Noto tried to get inside?" They hadn't allowed her father's former partner inside, but Mason, the insurance CEO, was here, dressed in a tuxedo, walking around the gallery like he owned it. Garek was right; something was off about the guy.

Ivan shrugged. "I will tell her about Noto later. Right now, she's busy."

She was working the room, charming patrons, lavishing praise on artists and, most importantly, selling art. His art. He was pleased about that for his sake, but he was even more pleased for her sake. Her gallery was a success.

Ivan whistled. "Are all your pieces sold?"

From sticking so close to Blair, he must have learned what the colored dots meant that were affixed to the nameplate for each piece.

Milek nodded. "Yes. Lionel Sims bought most of them." Blair had personally escorted the reclusive billionaire over to meet him. The guy had bought his art and confirmed his request to have the Payne Protection Agency protect those pieces and his other ones.

"So if you're not admiring your work, what are you looking at?" Ivan asked curiously.

"The wall."

Ivan snorted. "You're that bored that you're staring at a wall?"

"Better than at my own art," he remarked. "But this wall is bothering me."

"You and Blair both," Ivan said. "She wanted this one out. Then she would have had room for Z's dumpster."

"Why is it still here?" he asked. "For my work?"

"That's why she didn't take it out herself," Ivan said. "That and the contractor warned her that there was plumbing and electrical in it that he would have to tear up floors and other walls to move."

Milek furrowed his brow and studied it more. "I don't think there would be plumbing here."

Ivan shrugged. "I don't know. I'm not a contractor. I'm a bodyguard. What's bugging you about the wall?"

"I don't know. I'm not a contractor," Milek said with a smile. "But it just seems off."

Ivan shrugged again. "There are a lot of walls in this place that aren't holding up anything, so they're probably not plumbed, if that's what you mean."

"It's definitely not plumbed," Milek said. "It's thicker on this end than the other. Like wider boards were used than two by fours."

"Again I'm not a contractor," Ivan said. "But what are you thinking?"

"That a thick wall might be hiding more than plumbing and electrical," he said. "You got me thinking the other night when you told Detective Dubridge that someone could be trying to scare Blair out of opening up the gallery."

"But it's open," Ivan said. "If they really didn't want that to happen, wouldn't they have tried to blow up the place again, like really blow it up, or burn it down?"

"But maybe there is something in here that they didn't want damaged or discovered." Milek figured whatever that was had probably been hidden in this wall. "We need a sledgehammer to take it down. Is there one lying around here? One the contractor left?"

"If the contractor left one, Blair probably would have already taken down the wall and risked dealing with a broken water pipe and live wires," Ivan said. "I can get one. But later. Not now."

Milek glanced at the people still milling around the gallery. "I didn't intend to take it down now. I know this isn't the right time." But he was impatient to find whatever this odd wall might be hiding.

"Blair deserves this night to go well," Ivan said. He wasn't staring at the wall like Milek had been; he was staring at the beautiful gallery owner. "She has so much invested in this, money and work wise."

"It has paid off for her," Milek assured Ivan. "As well as selling so many pieces, I've heard the buzz. The art world, these patrons and critics, they're impressed. And take it from me, they're not easy to impress."

Ivan chuckled. "That's why you've sold out already."

"I sold out because of one collector."

"A man I still don't trust," Ivan said. "Maybe we need to get you a personal bodyguard, too. Won't your pieces go up in value if you die?"

Milek chuckled. "Yes, of course. But I am not easy to kill. Just like you, Ivan Chekov."

Ivan shuddered. "Yeah, I'm smart enough to know that's just dumb luck."

And eventually luck ran out.

Chapter 24

There was something in that damn wall. Ivan was certain of it. And he probably would have kept staring at it like Milek, if not for having something, someone, better to stare at. Blair was gorgeous, not just because of her dress and hair and natural beauty, but because she was in her element. She moved like a ballerina through the crowd, graceful and charming and almost ethereal.

"She's breathtaking," a man remarked.

Ivan turned to find Lionel Sims staring after her like he'd been. "Yes, she is," he agreed. Every time he looked at her, he lost his breath for a moment because he just forgot to breathe. He forgot everything but her and what it was like to be with her.

He needed to be with her again.

"She looks so much like her mother," Lionel said. "Sounds like her, too."

"You knew her mother?"

Sims nodded his bald head. "Yes, I knew her father first and then met her mother." He smiled. "She was like some bohemian goddess. I never understood how Elliot Etheridge had attracted her. They had nothing in common. But he tried to make her happy." He glanced at Ivan now. "I guess that's all a man can do, right?"

"Is that why you bought all of Kozminskis' art?" Ivan asked. "And loaned her those pieces from your private collection? You're trying to make her happy?"

As if she'd felt their attention on her, Blair pivoted on a heel and started toward them.

"I don't have to make her happy," Sims said. "I just have to keep my word to my dead friend and offer to help her however I can."

As she joined them, Sims leaned forward and kissed her cheek, but not in quite the creepy, possessive way that Z always tried. Then he turned back to Ivan. "You're the one who needs to make her happy, and keep her happy, if you intend to keep her."

"Nobody is responsible for someone else's happiness," Blair said.

And I don't have her...

That was what Ivan wanted to add, but Sims kissed her other cheek and slipped away, into the crowd that was just beginning to thin.

Blair wasn't his to lose because he'd never really had her. She had always belonged to this place instead.

But he found himself asking the question. "Are you happy?"

She drew in a deep breath and nodded. "I think the night has been a success despite not everything going exactly to plan." And she glanced toward that wall where Milek's work hung, by which Milek hovered.

"But are you happy?" he asked.

She released her breath in a shaky sigh. "I will be," she said. "Once whoever killed Jean-Paul is caught."

She'd displayed one of his pieces that the executor of his estate had agreed to loan her.

Ivan still wasn't sure that the man was a victim or an accomplice.

"Do you really believe that?" he asked.

"That a killer being caught will make me happy?"

"No, I know that would. It would me, too," he agreed. "But about not being responsible for someone else's happiness?"

She nodded. "My dad did so much to try to make my mother happy. But it hadn't worked. In the end, she'd left him, anyway. It didn't matter what he'd done for her, how much he'd killed himself trying to make her happy. She still wasn't happy enough to stay with him, with us..." Her voice cracked with emotion, and she blinked. "That was all a long time ago."

"But the pain never went away," he said. "She hurt you as well as him. She abandoned you." Willingly, not like his parents. "She's responsible for your unhappiness. So why is no one responsible for your happiness?"

She smiled. "Are you a philosopher now?"

He shrugged. "Just things I wonder about." Because even though he agreed that she wasn't responsible for his happiness, she made him happy. Her smile. Her laugh. Her indomitable spirit. Her kisses.

He wanted another one, but she looked about to flit off again as she scanned the gallery. "What is Milek staring at?" she asked.

"The wall."

"That damn wall."

"Exactly," he said. "He thinks there's something in it."

"Yeah, plumbing and electrical, according to the contractor."

That was what the man had told his crew and had advised them not to touch it. They'd checked out the company once, but maybe they needed to take another, closer look at the man's financials. Somebody could have paid him off just like Viktor Chekov had paid off cops and prosecutors and even judges to keep himself out of jail.

His uncle was another person who was responsible for a lot of unhappiness. For a lot of horrible things.

"Milek thinks there might be something else in that wall," Ivan said. "Something that someone doesn't want found."

She shivered. "What do you think?"

"Money? Art?" Ivan shrugged. "Your father and his partner did a lot of business out of this space."

She shivered again.

"Are you cold?" he asked. "Do you need a sweater?"

She smiled. "A sweater wouldn't warm me up right now."

"I could," he whispered. "If you'd let me close to you again…"

"You've been hanging on me all night," she said, but she smiled as she said it, like she hadn't minded.

But he wasn't talking about just physical closeness. He was talking about the wall she'd put up between them, the one she'd hidden her heart behind. He understood, though, that she was scared to give it to anyone again. She didn't want to be abandoned like her mother had abandoned her and her dad. Maybe she worried that Ivan wouldn't stick around.

He wished he could guarantee that he would, but if his uncle was faking the dementia and sent someone after him, he might have to leave again, to protect anyone close to him from getting hurt.

She didn't want to be hurt.

And that was the last thing he wanted to do. He wanted to protect her, even if the person he had to protect her from was himself.

* * *

That wall had been bothering Blair since she'd been given possession of the building. She'd wanted it down. It had bothered her, had seemed out of place. Had it always been there?

She couldn't remember it from years ago, when the gallery hadn't been open that long, when her mother had been with them yet.

So it probably wasn't as structural as the contractor had claimed it was. The architect who'd drawn up the plans hadn't thought it was. She should have insisted that it come down, and now, she could barely wait for her guests to leave, to take it down.

It was as if she could hear it now, like a clock ticking away or a heart beating. She shivered at her Edgar Allan Poe–inspired fantasy.

She'd rather have fantasies like Ivan had had about her, in a skirt, and the back room and that table. She wanted to be with him, alone in her bedroom, instead of this gallery. Maybe she should just insist on leaving now, that she was too tired to deal with whatever might happen when they took down that wall.

Pipes might burst. Lights might go off. That was what the contractor had threatened would happen. And if any of those things happened, she really didn't have the energy to deal with those kinds of catastrophes tonight. But she also wondered, like Ivan and Milek did, if something was in that wall, something that someone didn't want found.

Once the door closed behind the last guest, whom Viktor Lagransky, dressed as a valet, would escort to their vehicle, she was alone with Ivan and Milek.

And that wall.

Ivan had come up with a sledgehammer from somewhere. Probably one of the other bodyguards had brought it to him. They'd been in and out all night, providing backup, as if they'd been worried that something was going to happen tonight.

That someone was going to do something to destroy the gallery or stop it from opening. But now, Ivan was the one holding the sledgehammer that might do exactly that.

"What about water or electricity?" she asked with concern.

"I shut off the water main in the basement," he said. "And I shut off the breakers to this part of the gallery."

She'd started dimming the lights an hour ago to get the guests to leave, so she hadn't noticed that the ones around Milek's art were out. His art was off the wall now, too, stacked against another wall on the other side of the room.

How had they moved so quickly? But bodyguards had to move quickly to protect the people they'd been hired to guard. She couldn't help but think that Ivan was going to hurt her instead of protect her, though. And she braced herself as if he was going to swing that sledgehammer at her, wrapping her arms around herself before she nodded. "Go ahead. Do it. Take it down."

The first blow cracked the drywall like a rock cracking a windshield. Lines spread out from the hole in the middle of the wall like a spiderweb. The second blow knocked the drywall loose so that chunks of it dropped to the polished concrete floor. The third blow splintered the boards holding the wall in place, knocking it more askance than it had already been. And then, from between some of those widely spaced boards, something, wrapped in plastic, fell half out, like a jack-in-the-box falling half out of the box someone had cranked up, like Ivan had cranked up the wall.

The plastic parted and something tumbled out of it and

rolled a half a roll across the concrete floor. And Blair stared down at the skull that stared back up at her through hollowed eyes.

A gasp slipped out of her lips.

Then something else slipped out of that dangling plastic and fell into the drywall dust that had accumulated around the broken wall. A locket. A heart-shaped locket. The metal had tarnished with age and probably from being in that wall. It wasn't silver or gold, just plated metal. Blair knew because she'd bought that locket in her school's secret Santa workshop, and she'd given it to her mother for Christmas.

Her knees began to shake as she realized what this meant. Her mother hadn't left them, hadn't abandoned them; she'd been here the entire time, walled up in the gallery that her father had opened to showcase her talent. Instead, it had taken it and her and hidden them away all these years.

Her knees gave out, and she might have fallen if not for Ivan's arms catching her. He pulled her against his chest and held her, as if he already knew.

But she whispered, anyway, "That's my mother. That's my mother..."

Woodrow had been at the gallery earlier, with Penny. She'd looked beautiful, as vibrant as ever with her auburn-colored curls dancing around the shoulders her strapless gown had left bare.

They'd left early because Milek's art had already been sold and because Woodrow hadn't been able to wait to take that gown off her. But now, he was back, staring down at the skeleton the coroner's attendants and crime-scene techs were carefully removing from the wall that Ivan Chekov had busted partially open.

"Must be murder," he murmured to Dubridge and Officer Carlson, who watched the techs working.

"You don't wall someone up like that because they died of natural causes," Carlson remarked, then blushed, probably with embarrassment of her sarcasm.

Woodrow kind of liked that she wasn't an ass-kisser like some other officers. That sarcasm was probably why Dubridge liked and trusted her, too, despite the reservations Woodrow had had about her.

This body had been here since Carlson was a kid, so she definitely had nothing to do with this. Or probably with anything else.

"Ms. Etheridge believes it's her mother because of the locket." Dubridge held up the plastic evidence bag containing it. It was open, showing two pictures inside, one of a little dark-haired girl and another of a young couple, their arms wrapped around each other. Blair Etheridge on one side, and her parents on the other.

"Height and build match, too, and the hair that survived all those years of entombing is also black like hers," Carlson said. "Is whoever killed the mother trying to kill the daughter now?"

Woodrow looked at Dubridge for the answer, but the detective just shrugged. "It could be why someone was trying to scare Ms. Etheridge away from here. They did not want the body found."

So hopefully it would lead them back, through DNA or something else left behind, to the killer.

"There's still the matter of those forgeries and the dead artist," Carlson said. She glanced over at Milek Kozminski and the other bodyguards from their agency. "And the involvement of the Payne Protection Agency."

"Yeah, thanks, Chief, for calling me back early from my

family leave," Dubridge said. "I thought crime waves were going to be a thing of the past since Luther Mills died."

Dubridge had shot him dead, which was probably the only way the drug dealer would have stopped being a threat. What about Viktor Chekov?

Was he still one?

Did any of this have to do with him?

Chapter 25

Thanks to the chief showing up at the gallery, Ivan had been allowed to take Blair back to her place. They would give their statements tomorrow, after Blair had had a chance to recover from the shock of finding her mother's dead body in a wall of her gallery.

After identifying the body, she'd been quiet at the gallery and throughout the entire ride back to the carriage house. But once the door closed behind them, she turned to him and said, "That's obviously what someone didn't want me to find."

Ivan nodded. "Yes." And he wished like hell that she hadn't found it, although maybe it would be better for her to know that her mother hadn't abandoned her.

"Noto, my father's business partner, that must be who it is," she said. "He must have killed her and put her in there so that my father wouldn't find her body."

"Wouldn't your father have been there, too? Wouldn't he have known?"

"He traveled a lot," she said. "Finding artists, finding pieces for private collectors."

"Who would have been watching you then," he asked, "since your mother wouldn't have been able to..."

She flinched. "I—I remember a babysitter..." She closed her eyes.

Ivan wasn't sure if she was trying to remember or trying to forget something. He stepped closer and put his hands on her shoulders. "It's okay," he said. "I'm here for you."

Her lips curved into a slight smile. "Of course. You're my bodyguard."

"I would be here even if I wasn't," he said. "I care about you." Hell, he loved her. And he wasn't sure what to do about that because he was pretty sure she'd been telling the truth about not wanting a relationship.

Right now, he wanted to give her only what she wanted. "You can cry. Scream. Hit me…whatever you need to do to deal with what we just found…"

The truth. Her mother hadn't left her.

But he didn't think she wanted to consider what that might mean, that her father might have been the one who'd killed her and put her in that wall.

"I don't want to hit you," she said, and finally she opened her eyes. Instead of tears, there was something else in her gaze as she stared at him. Desire.

He wanted her, too, but not like this. "You've been through a lot tonight. A lot of emotions." He should have waited to open that damn wall; he should have let her enjoy her grand reopening celebration.

"Lust," she said. "I've been lusting after you all night." She reached up and tugged on the end of his tie, pulling the bow loose so that it dangled around his neck.

"Blair, you're hurting and vulnerable."

"I'm numb," she said. "And I want to feel. I want to feel you…like you were feeling me up all night, running your fingertips over my back. You were driving me crazy. I want to drive you crazy now." She pulled the studs through the buttonholes, parting his white dress shirt.

She was driving him crazy.

"Blair..." He got her name out through gritted teeth as she leaned forward and kissed his chest. His heart leaped beneath her touch.

She smiled. "You said I could do whatever I want right now," she reminded him. "I want to do *you*." Her fingertips trailed down his chest, over his abs, to where his erection was testing the fly of his tuxedo pants.

He groaned. "I don't want to take advantage of you."

She laughed. "You're not. I'm taking advantage of you." She unbuttoned his pants and slid down his zipper.

He groaned again, fighting for control. But it was all hers right now.

Maybe that was what she needed. To feel in control as her entire world, her reality, spun out of her control. What she'd always believed had been a lie.

Maybe she wanted his world as upended as hers was because she drove him out of his mind, first with her fingers. She slid them inside his boxers and around his erection, then up and down, his cock pulsating inside her grasp.

And he nearly panted for breath.

"I need this inside me," she said. "I need you." But she released him and stepped back. Then she turned around, showing him all that bare skin that had teased him, and probably every other man in the room, tonight.

She couldn't be wearing a bra under such a gown. And as she slid the sleeves down her arms, the dress dropped to her waist, her breasts free.

He kissed her spine, like he'd wanted to do all night, trailing his tongue down the entire length of it. And as he did, he cupped her breasts in his hands, holding them, teasing them. "You are so beautiful," he whispered against her neck.

She shivered, and her nipples pressed against his palms.

He turned her around and leaned over, swiping his tongue across first one nipple and then the other.

She moaned and clutched his head in her hands, holding him against her. He drew her nipple into his mouth and flicked his tongue across it again. "Oh, yes..."

There was a zipper on one hip. He pulled it down so that her dress fell away. She wore only a G-string beneath it, and then that was gone. He dropped to his knees and pulled one of her legs onto his shoulder. Then he made love to her with his mouth and his tongue.

She cried out, her body convulsing. But it wasn't enough for her. She went wild, tearing at his clothes until he was naked, too. Then she pushed him onto his back and straddled him, and she rode him fast and wild until her body convulsed again.

He came, crying out her name at the intensity of it. And she collapsed onto his chest that was heaving with his pants for breath. And his skin got damp from the tears leaking out of her eyes. He wrapped his arms around her and held her as she cried. And he felt like crying, too, for her pain and loss, and for himself.

Because he loved her, and he knew that she was probably going to reject that love. That she was too scared of getting hurt, of being left, to trust him or anyone else with her heart.

Voices, raised in anger, penetrated the fog of Blair's sleep.

"I saw how you were looking at him. And how he was looking at you."

Then there was the sound of skin slapping skin. Hard. And a cry.

And Blair jerked awake. Was that a nightmare or a memory? Her parents hadn't been happy. Even as a child Blair had known that, but was it because of her dad telling her that or because of what she remembered?

Ivan, lying next to her, murmured in his sleep. "Blair…"

"Shh," she whispered. "Go back to sleep."

Maybe now that the body had been found, he could get some rest. She had to be safe now; what the killer hadn't wanted found had been uncovered. And whatever evidence he might have been trying to hide with it.

So it couldn't have been her father who'd put the body there, who'd killed the woman he'd been obsessed with… even after she was gone. He'd loved her so much. Or had he?

Her memories were the memories of a child, not of the woman she was now. The woman who finally understood what love was because she'd fallen for Ivan. That scared her as much as that memory had.

She couldn't lie next to him without reaching for him, without taking the comfort he'd given her earlier. Every time he touched her or held her, she fell deeper in love with him.

So deep that she might be drowning under the weight of all her emotions. She had to fight her way to the surface. She had to think and couldn't do that lying next to him. So she crept out of the bed, grabbed some clothes and hurriedly dressed.

Milek and Garek must have come to the same conclusion she had, that she was probably safe now that the body had been found. Because when she snuck out of the carriage house, she didn't see any black Payne Protection SUV in the driveway. Just her little one with its passenger's side window replaced. The Kozminskis might have considered that Ivan would be enough protection for her, but she didn't feel safe with him. He was more a threat to her than anyone else right now.

Because she loved him so much, she was tempted to beg him to give up his job, to stay safe, to make sure that he never left her. But that wasn't fair. She had to deal with her fears on her own; she had to deal with her past.

She hopped into her vehicle, grateful that she had the keys in her purse, and started it up. Then she opened the gate and headed off toward the gallery.

River City PD must have finished processing the scene because the building was dark. But the crime-scene tape stretched across the door was broken, dangling against the jamb.

Had someone had to go back inside?

Officer Carlson?

Blair could imagine her going back to check something, to make sure she hadn't missed any clue. She wanted to solve this case, but Blair suspected that was more to do with the young woman's ambition than her sense of justice.

Her mother deserved justice. But could she get it now? So many years after her murder? Especially if her killer was already dead?

Blair pushed open the door and stepped inside. No alarms went off. Someone had disengaged the system. Or maybe they hadn't engaged it at all because the police had been here.

Blair reached out and snapped on the lights and she could see that an officer was still there, lying on the floor. Someone had knocked out Officer Carlson. And her gun was missing from her holster. She dropped to her knees to check the young woman for a pulse. It was there, beating faintly beneath the skin on the throat.

Then Blair heard something and looked up into the barrel of a gun directed right at her. The man for whom she'd been named, Blair Noto, held the weapon. She didn't know if it was his or the officer's. It didn't matter—either one would kill her.

"I knew it was you," she said. And instead of being scared, she felt a strange sense of peace. Her father hadn't killed her mother; this man had.

Now, she just had to figure out how to make sure he didn't kill her. She had to keep him talking, either until the officer regained consciousness or someone came to check on her.

Ivan.

He would realize she'd left; he would come to rescue her. To protect her. She hoped. Because she knew that if he was too late, if he found her like he'd found his dad and Jean-Paul, he would be affected. He'd told her that he cared about her, and she believed him, especially with the way he always looked at her, with such love. That was the way her parents had looked at each other, even when they'd fought.

But this man…

He was looking at her now the way he used to look at her mom, and revulsion raised goose bumps on her skin. She looked back at him with the hatred and resentment and anger she felt for him.

Looking at her was like looking at a ghost. She looked so much like her mother. So much that it chilled him. Had she come back from the dead to haunt him?

And the way she looked at him was exactly like how her mother had, like he was disgusting, like he was beneath her. "Good thing I took the officer's gun," he remarked. He intended to kill whoever came through that door with it, and then maybe he would kill the officer, too.

It had been easy enough to knock her out as she'd poked

around the gallery, like she would find some clue the crime-scene techs hadn't already found.

It was probably all over. He'd tried to keep that body concealed, like he'd concealed it from his partner all those years ago. By the time Elliot had returned from a work trip that he'd taken with his daughter, the odor had already been gone, and if there'd been any of it left, the remodeling he'd had done while Elliot was gone had explained it away.

Paint fumes and chemicals.

The idiot hadn't questioned it or the note he'd made her write, the note telling her family she was leaving them.

"I might have shot you if I had Officer Carlson's gun," Etheridge's daughter admitted. "You put me and my father through hell."

"How do you know that your dear old dad didn't kill her?" he asked. "He was insanely jealous of her and of every man that looked at her. And men looked."

"You were supposed to be his best friend," she said. "You were supposed to be loyal to him."

"You don't think I was?" he asked. "I took the blame for the money laundering. I worked out a deal that kept him out of it."

"Because you'd killed my mother."

She was as smart as she was beautiful.

"She was supposed to leave with me," he said. "When I found out that they were going to arrest me, Chekov gave me money to run away. Elliot was already on that buying trip with you. He couldn't bear to be apart from you and her. She was in the middle of some creative period, so she stayed behind. I thought to be with me. But she laughed at me, laughed at the thought of leaving with me."

The girl released a breath that sounded as if she'd been

holding it for a long time, and her shoulders slumped slightly as if a burden had come off.

He wished he could feel that way, that he could let it all go. But he would never get over how she'd looked at him before he killed her and after…and all the times he saw her face in his dreams. "Maybe if I kill you, it'll get rid of her," he remarked. "Maybe she'll stop haunting me then."

He'd just wanted to keep his namesake from reopening the gallery. Hell, he'd paid the contractor to stall and delay, but the guy had warned him that she was probably going to take down the wall, anyway. So he'd had to stop her, that was why he'd tried to kill her.

Now, he had to stop her mother's ghost. He slid the safety off and cocked the gun.

Chapter 26

The cocking of the gun was like a knife in Ivan's heart. He'd already been worried that he was too late when he woke up and found her gone. He knew where she'd gone, though. If only the police had still been here processing the scene…

Officer Carlson was here, but she was clearly no help even if she was still alive. He hoped she was. She didn't like the Payne Protection Agency very much, or at least the Kozminskis' branch, but he had no problem with her. She was just doing her job. And that was probably why she was still at the gallery.

Blair crouched over the young woman's body as if she was protecting her. But she was the one who needed protection and her bodyguard was failing her as much as the cop was right now. He had to act fast. He had to do something before the killer killed again.

He had his gun drawn, his sight set on Noto. But if the older man managed to squeeze the trigger even after Ivan struck him, he would kill her. He had to get that barrel moved away from her, toward him. So he made his presence known; he cleared his throat.

And that barrel swung toward him and fired. Something struck him, knocking him back, burning, but he ignored the pain and raised his gun and fired. Again and again, before he dropped to the ground.

"Ivan! Ivan!" Blair called to him.

But her voice got fainter and fainter, as if she was drifting away. Or maybe he was…

Maybe he was dying. The pain in his chest certainly felt like he was, and he couldn't breathe now. He couldn't tell her what he wanted to tell her.

He loved her.

And he didn't want to leave her like her mother and father had. He didn't ever want to leave her.

Blair had never been as scared as she'd been when her father's former business partner fired that weapon. She hadn't been afraid for herself; she'd been afraid for Ivan, afraid she was going to lose him just like she'd feared. But he opened his eyes and stared up at her from his hospital bed.

"Am I dead?" he asked, his voice gruff, probably from the tube that had been down his throat.

The bullet had broken one of his ribs and collapsed his lung, but he was going to be alright. And knowing that he would be, she would be alright, too.

"No, no, you're not dead," she assured him.

"So you're not an angel?"

"Nope, Angel is a dog who misses you very much." Ivan had been in and out of consciousness over the past couple of days, since he'd been shot.

"I do love that dog," he murmured.

She smiled.

"And I love you," he said.

"I love you, too," she said.

"You sure I'm not dead?" he asked. "Or at least dreaming?"

She smiled again and tightened her grasp on his hand. "Can you feel that? Can you feel me?"

"Must be why my heart is racing."

"Your heart is just fine," she assured him. "The bullet collapsed your lung, but the surgeon got it out and repaired all the damage. You're going to be fine."

He tugged his hand free of hers and cupped her cheek in his palm. He used his thumb to wipe away her tears. "Then why are you crying?"

"These are happy tears," she assured him. "You make me happy."

"I thought a person couldn't be responsible for another person's happiness."

She shrugged. "I don't know. I just know being with you, knowing you're going to be okay, that makes me happy." That was all that mattered, that he was okay now. He'd survived yet another close call.

Ivan Chekov was a survivor, just like she was. She didn't have to worry about losing him; she had no reason to keep her distance from him and every reason to keep him close. Because she loved him.

He blinked and the last of the sleep, or pain-med haze, cleared from his dark eyes. "Are you really okay?" he asked.

She nodded. "You saved me, as always."

"And Officer Carlson?"

She smiled at how sweet and considerate he was. "She has a concussion and a bigger chip on her shoulder than usual, but she'll be fine."

"And Noto?"

"He's dead. He killed my mother and Jean-Paul, too," she said. "It's over."

He swiped his thumb across her lips now. "No, it's just

beginning. You, me, Angel, your gallery…our lives are just beginning." But then his brow creased. "Unless…"

"Unless what?" she asked. "Please don't be worried that I'm going to withdraw again. I won't be scared, not with you by my side, my very own personal security."

He grinned but then the grin slipped away. "I don't want to put you in danger, though. If my uncle isn't faking…"

"He wasn't part of this. They matched all the bullet casings from the crime scenes to the gun they found on Noto, the one he'd knocked Carlson over the head with before taking hers. It's over."

He shook his head and sat up in his bed, then he pulled her up into bed with him, into his arms. She was getting tangled up in tubes and IVs, but she didn't care. She wanted to be close to him. She needed to be close to him.

She kissed him and smiled as joy and love filled her heart. "No, you're right. It's just beginning."

"It's not over," Garek told Milek as they sat in the chief of police's office. "Just like I told you."

Milek shook his head. "I told you that this was about the forgeries and insurance fraud."

"Is that what this is?" the chief asked Spencer Dubridge.

The detective shrugged. "I have no idea. I couldn't find a link between Noto and those forgeries. But he was once part of the art world. He didn't want that gallery to open, though, and that body to be found. So he probably paid Jean-Paul to stage that explosion to postpone the opening or scare Blair off. And then maybe the guy wanted more money, and he killed him."

"But where did the forgeries go?" Milek asked. "You searched everywhere linked to Noto and couldn't find them. They're still out there."

"We'll find them," Spencer said.

"Hopefully before someone buys them," Milek said.

Garek felt a flash of annoyance that, as usual, his brother was focused on the art. He was worried about the people. "I just want to know what is up with this damn insurance company. Is the CEO really using us to protect people or is he setting us up?"

Because then every one of Garek and Milek's new employees was going to be in danger, especially the one they wanted to get the closest to the CEO. But Blade was the one out in the field right now, protecting some pregnant widow.

But who was going to protect Blade?

Ivan had already gotten shot; Garek didn't want another member of his team getting hurt, or worse.

* * * * *